# Neat

# KANDI STEINER

Published by Kandi Steiner
Edited by Elaine York/Allusion Graphics, LLC/
Publishing & Book Formatting,
www.allusiongraphics.com
Cover Photography by Perrywinkle Photography
Cover Design by Kandi Steiner
Formatting by Elaine York/Allusion Graphics, LLC/
Publishing & Book Formatting, www.allusiongraphics.
com

# Neat

# SCOOTER WHISKEY
# DISTILLERY

*Here's to the ones who don't have it all figured out,*

*to the ones focused on the journey,*

*and not the destination.*

*To the messes —*

*because life's too short to always be put together, anyway.*

SCOOTER WHISKEY
DISTILLERY

# Chapter One

**LOGAN**

I was made to be a tour guide.

I know, it sounds crazy, right? What little kid looks at the endless list of possible career choices and thinks, "When I grow up, I want to walk tourists around an old, dusty whiskey distillery in perhaps the smallest town in Tennessee and tell them stories about how the Scooter brand came to be."

The likely answer? Not a single kid — except for me.

I could blame it on a number of factors — like that my dad worked at the distillery, and he was nothing short of Superman in my eyes. Or how my grandfather was a founding member of the distillery, of the Scooter Whiskey brand, of the distinct taste known around the world. Maybe I could attribute it to my weird fascination with history that developed at a young age, or my consistent need to learn something new every day and stash that information away to relay to someone else.

I loved reading books — especially biographies or history recollections. I loved watching documentaries, primarily centered around modern-day luxuries that we all take for granted and never wonder about how they came to exist. And, I loved checking the newspaper — every morning — for the latest technological advancement or forecasted "next big thing."

Essentially, I was a nerd — through and through — though I'd never portray that on the outside.

To everyone in my small town of Stratford, Tennessee, I was a Becker boy. I was trouble, never too far from a fight. I was the third oldest son of the late John Becker, a legend in our town, one taken too soon from all of us by a devastating fire at the distillery. And, I was a player, a man destined to never settle down, to hop from bed to bed for as long as the girls in town would let me.

That's what everyone saw me as on the outside, and only my brothers knew the real me.

I had three brothers — Michael, Noah, and Jordan.

Mikey was the youngest, a senior in high school, and he worked at the distillery with my older brother, Noah, and I. Mikey was in the gift shop for now, but I had a feeling that would change once he graduated. He was smart, and talented as hell on the guitar. Something told me he'd be moving on to an entertainment position of some kind, and that the distillery would be lucky to have him if he stuck around past graduation.

And Noah? Noah was the most well-known barrel raiser at the Scooter Whiskey distillery. He could put a barrel together faster than anyone I knew, and it'd been years since he'd had one that sprung a leak. He started as the youngest, and quickly moved his way up to a leader on the team. He loved to push my buttons when I brought a tour through his part of the warehouse, almost always pulling some sort of prank — like a sawed-off finger.

And I fell for it. Every single time.

Jordan was our oldest brother, and the only one who didn't work at the distillery. He was adopted before I was born, and though his skin was a darker shade than that of mine and my brothers, his hair coarse and black as night, he had always been our brother through and through — no "adopted" necessary to put before that title. He was the Stratford High football coach, and in my opinion, the best damn one our town had ever seen.

My brothers had quite the reputation around town — especially after our father died in the distillery fire when I was seventeen. No matter what we did, it seemed trouble always found us. Sometimes it was just a small bar brawl, other times it was stealing the mayor's daughter away on her wedding day — which was our latest scandal, thanks to Noah.

The town could say whatever they wanted about my brothers, but at the end of the day, they were the ones who knew the truth about who I was — and who I *wasn't*.

They knew that when those fights everyone loved to talk about happened, the only reason I was involved at all was because I was trying to play referee, to break it all up before anything even started. I only jumped in when I absolutely had to — which, sadly, with my brothers, happened to be a lot of the time. And yes, it was true that I hadn't held a single, long-term relationship in my life, but that wasn't because I didn't want to — it was because there wasn't a single woman in Stratford who could keep my attention.

My mind craved stimulation — late night talks about deep and unexplored topics, book discussions and conspiracy theories, questions I'd never been asked and beliefs I'd never been introduced to.

I was waiting for a woman to surprise me, and thus far, there had been none.

Well... there may have been *one*.

I tugged at the collar of my Scooter Whiskey Carhartt jacket at the thought of her, gripping the handle on the large door that led to the barrel-raising area of our distillery. I held the door open for the tour group following behind me, forcing a smile in spite of the turning in my gut at the thought of the one girl I was trying *not* to think about.

"Right this way, folks," I said, ushering our guests out of the cold and giving each of them an encouraging nod as they filed in. "Remember, this is an area where photos aren't allowed. Go ahead and stow those phones away now. And if I see any of you sneaking a picture, my suspicions about you being sent by those posers in Kentucky will be confirmed and I'll have no choice but to yank you out by your ear."

Several chuckles rang out at that, group after group squeezing past me and lining up against the wall inside to wait for me to continue.

I found Noah as soon as the metal door clanged shut behind me. He had bright orange ear plugs stuffed in each canal and protective eyewear over his eyes as he worked on situating the staves of wood in the metal ring to make a barrel come to life. He glanced up at me, a mischievous grin on his face, but he looked back down at his work before I could give him a warning glare not to fuck with me.

He knew that today of all days was *not* the time to give me shit.

"Alright, folks," I said, turning to face the group as they looked around. "Take it all in — *this* is where the real magic happens. If you recall the video we watched earlier, you'll recognize these fine gentlemen behind me as our Scooter Whiskey barrel raisers. Every single day, this small team of four bring five-hundred Scooter Whiskey barrels to life."

Noah, Marty, Eli, and PJ all waved from where they were working, offering the group welcoming smiles before their heads were down again, and they were back to work.

"Why can't you take pictures in here?" one of the men in the group asked. From chatting with him on the walk over from the gift shop, I discovered that he was passing through with his wife and sister-in-law on their way home from a Thanksgiving visit to Illinois.

"Good question," I said, pointing directly at him before I addressed the group. "We're one of the last distilleries that still make their own barrels, and we don't want our secrets getting out. Most get theirs from wineries nowadays, but we still take pride in making and charring our own — which is why with every bottle of Scooter Whiskey you drink, you get those familiar notes of vanilla and oak."

Murmurs rang out, each family within the group leaning in to talk to each other as they looked around at the barrels with more admiration.

"And these four guys are the ones responsible for every single barrel?" a woman asked.

I opened my mouth to answer, but before I could, a hand clapped down on my shoulder, and my brother took over. "Yep. My team and I are here five days a week, and we each raise anywhere from one-hundred-and-twenty-five barrels to one-hundred-and-fifty barrels every single day. Which means we get about twenty-five-hundred barrels out every week."

The crowd buzzed with a mix of *ooh's* and *ahh's*.

Noah grinned, and I couldn't help but smile, too. I loved that I got to work with my brothers, that they were a part of my every day. Noah was older than me, but just a smidge shorter — which always ticked him off. I was lean where he was stout, and our hair was the same sandy brown — though mine was a bit longer. And Noah had Dad's blue eyes, whereas I favored the hazel gold of our mother's.

"That's amazing," the woman breathed, and her eyes fell over my brother, from his arms to his midriff and lower. "Explains why you're built like an ox."

She said that last part almost so softly that I couldn't hear it, but I had — and I knew Noah had, too. If the poor girl had been a year earlier, she might have had a shot at ending her tour through town in my brother's bed. But, as it was, his heart was tied up in a redhead currently stationed across the country in Utah doing her first year in AmeriCorps.

Ruby Grace Barnett — the mayor's daughter who was supposed to marry someone else this past summer, but had ran way with my brother, instead.

Like I said.

Trouble.

Noah smiled, tipping his hat at the group before he turned. He squeezed my shoulder. "No pranks today, promise," he said. "I know you've got plenty on your plate."

My lips flattened. "Yeah."

"Has she come in yet?"

"Right after this tour."

He whistled. "Well, good luck. Come by my place later if you need a drink to decompress." He squeezed my shoulder one last time before letting it go and heading back toward his station, and though my stomach was twisting violently again, I turned to the group, continuing on with the rest of my spiel about the barrels before I led them through the door again and back out into the cold November air.

We were just a few days past Thanksgiving, and Stratford was well into the holiday spirit. Christmas lights were strung from every building at the distillery, and the entire town was dressed in lights and garland to match. The tree in the center of town was large enough to see from the end of Main Street no matter which way you were coming, and with all that around me, I waited and waited for the holiday spirit to find me.

It hadn't — not in years — not since my father passed away.

I inhaled the cool Tennessee air, the familiar scent of oak and honey wafting in on the breeze, but it did nothing to calm my nerves as I led the tour toward our final stop — the tasting. For the next twenty minutes, I'd be helping that group taste whiskey for what was likely the first time in their lives. Sure, they'd taken *shots* of whiskey, but they'd never stopped to smell it, inhale the special aromas, taste each flavorful note, and enjoy that familiar whiskey burn on the way down.

Twenty minutes.

That's how long the tasting would last.

That's how long I'd have before I'd be faced with the girl I'd been trying to avoid all morning, and for most of my life, if I was being honest.

Mallory Scooter.

*Scooter* — as in the name on the jacket I wore, the one in large letters on the building we walked inside, the one sprawled in the top right-hand corner of my paycheck each week.

*neat*

And the one my family had been at war with for decades.

To fully explain my jitters as I waited in my office for Mallory Scooter to arrive for her first day on the job, we have to go back in time a bit.

You see, Robert J. Scooter was the founder of the Scooter Whiskey distillery. And though it's *his* name on the bottles and the building alike, he had a pivotal partner in crime — my grandfather, Richard Becker.

Granddad was the first barrel raiser at the distillery, the one who fine-tuned the process and made it the instrumental one it is today. It was the beginning of the partnership and, more importantly, the *friendship* between Robert J. Scooter and my grandfather, and it was one that lasted all the way up until the founder's death.

And that's when shit hit the fan.

There was nothing in Robert J. Scooter's will about my grandfather, about leaving any part of the company to him — even though it was Grandpa who had helped build and establish the Scooter brand.

The distillery and brand as a whole was left to Robert's family, namely to his oldest son, Patrick — who is the CEO of the distillery today. It wasn't long after Robert passed that my grandmother died, and my grandfather right after. We'd always been told he'd died of a broken heart, and while most would argue it was because of grandma, we all knew a big part of it was the Scooters.

After Granddad's death, my dad stepped up and kept the Becker name alive and well at the distillery. He had been young when he started, and not too long after the changing of the hands, he was made a member of the board.

That's when the real trouble started.

While the Scooter family wanted to blow full-steam ahead toward innovation, my father was hell bent on keeping tradition. He wanted to remember and honor what had made Scooter a household name to begin with. The more he pushed, the more they pulled his reins. Eventually, he was reduced to nothing more than a glorified paper pusher — and when they assigned him to clean out Robert J. Scooter's office, it wasn't only a hit to his ego.

It was a hit on his life.

There had only ever been one fire at the Scooter Whiskey distillery. It happened in that office.

And my father had been the only one to perish in it.

To this day, my mom, brothers, and I have had to live with the mysterious death of my father and no viable explanation as to why it happened. The town buzzed about it — some wondering if foul play was involved, others tsking him for the bad habit of smoking — which the Stratford Fire Department swore was the cause, and which my mom insisted wasn't possible because he didn't smoke.

It was a mess — a giant, steaming pile of mess.

It was also another stave of wood hammered between the Becker family and the Scooter family.

Noah, Mikey, and I worked at the distillery for many reasons — but the main one was to keep our family legacy alive. And though Patrick Scooter and his family played along, there was always an underlying tension, like we were some kind of infection they couldn't be rid of.

But to fire us would be to stir the pot of rumors that they had something to do with our father's death, and for

*neat*

us to quit would be turning our backs on the distillery our family had a rightful hand in owning and operating.

Even with all that being said, I shouldn't have been so worked up over the fact that Patrick's youngest — Mallory Scooter — would be walking through my door any minute now. I shouldn't have been working my stress ball overtime, tapping one foot under my desk, biting the inside of my cheek as I ran over the words I would say when she got there.

Sure, she was the founder's granddaughter and the current CEO's daughter.

Sure, she beared the last name of the family I couldn't escape.

And sure, she hadn't *earned* this job — not the way I had. It'd been handed to her, just because of the blood flowing in her veins.

But it wasn't even any of that that mattered.

What *did* matter was that I was the lead tour guide, and rightfully next in line to be manager — and I had a sneaky suspicion she was hired to thwart that.

Another thing that mattered — perhaps what mattered *most* — was that I'd had a secret crush on Mallory Scooter since I was fourteen years old.

No one knew that last part — not even my brothers, who knew *everything* about me. I'd never told a soul that I found her outspoken sass and open rebellion against her family and this entire town a huge turn on. I'd never once stared at her longer than appropriate, never showed the fact that my palms were sweaty every time she came around.

We were the son and daughter of a bitter rival sparked to life decades ago and still burning hot today.

There was no option for me to entertain my infatuation with her, and I'd known that. I'd steered clear of her with little effort over the years. It was easy to do in high school and even easier to do once she left for college. The few times she had come back home made it more challenging, since I knew she liked to hang out at the same places I did. Still, I'd avoided her in every way possible, shoving down any and every urge I had to get to know the blue-eyed girl with the septum piercing who I'd watched scribble in her sketch book from afar all through high school.

But now, I would be working with her every single day.

What was worse, I'd be training her — and likely to take the job *I* was rightfully owed.

*That* was why I couldn't sit still, why frustration and giddiness battled inside me as I waited for her to show.

I wanted to see her.

I *hated* that I had to see her.

I couldn't wait to talk to her after all this time.

I couldn't bear the fact that I had to talk to her *at all.*

Not a single emotion made sense as they fought that war within me, and logic didn't have enough time to show up and calm them all down before there was a knock at my office door.

I dropped the stress ball in my hand just before it swung open, and I followed that bright yellow, spongey ball as it rolled all the way across the office and knocked gently against the toe of dirty, white, high-top Chucks.

I'm not sure how long I stared at those shoes, only that it was a little *too* long. Because by the time my brain finally processed that I should stand and clear my throat and make my way around my desk to greet my guest, she was watching me with an arched brow and flat, beautifully painted lips.

"Logan Becker?"

I forced a smile, ignoring the way my name sounded rolling off her tongue. I couldn't remember if I'd ever heard her say it before, though I was almost certain I hadn't.

I'd have remembered.

She had a slight Tennessee lilt, which seemed a little out of place, given her appearance. She paired those high-top white Chucks with jeans that had more holes than fabric, revealing slivers of the tattoos on her thighs. Her t-shirt was black, with a band name I didn't recognize, and more tattoos peeked out from under each sleeve. She had a blue and green flannel tied around her waist, accentuating a waist I wagered was just right for me to fit my hands around. Her hair — which had been purple just last week — was now a platinum blonde, parted down the middle and framing her face in a tight, shoulder-length bob. Her lips were painted a dusty rose, her blue eyes lined and shaped like a cat's, and that septum piercing she was so famous for around town glittered in the fluorescent light of my office.

She was everything that every other girl in this town wasn't.

And I *loathed* that it made me want her so fiercely.

Mallory arched her perfectly drawn eyebrow even higher as the silence stretched between us without me answering.

"Uh, yes," I finally said, stepping away from my desk and extending a hand for hers. "That's me. And you must be Mallory."

She popped the gum inside her mouth in lieu of an answer, which made my eye twitch before she took my hand and gave it a firm shake.

"You changed your hair."

The idiotic statement flew from my mouth just as she pulled her hand from my grasp. She still had that one eyebrow cocked up to her forehead, and she tucked her hands in her back pockets, watching me. "And you know that... how?"

I fought against the heat rising up my neck, praying it didn't show on my cheeks. "They provided a headshot with your file," I lied. "Your hair was purple in it."

The corner of her mouth quirked up, drawing my attention to the overly plump shape of them. She eyed me like she knew I'd lied, but thankfully, didn't call me on it.

"It was," she finally admitted. "But *Daddy* said the Scooter Whiskey tour guides had an appearance to uphold, and I was forced to dye it."

I didn't miss the sarcasm laced in the word *daddy*, and if I'd had any question as to whether or not she was here of her own accord or by the force of his hand, I'd just found my answer.

Mallory twirled a strand of her platinum hair around her finger to illustrate the new color, tilting her head to the side as she took a step closer to me. "What do you think?" she asked, lips rolling into a pout. "Do I look as good as a blonde as I did with purple hair?"

My next breath left my chest mid-inhale, which just made Mallory smirk more. She *knew* what she was doing — which meant I was doing a piss-poor job of hiding the fact that I found her attractive.

But with another pop of that damn gum inside her mouth, I snapped back into business mode.

My breath found me again, and with it, my common sense. I turned my back on her without a response, crossing to my desk and casually sitting in my chair before I pulled her file from where I'd placed it on the corner of my desk.

*neat*

"Please, take a seat, Miss Scooter," I said, my expression leveled, my demeanor cool once more. "We have a lot to discuss before your training commences."

## Chapter Two

**MALLORY**

Logan Becker's office was my own personal hell of a jail cell.

Not only was it a symbol of my surrender to my father and the first day at a job I had been trying to avoid my entire life, but it also *felt* like a jail cell — or, at the very most, an uptight library.

The walls were cream, the wood flooring dark and warm — but all that warmth was offset by the blinding fluorescent lights lining the ceiling. Not a single piece of art hung on the walls. In fact, the closest thing to art was the impressive wall of bookshelves behind his desk. They would have been beautiful, had they not been so meticulously organized that they felt more like a farce of comfort in a doctor's office than a display of stories worth reading. The books were lined up by height order, and then by color, and then, I was sure, without even looking closely, by author last name.

His actual desk was the same dark wood as the floor, held up by black, metal legs. His monitor sat on it, along with the file he'd just pulled — that I assumed had something about me inside — and a swinging ball pendulum that tick-tacked back and forth slowly.

The entire office was colorless.

I sighed, taking a seat in the chair across from him at his desk like he'd asked. He was still filtering through the file in his hands, so I looked around for something — *anything* — that wasn't boring and bland. My eyes settled on a photo of a family at a lake — four young boys, a father, and a mother. One of the boys rode on the father's back, ruffling his hair with his knuckles as they both laughed. The youngest boy was missing a front tooth, and the other two stood with their arms around each other's shoulders, and their mother's hands resting on their necks.

I smiled, thankful there was a human hiding somewhere under that robotic façade.

I knew Logan Becker.

Well, I knew *of* him. It was hard not to hear the gossip mill churning about the Becker family, no matter how hard I tried to avoid it — and I did. Logan had been in the same grade as I had growing up, but of course, he'd never talked to me. He was too busy dating every girl who'd look his way before dumping her and moving on to the next. And when he wasn't with a girl, he was with his brothers — probably getting into a fight or finding some other sort of trouble.

I also knew that ever since his father's death, he and his family didn't exactly favor mine.

My younger brother, Malcolm, caught on to that fact just as quickly as I did. But where I kept my distance and made it a point not to get caught up in the drama, Malcolm chose to thrive in it, instead. He'd been the root cause of more than a couple Becker brother fights — and honestly,

I couldn't say I blamed any of them for wanting to punch my brother in the nose after some of the comments I'd heard him make.

But that wasn't me.

I got out of Stratford as soon as I turned eighteen, and if it were up to me, I would have never returned.

Too bad life didn't work like that.

I stared at Logan's young face, smirking as I recalled the fact that he'd called me *miss*, like I was ten years younger than him, rather than his same age. Then again, the way he was dressed in his dark, slim-fitting dress pants and Scooter Whiskey polo, he certainly looked a lot more grown up than I did.

We were both the ripe ol' age of twenty-six, which — when I was younger — I assumed was the age where you had all your shit together. It took years of struggling through school only to discover that the amount of jobs waiting on the other side of that diploma were abysmal for me to figure out I was wrong.

So, yes, I could admit that I looked younger than him in the current moment, but part of that was on purpose — because I knew showing up for my first day of work at the distillery in what I wore every day would irk my father. The other part was just that I found no reason to dress in a way I didn't want to. I didn't care to impress my father or Logan or anyone else.

I had a job to do for my father, one that would give me my own dream in return. *That* was the only reason I was even in that stuffy office to begin with.

I popped the gum in my mouth, a bad habit I'd picked up after I quit smoking a few years back, as I waited for Logan to say something. At that sound, his eyes flicked to me, to my mouth, and back to the file in his hands again.

*neat*

His hands gripped it a little tighter.

"So, before we get started, I'll tell you a little about me and then I'd love to hear a little more about you," he said, his eyes still on the file. "Then, we can go over your training plan and I'll take you for a spin around the distillery."

I had to fight the urge to roll my eyes at that last statement.

My father *owned* the distillery, and every single member of my family worked there — save for my mother, who wouldn't be caught dead doing anything even close to work a day in her life.

"I'm Logan Becker, as you know," he started, and I smirked, sitting back in my chair and folding my arms over my chest as he recited what I was sure a speech he'd been practicing. "I'm the Lead Tour Guide for Scooter Whiskey, and I'll be the one training you over the next few weeks. I started at the distillery when I was eighteen and I've been working my way up the ranks ever since. I'm very knowledgeable when it comes to our distillery, to our whiskey, and to our process, so I think you'll find I'll be a great teacher."

I raised my brows. "I'm sure."

"Why don't you tell me a little about you?" he asked, dropping the file to the desk.

"Wait," I said. "Is that it? You didn't tell me anything about you. You told me how long you've worked here, and your job title."

"I think that's all that needs to be said right now."

"Are those your books?" I asked, ignoring his attempt to avoid telling me more.

Logan followed my gaze to where it rested behind him, then faced me once more. "They are."

"They're so... *organized*."

"I've been told I have a touch of OCD," he offered, picking up the file again. "So, it says here you attended the Tennessee School of Arts for seven years."

His brows shot up at that, and I knew he was thinking what everyone else did — *why so long?* But when you're in no rush to go back home, have nowhere *else* to go, and art has been your only escape your entire life? Well... seven years doesn't seem like a long time, at all. In fact, I'd argue it wasn't long *enough*.

"You have your Masters in Arts Management, with distinctions in photography and drawing." He frowned, eyeing me over the pages. "That's impressive. What brought you back here?"

"Did you miss it in all your research about me that the school I attended is in severe financial trouble and is no longer accepting new students because they're closing their doors soon?"

Logan didn't answer.

I shook my head. "Well, it's a fortune telling for my entire career, I think. Finding a job as an artist when you don't do graphic design or something similar is difficult. And so, here I am," I said, sweeping my hands over our surrounding area before I folded my arms over my chest again.

Logan opened his mouth like he wanted to ask me more, but thought better of it. He reached deeper inside the folder, instead, pulling out two copies of a very colorful sheet of paper.

"Alright, then," he murmured. "We'll get to know each other better at a later time. For now, let's go over your training schedule."

The Becker brothers were known for being as devastatingly handsome as they were mischievous, and

*neat*

I couldn't help but appreciate that fact as Logan started pointing out the various sections of my schedule. His skin was a mixture of olive and bronze, his hair a sandy brown shade that reminded me of the bark of an oak tree. His eyes were a bright hazel, almost like the golden yellow of a cat's, and ringed with a darker shade of olive around the rim. He was considerably taller than I was, which I noticed when he stood to greet me, and his body was lean and fit. I found myself wondering if he got up to run every morning, or if he spent his evenings doing calisthenics workouts in his back yard.

But of all his physical features that demanded a second look, it was his smile that was the most mesmerizing.

He'd only flashed it at me once since I'd walked in that office, but it'd been genuine enough for me to see the slight pinch of a dimple in his left cheek, to note the way those pearly whites of his spread across his entire face. His mouth was large, his jaw broad and sharp.

It was no surprise to me that he didn't let a girl tie him down. Why would you with a face like that?

"... and the yellow indicates lunch, which you'll see I've paired you with a different lunch buddy each day of the week for the first two weeks. I figured it's a good way for you to get to know some of the people who work here."

I chuckled, snapping back to the moment and finally noting the — impressive? crazy? — amount of colors on the spreadsheet in front of me. Every minute of my day over the next few weeks was mapped out in blues and oranges and yellows and greens and purples.

Logan paused. "Is something funny?"

I popped my gum, giving him a smile. "Just you. You're interesting, Logan Becker."

"Why, because I have an organized schedule for you as a new employee? Because I have my books in order?"

The muscle in his jaw clenched when I popped my gum again. "I'm not naïve to the fact that you're making fun of me, Miss Scooter, and I'll have you know that I don't appreciate it."

I laughed harder at that, but it was cut short when Logan's fists landed hard against the desk.

Everything on it rattled and shook, the little ball pendulum being thrown off track before it slowly swung back into rhythm. My eyes widened, and Logan's narrowed, his next breath coming hard through his nostrils like that of a dragon.

"Why are you even here?" he asked, furrowing his brows. "You're not taking me seriously, you clearly don't want to be here, you're dressed like a teenager and you have the manners of one, too. So, before you waste any more of my time, tell me — why are you here?"

It was the first time I'd seen Logan Becker's backbone since I walked in that office, and I'd be lying if I said it didn't turn me on in the strangest way.

*I'm here because I fucking have to be,* I wanted to say. *I'm here because if I do what my father wants, then I get what I want. I'm here because life isn't fair and the starving artist life sucks.*

"It's none of your business why I'm here," I said instead, leaning toward him over the desk. "And I wasn't making fun of you. I think it's endearing that you took so much time to create a color-coded training schedule. I apologize if I offended you."

Logan narrowed his eyes even more, searching my gaze like he was looking for some sign of sarcasm. When he didn't find it, he sighed, sitting back in his chair and pinching the bridge of his nose. "Look, I don't want to do this anymore than you do, okay? Training the new employee isn't exactly high on my list of things I'd like to do, just like I'm sure working as a tour guide when you have a Masters in Art isn't high on yours."

My gut twisted.

"But, this is where we're at. Okay? So, are you going to cooperate and let me show you the ropes or not?"

I just stared at him, wondering why I liked the severity of his expression now more than I liked the friendly one he offered before.

*Something about that scowl...*

"Good," he said when I didn't answer, tucking his copy of my training schedule back in the file and slamming it shut before he stood. "Come on, it's time for the tour."

He didn't look behind him to see if I was following, and before I could stand, he offered one last remark over his shoulder.

"And for God's sake, lose the gum before I have an aneurysm."

"So, this is another area where photos are forbidden," Logan said as we walked through the barrel-raising area. I noticed him give a slight head nod to his older brother, Noah, who eyed me with a scowl that told me he didn't like that I was there.

*You and me both, buddy.*

"Because—"

"Because we're one of the only whiskey distilleries who still makes their own barrels," I finished for him. "I know. You forget that my father owns this place."

"Trust me, I didn't forget," he murmured, and then continued on with his spiel.

I listened — or at least, pretended to — as I watched the team of four arrange staves of wood in perfect order within a metal ring to make a barrel. Noah slid the top ring down on a barrel he'd just put together, sending it down the line before he started the next, and I hated how much he looked like he loved his job.

Because I had a feeling it wouldn't be there much longer.

My father was all about innovation, about being the best of the best, being ahead of the times. Other members on the board had been fighting for tradition for years, urging him to keep the staples that made Scooter Whiskey a household name in the first place. But, those members of the board were thinning out, and slowly, Dad was turning the tides and showing why innovation should be at the forefront of their mind — especially with more and more craft distilleries popping up.

The team of four in front of me were some of the most important people in this distillery and had been for years.

And I couldn't be sure they'd have a job in six months' time.

Logan snapped his fingers beside me, and when I turned to face him, he cocked one brow. "Well?"

*Oh, shit. Did he ask me something?*

I smiled. "Uh... I'm sorry, could you repeat the question?"

Logan sighed at that, shaking his head slightly before making his way toward the back door of the warehouse. "Try to at least *pretend* you give a shit on this tour, could you?"

"I'm sorry," I said, jogging a bit to catch up with him. "Really, I am. It's just that I know this distillery like it's the house I grew up in... because, honestly, it practically was. This tour seems like a waste of time to me."

"You know the layout," Logan agreed, holding the back door open for me before we both slipped back out into the cold. Logan zipped up his jacket while I flipped up the hood on mine, tucking my hands in my pockets against the chilly wind. "You know the name and the processes. But, do you know the history? The selling points? The fun facts and figures that tourists will want to hear? The stories that will stick with them and have them telling their friends about the amazing tour they had when they get home?"

"Like that my grandfather died from an infection of a finger injury that he never told anyone about? Or how we use the fresh spring water on our property and that's why our whiskey has a distinct taste that no one can emulate?" I challenged.

Logan paused where we were walking, facing me for the first time since we left the warehouse. "Those are both great examples. But, they're also facts that can be found online. Tell me something no one can find with a quick Google search."

I opened my mouth, paused, and shut it again.

I couldn't think of a single thing.

The truth was that I *should* have known more stories than Logan Becker — being that I was the daughter of the owner and the granddaughter of the founder. But, I'd been trying to get away from this town and the legacy my family had built in it since I was fourteen.

I'd blocked out almost every story I'd ever heard my father tell, and any time someone asked me about my last name, about this town and the whiskey distilled in it, I gave them base-level information that anyone could find out on their own — simply because I didn't *want* to talk about it.

I didn't want to be a part of any of it.

Logan nodded. "I'll take your silence as an admission that you don't have an answer. Come on," he said, steering us in a new direction. "We're almost done, and then we can end your torture for the day."

We walked through various warehouses — where the single barrels are held, where the tasting takes place at the end of tours — before he gave me a quick overview of the gift shop and lobby area. His younger brother, Michael, was in the gift shop when we passed through.

He looked just as miserable to be there as I was.

"Is something wrong with your brother?" I asked when we left the gift shop, making our way through the back halls that led to the tour guide offices.

"Noah?"

"Michael," I clarified. "I've been in the gift shop a few times with friends who visited from out of town, and he'd always been so cheerful. But today... I don't know. He kind of seemed like he was going to bite the head off the next tourist who asked him how to order a Scooter barrel."

Logan's face soured. "He's just going through a rough time. But... you're right. He wasn't being the friendliest. I'll talk to him."

I blanched. "Oh, I didn't mean..."

I was mid-apology when Logan stopped, glancing down the hallway at an office door I knew all too well. It was Grandpa's office, the first one to ever grace this old building. For years, it had been unoccupied. Then, it had been damaged from the fire that took place inside its walls. Now, the door that had been closed since that day, other than to clean out the fire damage and make sure it was safe again, was open.

There were men walking in and out of it, carrying old, damaged furniture out and bringing in new furniture that looked similar to it. I noticed them removing a large canvas art print that I used to love, one I stared at when I visited Grandpa. It was of a young girl in a bright yellow dress dancing on the beach, her dress mid-twirl, golden hair spinning around her.

It was burnt, and the only reason I could even tell it was that painting was from a bright splash of yellow in the middle that had escaped charring.

"What are they doing?" I asked.

Logan's face was long and pale as we watched the workers. "I guess they're finally cleaning it out..."

"They're moving stuff in, too. I wonder if they're going to build it how it used to be, make it part of the tour?"

Logan stiffened at that, and he didn't respond to my question before he continued walking down the hall toward his office.

My throat tightened as I realized what that would mean for him, if what I suspected were true. That was the office where his father perished. It had to be hard enough to be in the same building with it, let alone walk a group of tourists into it every day and tell them about the man who used to work there... *without* mentioning the man who died there, too.

I caught up to him, unzipping my jacket and slinging it over my arm. "I really do like your bookcase," I said, trying to lighten the subject.

Logan raised a brow, eyeing me from his peripheral. "You like to read?"

He didn't ask in a sarcastic way, more in a way that he doubted I actually liked his bookcase and was instead wondering if I was making fun of him.

"Not particularly," I admitted. "But, I love anything that brightens up a room. And in your office, that bookcase is about as bright as it gets."

Logan actually smirked at that, and I noted the dimple on his cheek before it disappeared again. "Ah, right. As an artist, I'm sure my office is too bland for your taste."

I wrinkled my nose. "You have no idea. You need to hit up a craft market in Nashville or something, get something other than cream paint on those walls."

"I thought about it," he said, which surprised me. "But, I'm kind of banking on a promotion soon, so I was going to wait until I got into the new office."

He swallowed once those words were between us, glancing at me with a touch of discomfort before he opened the door that led to the tour guide quarters for me.

The promotion he was referring to was one he obviously knew I wasn't oblivious to. My Uncle Mac was his manager, and had been very vocal that he planned to retire within the next year. Logan being the Lead Tour Guide now, it made sense that he assumed the position would be his.

And now that he'd said it out loud, I wondered if there was more to my father's deal than dear ol' Dad had let on. Was it a coincidence that he wanted me here, in this department, right when a Scooter was about to retire and a Becker was possibly to be promoted?

"Well, I think I've submitted you to enough torture for one day," Logan said as we passed through the tour guide lobby.

It was a small area, with two large tables where Logan told me earlier that they ate lunch and had team meetings. It was also a bland room, and he and my uncle were the only ones who had offices to themselves. Everyone else had a locker and a small area to place their belongings — which made sense, since they were all out giving tours each day and didn't need an office to do the planning and behind-the-scenes work like Logan and my uncle did.

neat

"You'll have the standard orientation for the next two days, so I won't see you much. You'll be watching a lot of videos and doing the mound of paperwork Scooter likes to dish out to new employees," he said as we walked back into his office. "But, on Thursday, we'll reconvene and pick up with your training plan."

I nodded. "Sounds thrilling."

Logan chuckled, but the small smile fell as he looked me over. It was like he'd been trying to avoid actually looking at me all day, but in that moment, he watched me like he didn't give a damn if it made me uncomfortable.

And it didn't.

I liked the way his pupils dilated the longer he looked at me, and the way his breathing shallowed, his jaw tightening. He didn't look at me like I was a pain in his ass then — more like I was a temptation he didn't want to fight against any longer.

I smirked when his eyes flicked to my lips — lips I'd painted a dusty rose with my favorite tube of lipstick that morning — but he pulled his gaze away quickly, filtering through some papers on his desk as he cleared his throat.

"You'll get your uniform tomorrow, too — which I'm sure you'll be equally as thrilled about. Other than that and the orientation, I don't think there's anything else to go over before we meet again on Thursday." He tucked the papers inside the folder with my name on it, but still didn't look up at me. "Do you have any questions for me before you go?"

For as much as I didn't want to be there earlier, for some reason, I now found I didn't want to leave.

I walked to the bookcase behind him, and he avoided looking at me again until my shoulder brushed his as I past him. "Which one should I read?"

I glanced at the wall of color before looking back at him, and he looked more confused than I'd seen him all day.

"That is, if you can part with one piece of your perfectly put together puzzle here," I added with a smile.

Logan blinked. "You want to read one of my books?"

"I do. In fact, I want to read your favorite one. You said we should get to know each other better, right?" I shrugged. "I imagine reading your favorite book is a good place to start."

The corner of Logan's mouth tilted up marginally, and he took a step, reaching for a leather-bound book with gold letters on the spine.

"Wait," I said, wrapping my fingers around his forearm. He paused as soon as I touched him, the book hovering halfway off the shelf. "Something written in the last century, please," I amended. "I haven't read anything outside of required textbooks. Go easy on me."

I smiled, but Logan's face was completely blank as he stared at where my hand touched his arm. I pulled it back tentatively, not realizing how warm he was until I felt the brush of cold over me once we were no longer touching.

He replaced the book he had originally grabbed, reaching across the shelf in front of me for a hardback wrapped in a paper sleeve, instead.

"Try this," he offered, and as soon as I had the book in my hands, he took a step back.

"*All the Light We Cannot See* by Anthony Doerr," I mused, running the pad of my thumb over the beautiful cover. It was a blue-tinted photo of what looked like a coastal town in Europe somewhere, and a shiny, gold emblem boasted that the book was the winner of a Pulitzer Prize. "What's it about?"

Logan finally smiled again. "That's the point of reading it, Mallory — to find out."

I bit my lip against my own smile, and I wasn't sure if it was because he was joking around with me, rather than looking at me like I was a mosquito, or if it was because he'd said my name in a way that only a long-time friend would.

I wondered if it could be possible — a Scooter and a Becker being friends.

"Thanks for the tour. I guess I'll see you Thursday?"

He nodded, taking another step back so I could pass between him and the desk behind us. "See you Thursday."

His eyes darted to a space beside me, and I followed, chuckling when I noticed the now-blank space where the book had been.

"You're going to fix that before you leave, aren't you?"

"As soon as you're out the door."

I laughed, shaking my head as I slipped past him. "I'll leave you to it, then." I paused at the door, and couldn't help but smile at the difference in how I felt leaving as opposed to when I'd arrived. "Bye, Logan."

"Bye, Mallory."

Before I'd even made it out of the tour guide lobby, I heard him shuffling the books on the shelf.

# Chapter Three

## LOGAN

"That was one hell of a game tonight," I told my older brother, Jordan, Friday night as I heated up leftovers from dinner for him in our mother's kitchen. I opened the fridge and offered him a beer as soon as the microwave was started, but he shook his head, reaching into the cabinet behind him for a whiskey glass, instead.

I smiled, putting the beer back and opting for the bottle of Scooter's Winter Whiskey Mom had on the counter. It was a special release we did each fall that went away again in January, and it was one of Jordan's favorites. I poured him two fingers in his glass, and cheersed my own to his before he took a sip.

"It was more fun to watch than to coach, I assure you," he said, sucking in a breath through his teeth as the whiskey settled in his stomach. "We had too many errors. It shouldn't have been that close."

"Ah, but that's what makes it a good game," I offered, clapping my hand on his shoulder. "Have them run some drills on Monday, but tonight, we celebrate a win."

He tipped his glass toward me. "Hear, hear."

It was tradition for my brothers and I to get together at Mom's every week for family dinner, but during the fall, when dinner fell on a Friday, Jordan was always absent. He was the head coach of the town's high school football team, and that meant a game every Friday night for him. So, we'd have an early dinner, and then head to the field to watch the game. And after, we'd all meet at Mom's again, heat up some food for Jordan, and have family dinner round two.

Noah and Mom were at the table when Jordan and I made our way back to the dining room. Mom sipped on her sweet tea while the rest of us enjoyed our whiskey, and Jordan shoveled food into his gullet like he hadn't eaten in years.

"Careful," Mom warned with an amused smile. "The plate isn't edible."

Jordan made some noise that could have been a chuckle, if his mouth wasn't full, before shoving another bite in.

"Where's Mikey?" Noah asked.

Mom shifted, sliding her finger over the rim of her glass with a sad look in her eyes. "Back in his room. He was playing guitar for a while, but he's been silent for about an hour now... think he might be asleep."

My brothers and I exchanged worried glances of our own, wondering how long our youngest sibling would wallow in misery. His high school sweetheart had broken up with him last month, leaving school to chase her music dreams in Nashville. It had always been their plan to go after school ended... *together*. But, like we all feared, Bailey changed her mind and asked Michael for time and space to do her own thing.

It'd been the biggest betrayal to my little brother, who'd put Bailey above everything else — including his own dreams. Now, he was single for the first time in years, and just a half-a-year away from graduating high school with all the plans he *thought* he had thrown out the window.

"He'll be alright," I assured my mom, reaching over the table to squeeze her hand in mine. "He's heartbroken, but he'll bounce back. Just give him a little time."

Mom nodded, squeezing my hand in return and smiling as much as she could. Mom was a beautiful woman — always had been — and even in that moment, with her eyes rimmed with dark circles and her face long, tired, and worn, she was stunning. I loved how much of her I saw in me when I looked in the mirror — same hazel eyes, same full-faced smile. Noah was a spitting image of Dad, and sometimes I envied that he got so much of him, but I was proud to take after the strong woman who had raised us — when Dad was here, and after he passed.

"So, how did it go with Mallory this week?" Noah asked me, kicking his feet up in the empty chair Michael usually sat in. "Seemed like you two were ten seconds away from ripping each other's throats open in that tour run through on Monday."

Mom's face screwed up with worry, but she didn't speak, just sipped on her tea while she waited for me to answer. Something told me she was just as concerned as my brothers and I were that I was training a Scooter — especially one with a reputation like Mallory's.

Still, just the mention of her made my blood warm — and not in the way that my brother thought. From the moment she walked into my office that first day, I'd been fascinated by her. Hell, I'd been fascinated by her my entire life. But, that fascination was balanced out by my need to protect myself, by the fear that crept in every time I had a second to think and realized I could very likely be training the woman who would take the job I was rightfully owed in the end.

She infuriated me with her gum popping, her sarcastic remarks, her blasé attitude about being at the distillery — and yet, she still made my pulse race, made my hands ache with the desire to reach out and feel that silky, platinum blonde hair between my fingers.

"It was... fine," I said, deciding that was the best word to describe it. "She definitely had an attitude the first day, but by the time she left, she was playing nice. She was in orientation the rest of the week. I saw her briefly yesterday, and took her around for her first shadow tour earlier today." I shrugged. "It's weird. It doesn't seem like she wants to be there, but Mallory Scooter has never been one to do something she doesn't want to do. So, I can't really figure out why she's all of a sudden starting a career at the place it seemed like she'd been avoiding her whole life."

Jordan leaned back from his now-empty plate, his hand resting on his stomach now that he was up for his first breath of air since he started eating. "I saw her and her father checking out that empty shop at the edge of the Main Street shopping center on my way to the field today," he said. "I wonder if that has something to do with it."

"The spot where Rita's dress store used to be?" Noah asked.

Jordan nodded, reaching for his whiskey. "That's the one. They were walking around with Tracy from the real estate firm in town."

I frowned. "That doesn't make sense. Why would she be buying a store when she just started this new job?"

"Maybe it's Patrick who's buying it, and she was just hanging out with him?" Mom suggested.

"I don't know. She doesn't strike me as the kind of girl who would just hang out with her father willingly," I mused, running my fingers over the stubble on my chin. "Anyway, I feel like she's going to give me some trouble, but she's nothing I can't handle."

Mom laughed bitterly. "Oh, I have more than a feeling she's going to give you trouble. That whole family is just... just..." She shook her head, lips pursed together and face turning red. Mom was always a lady first, and I knew she was biting her tongue to keep from saying a whole string of curse words and other foul things about the Scooters.

Jordan reached over and squeezed her wrist, which brought her a new breath. She smiled, patting his hand and sipping her tea again without another word said.

"I'm sorry you have to work with her," Noah offered, sipping on his own glass of whiskey on the rocks. "I wouldn't be able to do it, work so closely with a Scooter. I get amped up enough when Patrick walks through the warehouse. I can't even imagine if I had to train Malcolm or something."

Malcolm was Mallory's younger brother, and a giant pain in our entire family's ass. Whereas most of the Scooter family held it together around us, playing nice and pretending like we all still got along after the death of my grandpa and Robert J. Scooter, Malcolm thrived in the drama. He loved to push our buttons — especially Noah's.

He was one stupid remark away from having his nose broken, if he didn't watch it.

"I agree," Mom said, her face souring. My mother didn't speak ill on anyone, but with the Scooters, even *she* had a grudge. "Honestly, I wouldn't be upset if both you *and* your little brother got out of that distillery altogether."

"We can't do that, Mom," Noah said gently, reaching over to squeeze her wrist. "Dad helped build that distillery, that brand... hell, *this* entire town. We're honoring him by keeping the Becker name alive in this company's history."

"I know," she said, brows folding together as sadness creeped in. "I know. And I know he's looking down on every single one of you, and he's so proud." She patted Noah's hand where it held her. "I just worry, is all."

"That's your job as our mother," Noah said.

"And we make it an easy job to do," Jordan added.

We all chuckled at that.

"Thanks, guys. But no need to worry. I've got it under control." I said the words as if I, too, was bothered by the fact that I had to be around Mallory Scooter. I'd avoided her my entire life, knowing I couldn't get caught up in a girl who was so off-limits it wasn't even comical to consider a world where I could try my luck with her. I still lived in that world, and I knew there was still no way in hell I'd ever have a chance... but being forced to spend time with her, to get to know more about the girl who'd always been a mystery to me?

It wasn't the *worst* thing I could think of.

It would, however, have been easier if she was as rude all the time as she was when she first walked into my office that Monday. Part of me wished we could live there — in the place where I annoyed her and she infuriated me. Because when she asked about my books, about my family, about *me*... I liked it.

And I wanted to know about her, too.

"Well," Mom said, smoothing her hands over the napkin in her lap before she placed it on the table and stood. "I think it's about time for a dance."

Noah and Jordan smiled as I stood, rounding the table and offering my hand to Mom. "I think you're right, Momma. May I have the honor?"

She placed her hand in mine with a warm smile, and Noah crossed the living room to the old record player Dad had bought before we were even born. There was a moment of fuzz and static, and then the first notes of Eric Clapton's "Wonderful Tonight" sparked to life, and Mom released a breath, closing her eyes a moment before we both began to dance.

I wasn't even a thought in the universe on the night my mom danced with my dad to this song, her in her long, cream wedding dress and dad in his blue jeans and white button-up shirt. But, I'd seen the video, the photographs, and I knew that the smile my mom wore each time one of my brothers or I danced with her was the same one she wore that night.

She and Dad used to dance every night in our kitchen while she cooked, or in the living room after dinner. It wasn't always to this song, though it was a favorite. After Dad passed, my brothers and I decided to keep the tradition alive.

Not just for her, but for us, too.

In the months that first followed Dad's death, our entire family fell apart. Mom had taken to drinking herself numb, my older brothers were fighting over who was the new man of the house, and Mikey and I were retreating into the things that brought us most comfort — me into books, him into music. It was the first and only time I'd ever seen our family machine break down.

The night I asked Mom to dance after dinner was the first night we started to come back together.

It'd been nine years since my father's death, nearly a decade without him being here with us, and yet I still felt his presence as if he'd never left at all when we were all inside that house.

That's the thing about losing a loved one. In one way or another, they stay with us forever. They're never truly lost, never truly gone — as long as we choose to keep them alive in our hearts.

Still, the mystery of his death was one that haunted every member of my family. Almost a decade had passed, and we still didn't have answers for the flurry of questions we asked ourselves every night.

Part of me hoped we would find those answers one day.

The bigger part of me knew we never would.

So, I shut those thoughts out, focusing instead on the music filling our home as I spun Mom out before dropping her down in a dramatic dip. And in the back of my mind, I wondered what it would be like to dance with my own wife to a song that we'd call our own, one we'd lean on in the good times and the bad as we went through life together.

Then, for some odd reason, I wondered if Mallory Scooter liked to dance.

The thought was gone with the next spin.

## MALLORY

*Mine.*

All my life, I'd wanted to look at something — *anything* — and feel that one, possessive, all-empowering word ringing true to my bones.

When I was younger, I'd wanted a dog — and we'd gotten one. But it wasn't *mine*, it was ours — my brother's, my dad's, my mom's. I'd had a room to myself growing up, but it had been decorated carefully by my mother, without a single representation of who I was. When I got my car, it was the one my father had driven for five years and then handed down to me. Even when I was at college, I shared an apartment with three girls I didn't know, and the space never felt like mine.

Now, standing in the middle of the gutted retail space that I would transform into an art studio, I looked around and tried to feel it.

*Mine.*

*This place is mine.*

I should have felt it, because for all intents and purposes, it *was* mine — along with the small studio apartment above it. It was free for me to do what I wanted with it, to bring my dream of owning my own studio to life.

I could look around and picture it all.

I saw the windows, floor to ceiling, letting in natural light and giving passerby's a view of the art being made inside. I saw the back room that I'd convert into a dark room, where photographs would slowly materialize. I saw the stage for live models, the easels surrounding it, imagined artists of all ages gazing up at their subject before dipping their paint brush to begin. I saw craft classes for children, saw date night painting projects for couples, saw wine night sketch classes for girls' outings. I envisioned students taking classes with me for years, honing their craft, becoming stronger and more creative as the years passed.

The options for what would happen inside that empty room were endless.

And still, it didn't feel like mine.

Because it came at a price.

It was my father's name on the check that secured that piece of real estate for me. It was because of him that I had a place to live on my own, and a business to bring to life.

And in order to keep it, I had to play by his rules.

Every time the thought assaulted me, my fists would clench, my nose would flare, and I'd close my eyes and try to find a breath that didn't burn on the way down. There was nothing I could imagine being worse than being in debt to my father, than being under his thumb again like I had been before I turned eighteen.

And yet, here I was.

I was still looking around, trying to find a sense of ownership when my best friend plowed through the front door with a bottle of champagne in his hand.

"I brought the bubbly!" Chris exclaimed, floating into the vacant shop with the same grace that he made an entrance everywhere he went. He was dressed impeccably in his beige cable knit sweater, accented by a thick, plaid scarf that hugged his neck and the tweed jacket shielding him from the Tennessee winter wind outside. I'd never seen my best friend in jeans, not in all the years I'd known him, so it was no surprise that he was in navy dress pants and brown leather ankle boots. His blonde hair was parted to the left, styled neatly, and his face clean shaven — which accented what I referred to as his Superman Jaw. His chocolate eyes were warm and inviting as always, accented by the flurry of freckles that dotted the apples of his cheeks.

I lifted one eyebrow at the bottle in his hands. "I'm sure you brought that bottle to celebrate the shop, and not at all because it's Saturday and you love brunch more than the cast of *Friends* loves coffee."

"Think of it as two birds, one bottle," he said with a mischievous smile. "Now, we just need two champagne flutes and a—"

Chris stopped mid-stride on his way over to where I stood in the middle of the room, his eyes dropping to the mound of matted fur in my arms.

"Mallory... what in the ever living *hell* is that?"

I glanced down at the subject of his disdain with a smile, running a hand over the little fur ball until I found an ear. I scratched behind it, and a soft purr rumbled against my chest.

"This is Dalí," I explained, and as if he already knew his new name, he peered up at me with green, glowing eyes that then turned to Chris.

"What the fuck is a *Dalí?*"

I rolled my eyes. "He's a cat, silly. Here," I said, holding Dalí out toward him. "You can hold him. He's really docile."

"*Why* do you have a cat?" he asked, leaning away with one brow climbing higher and higher on his forehead as he assessed the creature in my hands. "And *how* do you have a cat?"

"He was a stray. He wandered up when I was moving my stuff upstairs last night. I gave him some food, a place to sleep that wasn't freezing... isn't he cute? He reminds me of Salvador Dalí with his little mustache," I said, running my fingertips over the fur around the cat's mouth. "I thought he could be a sort of Shop Cat."

Chris blinked. "Only you, Mallory. Only you."

He rounded to stand on the other side of me, still watching Dalí like he was a dragon and not an adorable, fluffy, calico cat.

"*Anyway*," he said, unwrapping his scarf and letting it hang over his shoulders. "Can you put Mr. Dalí down and go grab us some glasses? We have celebrating to do!"

I sighed. "I can, though I'm not sure I'm much in the mood to celebrate."

"How could you not be? You have an *art studio*, Mallory. This has been your dream since you were in high school."

"But it's not mine," I reminded him, placing Dalí on the floor. I gave him one last pet before he sauntered off, finding a spot by the window where he could soak up the sunshine streaming in. "It's my father's."

Chris waved me off. "Logistics. His name was on the check, but it'll be *your* name on the door. And besides, you only had to sell him five years of your soul in exchange for something that you can build and enjoy for a lifetime." He pointed the bottle at me. "I'd say that's a deal worth making. Now, glasses. Stat." He started peeling back the gold paper around the cork. "Mama needs some champs."

I chuckled, jogging up the stairs that led to my small studio apartment above the shop. It was almost as vacant as the shop below, aside from my art from over the years that laid against the walls, waiting to be hung, the new bed I'd splurged on, and a random pile of shit I'd picked up from the local thrift shop. Mom had offered to take me shopping for furniture and essentials, but I'd declined.

I was already in enough debt to them as it was.

Because I knew my best friend was coming over, I'd been sure to make two champagne glasses first on my list at the thrift store. I plucked them free from one of the boxes, unwrapping the brown paper around them and rinsing them off in the sink. I glanced around at the assortment of boxes waiting for me to unpack them before my eyes landed on the one and only book in the entire place.

I paused, smiling as I thought of the boy who'd given it to me. I'd only read thirty pages so far, but already, I could tell there was more to Logan Becker than I ever imagined before.

You could tell a lot about a person by reading their favorite book.

I made a mental note to pick it back up before bed tonight, so I'd have something to talk to my new, grumpy boss about on Monday. Then, I made my way back downstairs.

"Two champagne flutes, as requested," I announced, setting them on the folding table left behind by the previous owner. It was the only piece of furniture in the shop, save for the metal folding chair beside it.

Chris popped the bottle of champagne open, both of us smiling at the familiar sound. He poured me a glass first, and then one for him before setting the bottle down and holding his glass in the air.

"To my amazing, hard-working, talented-as-fuck best friend and her dream becoming a reality," he said. "May this studio be everything you've ever wanted and more."

I touched my chest. "You're so sweet. But no, you can't host a grand opening."

He was just about to take a sip, but he paused, poking his bottom lip out. "Oh, come on. *Please?* You have to get the word out somehow. Just let me throw one, eensie-weensie grand-opening party with some glitter and booze and then I swear, I'll never ask to host an event again. I'll let you make the studio as boring and emo as you want."

I chuckled, rolling my eyes before I clinked my glass to his. "Fine. But no glitter, and *no* techno music."

"Your loss," he said on a shrug, taking his first sip before he did a little twirl, taking in the studio in all its naked glory. "So, work at the distillery five days a week, and you get to run this bad boy on the evenings and weekends. That was the deal you made with good ol' Patrick Scooter, am I right?"

"Yep," the word rolled over my lips with a pop. "Which basically means I'll be doing what I loathe more than anything for seventy percent of my life, and what I love for the other thirty."

"Life is about balance," Chris offered with a teasing grin. He leaned a hip against the folding table, watching me over the rim of his glass before he took another sip. "How was your first week at the glorious Scooter Whiskey distillery?"

"Annoying. I have a stupid uniform, and had a two-day orientation that I'll never for the life of me understand why I didn't get to skip, considering who I am." I sighed. "Oh, and, you'll never guess who's training me."

"Logan Becker."

I opened my mouth to tell him who, only to pop it closed again. "How could you possibly know that?"

Chris cocked a brow. "It's Stratford, honey. Not like this town doesn't know everything about everyone. Logan has been the Lead Tour Guide for two years now. Of course, he's training you."

"Huh," I mused. "Well, then you can also imagine how awkward it is."

"Oh, you mean because your families used to be best buds back in the day and now loathe each other?"

"Don't be cute."

"Impossible not to be," he said with a wink. "But honestly, it can't be that bad. You are both far removed from your parents' drama, aren't you? Logan Becker always struck me as the most level-headed of those brothers. He was always the one trying to stop them from fighting."

"But he never backed down from one, either."

"Touché." Chris took a drink of champagne. "Was he an asshole to you?"

I thought that question over, battling with whether the answer was yes or no. He *was* a bit rude, especially when he asked me why I was even there at all. Then again, with the way I dressed that first day and the prissy *better than everyone* attitude I walked in with, I couldn't blame him.

"No?" I finally said, taking my own sip. "I mean, I can tell he doesn't want me there — but I think it's just because of who I am, and the fact that my uncle is retiring soon, and he's had his eye on that job for years."

"You think they'll make you manager over him?" Chris shook his head. "That doesn't seem right. You're just starting."

"I don't know," I answered honestly. "Dad never said anything about that in his deal, but..."

We both fell silent, because I didn't need to say it out loud for Chris to know that my father wasn't known for playing clean or fair. He knew what he wanted, and he stopped at nothing to get it.

If me being manager was in his plan, it didn't matter if I knew about it or not — it would happen.

"Logan Becker," Chris mused. "*God*, I had the biggest crush on him in high school. He was always so broody, in like... a nerdy kind of way. You know? Like, he was always reading in a corner, being mysterious and shit." He sighed. "There's just something about a boy with a book in his hands."

I chuckled.

"What?" Chris said, crossing his arms, the top hand still dangling his champagne flute like a charm bracelet.

"Like you don't recognize how down-home hot that boy is."

I shrugged, pushing off from where I was leaning against the table next to him to pace. "He's not hard to look at."

"Bullshit."

"Fine," I huffed. "Yes, he's hot. But, he's *Logan Becker*. That boy has had more girls in his bed than I've had pairs of Chucks — and that's saying something. It's not like he's anywhere near my type, or that I'm anywhere near his. We were in the same grade and never said more than two words to each other."

An amused grin split my best friend's face as he took another sip of champagne. "I never said anything about dating him, Mallory... but apparently that's a subject that's been on *your* mind."

He cocked a brow as I stood there like a guppy, mouth open, catching flies.

I rolled my eyes, trying to play it off. "I was just making a statement."

"Mm-hmm. You know, this actually would be kind of perfect." He gasped. "Oh, my God. It'd be like a modern-day *Romeo and Juliet*! Oh, *please*, can you do it? Date Romeo, Mallory. It'd be so fun!"

"You do realize that play is not romantic in the slightest, and that both Romeo and Juliet die in the end."

He waved me off just like he had when he first arrived. "Logistics."

"Logan Becker will never be my Romeo," I said definitively. "Now, can we get back to the subject of how the hell I'm going to survive the deal I made with the devil that is my father?"

Chris chuckled, standing straight and wrapping me in a bear hug with his glass of champagne still firmly in hand before he rested his chin on the crown of my head. "Oh, darling. Don't think of it that way, okay? This is a trigger for you. You hate to feel manipulated or controlled in any way, and that's what this feels like. The one man you've been trying to establish your independence from is the one man you can't seem to escape."

I sighed.

"But, that's not what this is," he continued. "You're a bad ass business woman, and you made a *business* deal. It's five years of sacrifice, and then?" He pulled back with a supportive smile. "Then, you're free — and this place really *will* be yours."

I swallowed, looking around as emotion threatened to surface. I didn't *do* emotions — but standing there inside of a blank canvas I'd been painting in my imagination since I was a little girl, I couldn't help but tear up.

"So, first thing's first, show me your uniform so we can make it cuter. If you *look* good, you'll feel good," he said, releasing me and draining the last of his champagne before he refilled it to the top. He spun, looking around at the empty space with a mix between an optimistic smile and a timid grimace. "And then, we start on this mess."

# Chapter Four

## LOGAN

On a normal Monday morning at the distillery, I'd be happy to be back at work. Of course, I'd be missing the weekend just like anyone else, but for the most part, being at work never bothered me. Even when I was a newbie and had to work tours on the weekends, I never complained. I was in my element when I was talking about history, and I was always happy to do it.

But today wasn't a normal Monday.

Today was the day Mallory would shadow me, which meant I'd be spending all day long with her. And as much as I'd spent the weekend pretending like that didn't faze me, like she was just another new guide and it would be business as usual, the unease in my stomach that Monday morning proved it'd all been bullshit.

Still, I schooled myself as much as I could, revisiting her training plan and making notes on important things I wanted to cover. That was my M.O. — throw myself into what I could control to avoid what I couldn't.

I couldn't control the fact that I should have hated Mallory Scooter, but I was intrigued by her, instead.

I couldn't control the fact that I had to train her when she didn't even want to be here.

And I couldn't control the fact that she was most likely here to take the job I'd been working my ass off for years... no matter how much that fact killed me.

All I *could* control was how well I trained her, how well I demonstrated that it was *me* who was made for the management job, who was destined to lead this team of tour guides — not her. It wasn't much, but it was something I could throw my all into.

If they gave that job to her instead of me, I wanted everyone in this company to know the wrong decision had been made — including the ones who made it.

I was still making notes in the margins of the day's agenda when there was a knock on my doorframe, and I looked up to find Mallory leaning against it, arms folded and an amused smirk on her face as she eyed my stack of highlighters.

"Mornin'," she said. "I see you're already color coding the day."

"And I see you're already making a habit of being late," I countered, checking the time on my watch. She was supposed to be in my office at eight, and it was eight twenty-two. "Have a seat, I'm just finishing up my thoughts here and we can go over the plan for the day."

"Can't wait," she muttered, and it wasn't until she unfolded her arms and made her way into my office to the chair across from me that I realized what she was wearing.

My eyes bulged — so much so that I knew there was no use in trying to hide the reaction. Her tight midriff was exposed by the tour guide polo that she'd maimed with scissors, cutting it into a crop top. A belly button ring glittered under the fluorescent light as she took a seat, and she crossed her right leg over the left, looking around my office like there was nothing out of the ordinary. She'd cut the hem of the sleeves, too, which caused them to roll slightly and show more of her toned arms. Tattoos crawled around the bicep of her left arm, and black script lined the skin of her right forearm. There was even the tail end of something peeking out from under her top, something that appeared to line her ribs and dip down to the top of her navel.

*Feathers*, I realized.

And for a split second, all I could think about was lifting that shirt to see the rest.

I blinked, clearing my throat and turning my attention back to my notes as I shot that thought down like a skeet disc.

"How was your weekend?" I asked.

"Oh, as thrilling as it can be in Stratford," she joked, still looking around my office. "How about you? You get into any trouble?"

"I'm a Becker," I answered, finishing my last thought on the agenda. "Trouble finds *me*."

"I did hear you all made an appearance at The Black Hole Saturday night."

The Black Hole was the pet name for one of the more popular party spots in town, an old barn with a huge fire pit that was always crawling on the weekends.

"Did you now?" I mused. "And what is the rumor mill saying my brothers and I did this time? Rode a wild hog? Got in a fist fight with twenty, full-grown men? Drove a car into the creek?"

"Actually, they're saying Mikey threw his guitar in the bonfire, and that you took Sadie Hollenbeck home with you... for the fourth time in three weeks." She lifted a brow at that. "That's like a record for you, isn't it?"

I frowned. "Mikey's going through a rough time... and that guitar is old, anyway. Maybe he just wanted to give the fire something more to keep burning."

"Right. Because the mound of firewood wasn't enough." Mallory rolled her lips together. "And what about the part about Sadie? That true, too?"

The way she watched me, I would have sworn she was a little jealous that rumor had it I'd taken a girl home from The Black Hole on Saturday night. I would have sworn it — had I been naïve and ignorant of the kind of girl Mallory was. She'd never had a boyfriend in Stratford — not since middle school, anyway. I'd heard she'd dated someone in college, but he'd never come home for holidays or made an appearance at any of the hometown hangouts.

I didn't think there was a man interesting enough for Mallory Scooter, and I knew for a fact that she didn't give a fuck who was warming my bed at night — which, though the town gossip would apparently argue otherwise, was no one. I didn't invite women back to my place, though I was never opposed to going back to *theirs*.

Sadie was a good girl, and she was going through a tough break-up with her high school sweetheart — who everyone now knew had been cheating on her for years. He'd already moved on, but Sadie was a mess. So, last month, I listened to her cry at The Black Hole and convinced her that he needed a dose of his own medicine.

I then offered to *be* that medicine.

So, yes, I'd gone home with Sadie a few times — but we hadn't done anything we couldn't do in church. Mostly, it was her testing out her baking recipes on me and me playing shrink, trying to help her heal and move on from her asshole ex.

Still — Mallory didn't need to know all that.

"Maybe." I shrugged. "But a gentleman doesn't kiss and tell."

She snorted. "Right. And you're the gentleman in this case, I presume?"

I pressed a hand to my chest, leaning back in my office chair with feigned offense. "I can't believe you'd insinuate otherwise."

Mallory just rolled her eyes, nodding at the agenda I'd just finished. "So, what am I in for today, boss?"

My smirk climbed higher when she called me *boss*, but I subdued it, picking up the piece of paper and reviewing it with her. "You're shadowing me today, so we're going to do two tour groups together. The first one, I'll lead, and you can take notes and follow like you're part of the group. The second one, I'll give you a little more of a hands-on role, let you pour the whiskey at the tasting and answer some of the questions."

Her smile tightened. "Oh, joy."

"But, before we get started... you're going to have to change," I said, eyeing her midriff before I met her eyes again.

"Why?"

"Because it appears a bear got ahold of your uniform."

She glanced down at her shirt, lifting a brow at me like I was seeing something she wasn't. "I made it look better. I made it *fit,* honestly, because it was like a bag on me before."

"We have smaller sizes in the back," I told her. "And, it's pretty chilly today. Let's go back to the supply closet and get you a long sleeve, and we can see if there are any jackets, too."

"I'm not changing." She set both feet on the ground, crossing her arms in defiance. "I look fine. Just because you're offended by a woman's stomach doesn't mean I have to cover it."

"I'm not *offended*," I said flatly. "You're a tour guide, Mallory. You're representing the company, the brand, and you're meeting with tourists from all over. Plus, like I said, it's forty-degrees outside. You really want to walk around like that?"

"Like *what*?" she probed.

I threw my hands up. "You know what, fine. Wear whatever you want. You are Mallory *Scooter*, after all, aren't you? I guess the rules don't apply to the princess of Stratford."

A shadow of something passed over her face then, her expression unreadable.

I stood, snatching my clipboard off my desk and heading for the door without another look in her direction. "Come on. First tour is in ten minutes, it's time to greet our guests."

I was going to strangle her.

I was going to strangle Mallory Scooter.

And not in the sexy, playful way like I did my first girlfriend after high school, who used to love to be choked and fucked from behind. That was just a light pressure, a hand around the throat, gentle squeeze to get the adrenaline pumping and send a spike of pleasure through her bloodstream.

No, this was a different kind of urge — one that rang true somewhere right around *throttle her*.

We were nearing the end of the tour, and with every new stop along the way, the urge had grown larger. Mallory was a sideshow, popping her gum loudly and texting away on her cell phone — all the while wearing our company's logo on her chest with her fucking belly ring showing. She didn't pay attention, didn't take any notes, and whenever I asked her to assist with something, she rolled her eyes for everyone to see before obliging.

At least she was shivering whenever we were outside. Staying out there a little longer just to watch her suffer was about the only revenge I could get.

It was almost impossible to keep the group's attention on me with all her gum noises and incessant texting — not to mention her barely there uniform. I'd introduced her as our newest tour guide at the beginning of the tour, and everyone watched her like they were wondering if the money they'd paid was for nothing.

We were the face of the company, and Mallory made us look like a disaster on ice.

She was still chewing away on her gum, gaze fixed on her screen, when the tour group followed me to the building where we had the whiskey tasting at the end of each tour. I held the door open, smiling at each of them as they passed, but before Mallory could follow them, I hooked her by the elbow, swinging her outside and letting the door shut, effectively putting a barrier between us and our guests.

"Are you *trying* to look like an idiot, or is that just your natural state today?"

Mallory cocked a brow, blowing a small bubble with her gum before it popped on her lips.

I blew out a breath through my nose like a dragon.

"Careful there, might pop a blood vessel," she remarked.

"You're making a fool of yourself."

"I'm just acting like the *princess* that I am," she smarted off.

I released her arm with a scoff. "If there's a point you're trying to make, you can just go ahead and make it so we can all move on."

"My *point* is that a woman should be able to dress how she wants without someone trying to make her conform."

I pinched the bridge of my nose. "Mallory, that's not why I asked you to change. I agree, women *and* men should dress how they want to — on their own time. But when you work for a company, and that company has a uniform, you just have to suck it up like the rest of us and wear it when you're on the clock. That's all I was asking of you."

"Well, that's not how you said it. And besides, this entire training plan of yours is bogus. You're treating me like someone who just discovered Scooter Whiskey a week ago instead of someone who grew up living and breathing every aspect of this distillery. I don't need to shadow you to know how to give a fucking tour of my *father's* company," she reminded me, as if there was any way for me to forget. "You're a tour guide, Logan — not a brain surgeon. So stop treating this job like it's difficult, or special, or whatever else you think it is, and for the love of *God*, stop acting like I don't already know everything you can tell me about Scooter Whiskey."

My blood boiled so hot under my skin, I was sure I'd turned the color of a beet.

"I can do this tour in my sleep," she continued. "And honestly, I'm annoyed that I'm wasting my day following you around when I could be doing better things with my time."

I clenched my jaw, lips flat as I stared down at those icy blue cat eyes of hers. She was so tiny, and yet so fierce as she stared back up at me, chest puffed, not backing down.

I'd have found her cute if she wasn't being such a brat.

"You know what, you're right."

She narrowed her eyes, ready to fire back when my response hit her, and everything on her face fell slack. "What?"

"You're right," I repeated. "I don't know what I was thinking. Of course, Mallory Scooter doesn't need my help. Tell you what, you can lead the next tour."

She blinked. "Wait, really?"

"Of course," I said, glancing down at my clipboard and flipping through to check the times. "Let's just wrap up this tasting, and the next group should be here within an hour. We'll take a short break for lunch, and then you can lead the tour, and I'll shadow *you*. How's that sound?"

Mallory opened her mouth, shut it again, and finally gave a firm nod. "That sounds great. Thank you."

"Mm-hmm."

I didn't say another word, just left her standing there shivering in the cold while I made my way into the tasting building. I finished that tour with the smuggest smile on my face — one I was sure Mallory couldn't decipher, and for that, I was glad.

She thought my training plan was bullshit, that this job was easy and she didn't need any help? Fine. Time to show her the ropes the way my grandfather showed me how to swim — by tossing her into the pool without a floaty.

Sink or swim, Mallory Scooter.

Which will it be?

# Chapter Five

## MALLORY

I couldn't wait to knock that smug smile off his stupid, too-handsome-for-his-own-good face.

It didn't take me long to figure out why Logan was so quick to let me lead the next tour. When he idled in the back of the group, arms folded, clipboard hanging from one hand and cocky smirk on his stupid face while I gathered everyone together, he might as well have been wearing a flashing neon sign that gave him away.

He thought I would fail.

No — he was *certain* I would fail, and that I'd eat crow and apologize.

Well, he was mistaken.

His first mistake was commenting on what I wore. I'd rebelled against my father for the same reason when I was younger. He wanted me to dress conservatively, professionally, *"like a lady"* — and I'd told him to shove his opinion on what *I* wore right up his ass — especially when dressing conservatively didn't stop his piece of shit friends from ogling me once I had tits.

If my own father couldn't get away with it, there was no way in hell a Becker would.

His next mistake was calling me the princess of Stratford. I was no stranger to that nickname, and he knew before he said it that it'd push all the wrong buttons.

So, I gave him the *princess* he asked for. I'll admit, it was a little immature, being on my phone and chewing my gum purposefully loud to make my point. But, I was already annoyed that I had to be here, and while I was perfectly content to do like Chris had told me and just bite my tongue to get through it in order to keep my studio, Logan had soured my mood instantly with his comments.

Now, I didn't just want to get through it.

I wanted to annoy *him* as much as this entire situation annoyed *me* — by showing him that I could do his job with both hands tied behind my back.

"Alright, everyone. Thank you for visiting the Scooter Whiskey distillery. Can everyone hear me okay?"

The group nodded in unison, though everyone was watching me with somewhat confused faces. I noticed a few of them looking at my shirt, whispering to each other.

Okay, maybe slicing off half my shirt wasn't the most professional thing.

*Fine, Logan — you win that point.*

"I'm Mallory Scooter," I said. "Yes, as in the daughter of the owner, granddaughter of the founder. I'll be your guide today."

The faces of the tourists in our group lit up, a few of them exchanging excited glances. I looked back at Logan to see if he was bothered, but he still watched me with an amused smirk.

*Asshole.*

"So, if you'll follow me right this way, we're going to load up on that bus over there that will take us down to the first stop on our tour — the spring — which is where we get the fresh, delicious water that we make your favorite whiskey with."

Everyone smiled, chatter picking up as they followed me down to the bus. I smiled proudly at Logan, but he just jotted something down on his clipboard, piling onto the bus after the group and taking a seat in the back.

And from there, the tour went perfectly.

For about ten minutes.

Talking about the spring was easy. I'd heard my grandfather tell stories about how he'd first came upon it, how it had been on the land of a pastor — a pastor who, funny enough, had a hankering for good whiskey. It was actually the two of them who made the first batch of what would become known as the distinctly flavored Scooter Whiskey.

I told that story with pride, adding in a few fun jokes my grandfather had told me about the spring, and then we were off to the next stop on the tour.

And that's when things went downhill.

We were outside for longer than I expected — mostly due to me chatting more than was needed — and I was shivering so much from the cold, my teeth were chattering as I tried to explain the distilling process, and how the yeast from our process combined with the microcosms near the freshwater spring to form the Baudoinia mold they saw covering the trees around the distillery.

One of the women on the tour asked me if I wanted her jacket.

To add insult to injury, I completely bypassed a part of the tour in my effort to get warm, skipping the warehouse with our limited-edition single barrels inside, and going straight to the warehouse with the pot stills that initiate the distilling process. Logan had to remind me, and we had to turn back, making an unnecessarily long trek back to where we'd just left before circling around again.

The more that went wrong, the more wired I became — and the worse the tour got.

To his credit, Logan's snarky know-it-all smirk had softened, and where he was quick and happy to point out that I'd missed part of the tour earlier, his voice was gentler as he filled in the blanks for stuff I missed as the tour continued.

Still, I was proving his point.

And I hated it.

"This is one of my favorite parts of the tour," I explained when we made it to the barrel-raising warehouse. I schooled my nerves, reminding myself that I knew more about this place than almost anyone, and not to let a few hiccups rattle me. "Scooter Whiskey is one of the few distilleries that still makes and chars our own barrels. And this team of four is the incredible team that brings those barrels to life."

I gestured behind me to the boys, and they all waved before getting back to work. I didn't miss the questioning glance Noah gave Logan, but Logan just shook his head, as if to say *I'll explain later*.

"Now, you might remember them from the video earlier. If—"

"What video?"

I stopped, searching for the source of the question. It was an older woman, the one who had offered me her jacket.

"I'm sorry?"

"You said we should remember them from the video. What video?"

"I—" I paused, realizing I'd skipped over the small museum of history put together over the years. It included all the versions of our bottle, label, and the first blueprints for the distillery.

It also included the video I'd just referenced — that no one had seen, thanks to me.

"I'm sorry," I said with a smile, shaking my head. "I must have forgotten that stop. We'll circle around after this."

"So, you forgot that stop, and the stop earlier, and, apparently, the other half of your shirt," she said, eyeing my midriff disapprovingly before she looked at her husband. "You'd think the daughter's owner would be better prepared to give a tour — especially one we paid for."

There were murmurs of agreement from the rest of the group, and a few people looked away with discomfort.

I swallowed. "I'm very sorry about missing that, but I assure you, we'll go—"

"I don't need your assurance, dear. I need you to give us the tour we paid for. Yelp reviews said this was an amazing experience, and so far, it's fallen pretty flat. I don't know about these folks, but I'd like a refund."

There were more nods, more agreements, and something that felt a lot like embarrassment settled low in my stomach. If I'd have been a more emotional woman, I might have teared up, but as it was, I just stood there, frozen like a stupid deer in headlights, not knowing what to do or say to make it right.

My eyes found Logan, and he frowned, tucking his clipboard under his arm as he made his way to the front to stand next to me.

"I apologize for the mishaps in today's tour, ladies and gentlemen. Mallory is a new tour guide, and this is her first tour she's led by herself. As you can imagine, it can be a little nerve-wracking."

He touched my arm — just for a second — but it was the only source of warmth I felt in that moment.

"We'd be happy to provide refunds," he continued. "But first, let me tell you a little more about these barrel-raisers, and then we'll get to the best part — the tasting. Sound like a fair deal?"

There were some chuckles and murmurs of approval at the mention of the tasting, and as if it was the most natural thing in the world, Logan slipped on his charm and took over, doing his best to turn the tour around.

And I couldn't even stay to watch it.

I smiled as best I could at the group, letting them all pass me before I escaped out the back door of the warehouse and practically ran back to the main building. I crossed my arms over my exposed stomach, shaking my head as the disaster of a tour replayed over and over in my mind. By the time I made it back to the tour guide lobby, I felt something so close to what I remembered crying feeling like that I locked myself in the bathroom so I could get my shit together.

I wasn't sure how long I sat there, fully clothed on the toilet, elbows on my knees and face in my hands as I focused on breathing. In and out, inhale and exhale. No matter how I tried, I couldn't calm down, and it didn't take me long to realize why.

I had made a fool of myself, just like Logan had said.

It was time to eat crow, to apologize to him and take back everything I'd said. Suddenly, my shirt felt idiotic. It was my sad attempt to rebel in whatever little way I could against my father and the deal we'd struck, and it'd been the catalyst for this whole disastrous day.

I had acted like a child, and what was worse, I'd lived up to the nickname I loathed so much.

I sighed, taking a moment to splash water on my face before I left the bathroom in search of Logan. He was just setting his clipboard down in his office from returning from the tour, and when he turned and found me standing in his doorway just as I had that morning, he gave me a soft, sympathetic smile.

"You okay?"

He could have gloated — God knows if it were me in his shoes, I would have — but instead, he stood there with his hands in his pockets, his shoulders folded, eyes sad like he'd just kicked a bunny.

Like *I* was said bunny.

I shook my head, swallowing down what was left of my pride before my eyes met his again. "Logan, I—"

"WHAT THE HELL WAS THAT?!"

My words were cut off by my Uncle Mac blowing past me into Logan's office, eyes murderous, face red and puffy as he slapped a thick stack of papers down on Logan's desk.

"A tour of twenty-five, and every single one of them demanding a refund. I had to give out free shot glasses from the gift shop in an effort to stop them from ripping our distillery a new asshole on Yelp reviews," he fumed, pointing a finger directly at Logan. "I need an explanation, and I need it *now*."

Logan stood straight, chin high and chest broad as he addressed my uncle. "Mac, this was all my fault. I thought Mallory was ready, and I let her lead the tour. I th—"

"It's her sixth day on the job, and three of those days were spent in orientation, for Christ's sake. What were you thinking?" He didn't wait for Logan's response before he continued his rant. "Of *course* she wasn't ready, and you knew better than to let her do more than pour the whiskey at the tasting, let alone lead a full tour."

"Yes, sir," Logan agreed. "I thou—"

"I don't need any more excuses," Mac said, holding up a hand to silence him.

"Uncle Mac," I said, stepping in to defend Logan. It was my mess, after all. "This wasn't his fault. I insisted on leading the tour. I know more about this place than almost anyone, and I didn't want to shadow. I was bored."

"Oh *no*," my uncle cried dramatically, hands framing his face. "You were *bored*? Well, we can't have that."

"You've made your point," I deadpanned.

"Have I?" He took a step toward me then, and his eyes slipped to my navel, brows screwing together. "What in the hell are you wearing?" He turned on Logan again. "You let her lead a tour dressed like *this*?"

Logan opened his mouth, but just shut it again without responding.

I knew it was taking everything he had to not throw me under the bus.

I knew it was taking everything in him to take that verbal scolding from my uncle without standing up for himself.

"Look, I don't have time to listen to whatever it is that's going on here," Uncle Mac continued, gesturing between me and Logan. "But you just lost us money, and I have zero tolerance for that. Get your shit together and don't *ever* let me hear about someone in your group requesting a refund ever again. Understood?"

Logan and I both nodded, Logan's eyes on the floor and mine on his, begging him to look at me.

"Good." Mac glanced at Logan once more before heading toward the door, and he shook his head at me as he passed. "And for fuck's sake, get her a proper uniform."

I flinched when Mac left the office, slamming the door behind him and leaving me and Logan alone. I let out a long breath, shaking my head as I crossed the space between us.

"I'm so sorry, Logan. You were right, I wasn't ready to—"

"I think we're done for the day, Mallory," he said, not giving me so much as a glance as he rounded his desk and took a seat, a frustrating sigh leaving his lips.

I should have left it alone, but I just stood there, waiting.

Logan picked a pen out of the cylinder on his desk, writing something on his clipboard and effectively ignoring the fact that I was still there.

"Logan, please. Talk to me."

"About what?"

I scoffed. "Come on. I know what I did was immature, and I'm sorry. I just thou—"

"I know what you thought," he said, slamming his pen down. He stood, finally meeting my gaze, and when he did, I wished he hadn't.

His warm, hazel eyes were gone, replaced by a cool steel that I felt piercing me to my bones.

"You thought you knew everything. You thought my training plan was stupid, and that there was nothing I could teach you that you didn't already know. You thought I took my job too seriously, and that you were too good to be here."

My heart sank at my words being thrown back at me. "I didn't mean—"

*heat*

"You know, all this time I thought you were this intriguing girl," he said, rolling his lips together before he continued. "I thought Mallory Scooter was an enigma. You were always this fascinating creature to me, because you were unlike anyone else in this town. I thought you were different, elevated, just... I don't know. I couldn't ever put my finger on it, but you were something I'd never experienced."

Something happened then, a flip of my stomach, a flood of something warm and dizzying settling deep in my chest.

"Really?" I whispered.

"Really," he said. His eyes searched mine, like he'd lost his train of thought, but in the next exhale, he flattened his lips and shook his head. "But after today, I know I was wrong. You're just like everyone else. You have no regard for the people around you, you only think about Mallory and what serves *her*. So, thank you. Thank you for shattering the illusion I had of the mysterious Mallory Scooter. The veil has been lifted, along with the spell, and now I see you for exactly who you are."

That sting I felt earlier tripled, and my eyes glossed over — not enough to leak actual tears, but enough for me to feel a cool rush of wind all the way down to my toes.

I swallowed, trying to hold my head high as Logan waited for me to respond.

But I didn't.

What could I possibly say to that?

"Like I said, I think we're done for the day," he echoed, sitting back down and snatching his pen off the desk.

He started writing again, and I stood there — numb, ashamed — like a little kid put in her place. I wanted to apologize, but saying I was sorry felt just as foolish as my shirt did now. I'd gotten him in trouble, and he was pissed — he deserved to be. I wanted to make it right, but I didn't even know where to start.

So, I left, tucking my tail between my legs like the dog I was, without another word.

There were too many emotions flooding through me as I made my way out of that distillery like a zombie. I barely remembered the drive home — only that I could barely breathe, could barely think, could barely remember why I'd been so set on leading that damn tour in the first place.

I needed to calm down, to go to the place where I could be alone, where I could work through what had happened and get a lasso around what the hell was happening to my emotions.

I needed a pencil and a blank sketch pad.

I needed a camera and a sunset in the mountains.

I needed a canvas and a palette of paint.

And I needed to find a way to make it up to Logan Becker — and prove to him I wasn't the girl he thought I was.

Nothing cleared my mind and brought me peace as much as sketching did.

My left hand was covered in gray dust, fingers guiding the pencil over the page in my sketch pad as I kicked back in the corner of my very messy, soon-to-be art studio. More and more boxes of supplies I'd ordered had started to arrive, but I hadn't found the time or energy to go through anything yet.

My dream was in mountains all around me, and yet something was stopping me from unboxing it.

I couldn't think about that, though — not when my thoughts were consumed with Logan Becker and the hellish day I'd had at the distillery. And to escape *those* thoughts, I'd picked up a fresh new pencil, a blank sketch pad that I'd plucked from one of the boxes, and I'd turned my worries loose.

Sometimes my mind wandered while I sketched, but most of the time, it was just me and whatever I was creating — that image I was bringing to life. I'd lose myself in the comforting sounds of pencil against paper, of my hand skating across the page with each dark line or light shading. I had a soft indie playlist playing in the background, and the setting sun streaming in through the Main Street windows as my light.

A rush of cool wind blew my hair back off my shoulders, and it brought me out of my daze. I blinked, looking up at the front door, the first time my eyes had left the page since I'd sat down.

And then I sighed.

My parents were just inside the studio, looking around at the mess — Dad with his hands in the pockets of his dark jeans, Mom with her hands folded over her purse hanging off her shoulder.

Dad wore a cream cowboy hat over his white hair, his skin somehow tan even in the middle of winter. Wrinkles lined his long face, revealing more about the life he'd lived than any words could. He was tall and lean, a picturesque cowboy from an old western film. I half expected the sound of spurs clinking on his boots when he started making his way toward me, scanning the piles of boxes and yet-to-be-built furniture and supplies before his gaze found me.

"Looks like things are coming along," he said, a sympathetic smile touching his leather lips.

I closed my sketch pad, letting it fall on the folding table I'd had my feet kicked up on before I scrubbed my hands over my face. "I know it's a mess. I've been tired after work," I said that last part pointedly. "But I'll get started unpacking this weekend."

"I wasn't judging," he assured me, though his eyes told me otherwise.

I'd learned long ago that though my father always had the sweetest words for me, though he acted as if I was the pride and joy of his life — I was far from it. It was the same with my mother, who loved him unconditionally. And with my brother, who looked up to him like he was a superhero who could do no wrong. They thought they were his everything, that he'd go to war for them — just like I'd used to think.

But I'd learned better.

My father's main priorities were money, and that distillery, and this town of old men he had wrapped so tightly around his little finger.

*That* I was sure of.

"I bet it will be beautiful when you're all done with it," Mom chimed in, trying and failing to hide the wrinkle of her nose as she looked around the space. She wore a rose-colored pea coat that wrapped her up from shin to neck, and a fashion hat the same color hid her short, brunette-dyed hair. Her nude kitten heels tapped on the floor when she crossed to where Dad and I were. She smiled, folding her gloved hands in front of her and not saying another word.

That was what I'd come to know my mother as — a silent sidekick. Agreeable, polite, and ever the dutiful wife.

"I heard you had a rough day at the distillery," Dad offered, resting his elbow on one of the tall boxes that held shelves I needed to put together. "Everything okay?"

I waved him off, standing and making my way over to the one box I *had* unpacked — the one with the booze.

"I had a lapse in judgment," I murmured, grabbing the neck of a bottle of gin. I lifted it to my father to ask if he wanted some, but he just shook his head. I didn't even bother asking Mom before I shrugged, pouring a finger into a red Dixie cup. "I just tried giving a tour when I wasn't ready to. Classic Scooter know-it-all-gene biting me in the ass."

Dad smirked at that, folding his arms over his chest. "Ah. I've been struck by that a time or two."

*Didn't I know it.*

"Well, I didn't come here to make you feel worse about what happened," he said. "I just... I know you don't want to be there. But, remember, we have a deal."

I slammed back the alcohol I'd poured, my eyes landing on his with the swallow. "I didn't do this on purpose."

"And I believe you," he said, putting his hands up. "I just had to check. I know you have some sort of... *vendetta* against me."

I scoffed. "Dad. Please."

"Well, what other reason would you have to... to..." He gestured to me, as if I as an entire entity was a problem. "To dress like that, and ruin the temple of your body with those tattoos and piercings. And God knows you never *wanted* to work at the distillery."

"So you *did* come here to berate me."

"No," he said, a sigh of his own leaving his chest. "I just wanted to remind you that the reason you have this place is because we made a deal. And I don't want you to think that you can half-ass your part of it without me noticing."

"I'm not." I paused. "At least, I didn't mean to. And trust me, I ate a big helping of humble pie today."

Dad watched me, like he wasn't sure if he could trust me to be telling the truth.

*That made two of us.*

"I'll turn it around," I promised him. "Okay? I was just about to head out, actually. To go apologize to Logan."

Dad's face leveled at the mention of the name, and Mom snapped out of her daydream.

"Logan Becker?" she asked.

I nodded.

"Ugh," she huffed, shaking her head. "Those boys are such a menace. I don't understand why we put up with having them at the distillery at all, anymore."

"You know *exactly* why we do," Dad murmured to her, softly, but with a look stern enough to have her buttoning her lips. He turned his attention to me next. "Why are you apologizing to him?"

"Because he's the one I was a brat to today," I admitted. "And I got him in trouble with Uncle Mac. I need to apologize and make things right." I paused, lifting one brow at my father's unreadable expression. "You did know he's the one training me, right?"

Dad cleared his throat. "Of course." But the way he said it, I knew he didn't.

I smirked, crossing my own arms.

Uncle Mac must have left that part out.

"He's good at his job," I said. "Really good. And from what I can tell, every single one of the other tour guides thinks he'll be the one taking Mac's spot when he retires." I swallowed. "You think that's what will happen?"

My father shrugged noncommittally, already turning for the door, my mother on his heels. "We'll cross that bridge when we get to it. Anyway, I just wanted to check on you, but it seems like you're doing alright. Just... honor your promise to turn it around up there, okay?" He paused at the door, opening his arms. "Come give your old man a hug before you go out."

I crossed the room with heavy lead legs, hugging the man who had helped give me life like he was an acquaintance I was dropping off at an airport.

"Love you, kiddo," he said into my hair, placing a kiss there.

My heart squeezed, the young child inside me who had been Daddy's Little Girl longing for that connection again. But the woman who stood wrapped in that man's arms now knew his true colors.

Daddy's Little Girl would never exist again.

"Love you, too," I murmured.

Mom hugged me, too, before they were both gone, and as soon as they were, I jogged upstairs to get dressed and put on a fresh coat of makeup. Dad might have said every one of those words with a smile, but I read the threat beneath it all.

That was a warning to get my shit together before I lost the dream I hadn't even had the chance to unpack yet.

It was time to take the first step in turning it all around, just like I'd promised — starting with apologizing to Logan.

And I knew just where to find him.

# Chapter Six

**LOGAN**

"And then, I actually started to feel *sorry* for her," I said, gripping the tumbler of whiskey in my hand a little too tightly as I recounted the day's disaster to my older brothers. "She almost looked ready to cry, so I stepped in, took over the tour to get her out of the hot seat. And when I got back to the tour guide lobby, I was checking on her, asking if she was alright." I shook my head. "Of course, that was *before* Mac came in and ripped me a new asshole big enough to shit a brick out of."

Jordan chuckled. "Well, feeling bad for her doesn't make you an idiot. It makes you a good human being."

I made a noncommittal noise, taking a larger sip of whiskey than necessary just to feel the burn.

"She's a Scooter," Noah reminded me from the bar stool next to Jordan. "Does it really surprise you that she acted like a know-it-all asshole? I mean, isn't that like on her family crest or something?"

I sighed, not wanting to admit that I thought Mallory was more, that she was different. "I guess."

Jordan clapped me on the shoulder. "Don't sweat it, okay? So what, Mac got a little pissed. I know you hate conflict, but to be fair, that old man is always grumpy about something. He'll get over it, probably tonight, and things will move on."

"But I still have to train her," I reminded him. "And there's that whole thing about her most likely taking his job when he leaves."

Noah slammed his glass down. "If they give her that manager job that you've been lined up for for years, they're going to have an entire distillery full of people to explain their actions to. Everyone in that place *knows* you're the best tour guide. You have been for years. And she just started, for Christ's sake. And obviously doesn't even want to be there."

"But that's just the thing, they don't *have* to answer to anyone," Jordan chimed in.

"Yep. They own the place — literally." I sighed. "It doesn't matter if I'm the best. What matters is that if they want her to take that job, it's hers. Period."

Silence fell over us, long enough for me to take the last sip of my whiskey. I held the empty glass in my hands like it was a lifeline.

"Hey, we still don't know that that's what they have in mind," Noah said gently. "For all we know, they could just want her to be a part of the company, finally live up to the Scooter name she seems to have been running from all this time."

"Yeah, I don't think anything points to them making her manager. Not yet, at least," Jordan agreed.

"Nothing pointed to them murdering our father, either. But..." My voice trailed off, a sticky and uncomfortable knot forming in my throat at the words. Because the truth was, we didn't have proof that our father's death was the result of foul play — only suspicion. We knew our father didn't smoke, and that's what the fire was blamed on. We also knew he'd been causing waves on the board, and that Patrick didn't like it, so he'd shoved him into the founder's old office to sift through paperwork. And maybe those two things together didn't sound like enough to get suspicious over, but even if it couldn't be explained, we all felt it — my entire family — that something was off about that fire that took my father's life.

Jordan swallowed down the knot in his own throat, not commenting on what I'd said and choosing to try to comfort me, instead. "Just try to get through her training, and then you won't have to deal with her as much. She can do her tours, you do yours. You'll only have to see each other at meetings and at lunch. You can survive that."

I nodded, but didn't have a response. The truth was I may not have had a reason to believe they wanted her to be manager, but I had a gut feeling — and if Dad had taught me anything as a boy, it was to trust that.

Still, there was no point in dwelling on it now. If it was going to happen, it was going to happen — and I'd deal with it then.

For now, I was more upset at the shattering of the illusion of a girl I'd crushed on secretly for years — not that I could tell my brothers that. But seeing Mallory act the way she had — childish, combative, entitled — it was like a sign from God that there wasn't a woman out there who fit the image I had in mind for what I wanted in a partner.

Not that Mallory Scooter ever could have been *that* for me.

But she was a beacon of light, one that showed me there were gems out there, women who were different,

*heat*

unique, fascinating. There were women I could talk to about something other than the town gossip or the latest country song. There were women out there who didn't care what people thought, who danced to the beat of their own drum, who were *above* the bullshit.

That's what Mallory Scooter had been for me — hope.

And now, that hope had been reduced to ashes.

Maybe it was silly to put so much stock in her in the first place. Hell, I hadn't been around the girl in years. I didn't actually *know* her. I'd created this image of what I *thought* she was in my head and clung to it like a naïve teenage boy with a crush on a movie star.

Now, I'd seen the real human behind the image I'd painted.

Now, I knew the truth.

"Unrelated, but before this whole shit show went down, Mallory told me that Mikey threw his guitar into the bonfire at The Black Hole on Saturday night," I said, effectively changing the subject.

"He *what*?" Noah shook his head. "Dad bought him that guitar. He's had it forever."

"I know," I said. "Bailey fucked that kid up. *Bad.* Worse than I thought, for sure."

"He'll be okay," Jordan said — which was his response to practically everything. I swore nothing ever fazed him. The zombie apocalypse could be happening and he'd be cool, calm, and collected as he loaded his shot gun and assured everyone around him that everything was fine. "Besides, you'll never guess who came by Mom's earlier when I stopped by to bring her some groceries."

Noah and I exchanged looks before he spoke. "Bailey's back?"

"No, no," Jordan said quickly, then he smirked. "*Kylie.*"

"Ky?!" Noah and I asked simultaneously. I shook my head, recalling the girl who used to practically be a little sister to us. "They haven't hung out in a long time... like, since he and Bailey started dating."

"I know. I mean, I'm sure they talked at school and stuff, but maybe Bailey had a problem with them being so close?" Jordan shrugged. "I'm not sure, but she was there helping Mom with dinner when I showed up. Mikey was in his room, and when he did come out, he didn't seem any more cheerful than he has been. But... she was there."

"Hmm," Noah mused, circling the ice in his whiskey. "Well, if we can't pull him out of this slump, maybe she can. They were best friends before Bailey came along."

Jordan nodded. "I guess we'll see."

The jukebox cut out just as the local band that played almost every night at Buck's bar started their mic check, tuning their instruments and getting ready to play. Buck's was the only bar *in* town — though there were a few just outside of city limits on both the north and south sides. Still, it was the watering hole of Stratford, and even though it was a Monday night, the place was packed.

I stared at the empty glass in my hand, debating if I wanted another one. I was slightly buzzed, and part of me wanted to go home, watch the space documentary I'd bookmarked on Netflix and forget about the shitty day I'd had. But, the other part realized that the days of hanging with my brothers at a bar likely wouldn't last forever, and I was enjoying my time with them.

That thought won out, and I lifted my glass to signal to Buck that I was ready for another. As soon as my hand was in the air, another smaller, more delicate hand with black nail polish donning each nail was on top of it.

"Let me get this round."

I stiffened at the sound of her voice, face flat as I turned to look over my shoulder.

Mallory smiled, though it was a weak one — tinged with an apology she'd tried to give me earlier. Her platinum blonde hair was tied up in a messy bun that somehow looked perfectly designed, with little tendrils falling down to frame her face. Those cat eyes of hers were winged, her lips painted that dusty rose color I'd come to both love and loathe. The piercing in her septum moved a little as her smile widened.

"Please," she added.

Her eyes searched mine, and too many emotions warred inside me for me to decipher. I hated her. I wanted her. I needed her to leave. I longed for her to stay. The longer I watched her, the more I wondered if she could see right through me, if she could read every little thought.

Buck knocked on the bar, calling my attention back to him.

"Another?" he asked.

Buck was the owner of the little watering hole, his name painted on the brick outside. He wasn't just the bartender, though — he was everyone's friend, therapist, referee, and liquid pharmacist.

I nodded, sliding my glass toward him. "Scooter Signature. Neat." I tilted my head toward where Mallory stood behind me then. "Put it on her tab."

Buck lifted one thick, caterpillar eyebrow at Mallory. "Okay... and for you?"

"Gin and tonic, please."

He gave something close to a smile, still eyeing us like a Scooter and Becker together couldn't be trusted — he wasn't wrong — before he finally turned to make our drinks.

Jordan and Noah had been in their own side conversation, but I saw Noah nudge Jordan out of my peripheral, and they were both staring at Mallory now.

"Mallory, you know my brothers?" I leaned away from the bar so she could get a better view of them on the other side of me. "Jordan, Noah."

Mallory beamed, a smile bigger than I ever remembered seeing on her. "Of course. Hey, guys, how's it going?"

They murmured something that sounded like *fine*, offering strange smiles that did nothing to hide the fact that they were questioning why the hell she was here.

"I made an ass of myself and got your brother in trouble today," she explained. "Figured a drink or two might help make up for it."

Noah smiled a little more genuinely then, but Jordan's brows furrowed, and he offered nothing more before turning toward the shelves of alcohol behind the bar and sipping on his whiskey.

"How do you like working at the distillery so far?" Noah asked, aiming for amiability.

"It's... well, it's not what I expected." Mallory looked at me then. "I thought I knew what I was walking into, but I was wrong."

Noah nodded. "I'm not used to hearing those words come from a Scooter."

It was meant as a joke, but his voice didn't hide the fact that he was mostly serious with that statement.

Mallory chuckled. "No, I suppose you wouldn't be." Buck placed our fresh drinks on the bar in front of us, telling us to let him know if we needed anything else. Before I could take the first sip, Mallory grabbed both drinks in her hands and stood. "Play a round of pool with me?" she asked, her eyes pleading for a yes.

*neat*

Everything in my chest tightened — but not in the way it should have. I told myself it was because I didn't want to play pool with her, that I was annoyed she was here, that I hated her and was still furious for what she'd done.

The truth lay more somewhere around me being giddy at the prospect of getting some one-on-one time with her — *outside* of work.

I stood in lieu of an answer, which had her smiling again as she turned and made her way toward the free pool table in the back. I didn't dare glance over my shoulder at my brothers — who were no doubt watching us walk away — because I knew what I'd find.

Questions.

Concern.

Opposition.

And I didn't want to answer to any of it.

Mallory handed me my drink once we made it to the table, taking a sip of her own before she sat it down and started racking up the balls for us to play. She was silent for a long while, and I just watched her fill the triangle with stripes and solids, moving the balls around until she had the order she wanted.

"So, obviously I owe you an apology," she finally said, removing the triangle frame. She glanced at me through her lashes, stowing the frame away and grabbing a cue stick from the rack behind her. "You want to break?"

"Go ahead."

She nodded, chalking the tip before she lowered her chest toward the table, lining up the shot. She steadied her aim, sliding the wood between her fingers a few times before she fired the shot, sending the white cue ball down the green felt to bust up the balls at the other end. They scattered, landing one solid and one stripe in opposite side pockets.

"Stripes," she called, lining up for the next shot.

She missed, and when she was standing again and it was my turn, she leaned on her cue stick, picking up her drink for another sip.

"I *am* truly sorry for what happened today, Logan," she said as I picked out my own cue stick, chalking the tip. "I acted like a fool — like a know-it-all — and this is me eating crow. You were right, I was wrong. And I'm sorry I had to act out like that to learn the lesson." She paused. "I'm doubly sorry that I got you in trouble with my uncle."

I nodded, lining up my first shot. I sank the four ball in the corner pocket, finally looking at her as I rounded the table for the next shot. "Thank you."

Mallory smiled, and silence fell over us as I took the next few shots. When it was her turn again, she passed by where I stood against the wall, her arm brushing mine before she paused in front of me.

"I've been thinking," she said, voice a little lower now. "About what you said earlier. About me."

She was so close, just another inch and her chest would touch mine. Of course — the top of hers would hit the bottom of mine. She was at least a foot-and-a-half shorter than me.

I swallowed, looking down the bridge of my nose at her glowing eyes. "Yeah?"

"Yes," she answered. "I like that you think I'm different." Her eyebrows folded in. "Well, that you *thought* I was different. And I was hoping we could start over, that we could go back to when you thought I was this intriguing minx and not just the princess of Stratford — like everyone else in this town."

I smirked. "I never said I thought you were a minx."

"But you did," she fired back with a smirk of her own. Her eyes glowed a little fiercer then. "You still do."

I rolled my lips between my teeth, looking up at the ceiling like God himself was up there to help me resist this woman in some way. When I looked at her again, her smile had climbed, eyes dancing in the low light of the bar as she waited for my answer.

"We can start over," I told her, avoiding the minx assessment altogether.

She opened her mouth to respond just as the lead singer of the band came over the microphone to introduce himself and the rest of the crew. Mallory immediately cringed, plugging her ears with her fingers as she glanced up at the speaker that hung right above us.

We were both silent as the band talked on, and when they started playing, Mallory unplugged her ears, saying something I couldn't make out — no matter how hard I stared at her lips.

And trust me — I was staring.

"What?" I yelled over the music.

She said it again, but I shook my head, still not able to make it out.

Then, she grabbed the collar of my button-up plaid shirt and pulled my ear down to her lips. The soft, warm, velvet flesh of them brushed my ear lobe when she spoke.

"Wanna get out of here? Take a walk?"

Chills broke out over every inch of me — which thankfully was covered by the sleeves of my flannel shirt and the denim of my dark jeans. Mallory released my shirt, stepping back with a hopeful smile.

*Do not say yes.*

*Do not go on a walk with that girl.*

*Do not entertain whatever fantasy you have — not now, not ever.*

But I ignored every warning firing off in my head, nodding instead as I hung my cue stick on the rack and drained what was left of my whiskey. Mallory sucked her drink down, too, nodding toward the bathroom. "Just give me a minute," she screamed. "I'll meet you outside."

I nodded again, apparently speechless now that I'd agreed to leave Buck's bar with Mallory Scooter. When she was inside the bathroom, I made my way over to the bar stool I'd abandoned next to my brothers, tugging my jacket off the back of it.

"Where are you going?" Jordan asked.

"On a walk."

"Alone?" Noah probed.

"Why don't you mind your own business?"

Noah laughed, while Jordan's brows folded over his eyes so hard I didn't think he could see me when his hand caught the sleeve of my jacket in a fist.

"She's a Scooter," he reminded me. "Watch yourself."

"She just wants to apologize," I said, ripping my arm away from his grasp. "Besides, we work together. We need to get along."

Both of my older brothers watched me like I was a kid walking into a snake pit I didn't even realize was there. What they didn't know was that I *saw* the pit, I just didn't care.

Maybe the snakes weren't the venomous type.

Maybe they were garter snakes, like the ones Dad used to find in our yard all the time.

Neither of them offered another word, and neither did I. I slapped some cash down on the bar for Buck for the tab I'd run up before Mallory paid for my last drink, nodding a goodbye to him before I made my way toward the door. Mallory was just outside, and when I pushed through the door, she turned, smiling as a puff of white left her mouth with her first breath.

She was wrapped up in a black leather jacket and thick, burnt orange scarf. Her hands were in her pockets, eyes somehow different than they'd ever been before as she offered me a smile.

"Should I lead the way, or am I following you?"

**MALLORY**

Stratford was quiet, as it always was this late on a Monday night. Logan and I walked side by side, our steps in line, the only sound between us being the soft thumps of his boots on the sidewalk and the click-clacking from the heels of mine. Christmas lights were strung all along Main Street — curling up the light posts, adorning the limbs of each little naked tree, highlighting the storefront windows. Gold and garnet garland accompanied the lights on the posts, along with little signs that said things like *Merry Christmas* and *'Tis the Season.*

Even from where we walked at the north end of Main, you could see the lights from the big tree set up in our small town square at the south end of the main drag. That tree was erected every year on the Friday after Thanksgiving, Stratford residents always being more excited about seeing the ornaments and lights hung on that evergreen than they ever were about catching a Black Friday deal.

The holidays in this small town weren't just celebrated — they were honored like a sacred tradition.

I smiled, eyes trailing over the enthusiastic display the little boutique in town had put together in their storefront. It was like looking into a snow globe at the North Pole — complete with elves, Santa and Mrs. Claus, and all the reindeer.

"Do you like Christmas, Logan Becker?" I asked, pulling my gaze from the window back to the quiet man walking next to me. The same Scooter Whiskey Carhartt jacket he wore every day at work was warming him now, the hem of his blue and green flannel peeking out at the bottom. He wore an old baseball cap that I swore I'd seen him wear in high school, and his chestnut hair curled around the edges of it, giving him a young, boyish look.

A soft smile touched his lips, but he kept his gaze on the sidewalk. "Are you insinuating that I'm the Grinch?"

"No." I chuckled. "Although, now that you say it, I could see you painted green and slipping down chimneys to steal presents."

Logan glanced at me with a smirk before he let his gaze wander up and over my head, trailing the lights around us. "I used to love it," he said. "When I was younger. I always had this... I don't know, this indescribable feeling of excitement that would come over me around Thanksgiving. I remember putting up the tree with Dad, making cookies with Mom, wearing matching pajamas with all three of my brothers and watching all the classic Christmas cartoons on Christmas Eve." His eyes glistened under the lights, twinkling like stars. "I guess it's that Christmas Spirit everyone talks about. But... I haven't felt that in a long time." He frowned. "Honestly, Christmas just kind of floats by for me now. I see the decorations everywhere, I hear the songs, I see the movies on TV, but... it's just not the same. I don't feel it anymore."

"Since your Dad passed?"

His frown deepened on a nod.

We fell silent again, and I did the math in my head, trying to remember the details of an event the entire town was always trying to forget — my family, especially. There had only been one death at the Scooter Whiskey distillery — and it was John Becker. I was eighteen, and we had just graduated high school. Mr. Becker was at the ceremony, and died weeks later.

Logan was seventeen, I realized. I remembered he was always one of the young ones, and one of the only ones who couldn't join the senior ditch day when we went to Nashville to bar hop all the places that let you in at eighteen.

My heart lurched in my chest. I wasn't close with my parents — not my weak, spineless mother and certainly not my greedy, pretentious father — but even so, I couldn't imagine losing either one of them.

"What about you?" Logan asked when the silence had stretched into awkwardness. "Are you a Christmas fanatic, Mallory Scooter?"

I smiled a sour smile at the mention of my full name, a name I'd tried to escape my entire life, a name I realized I'd never be rid of.

"I'm not a fanatic about anything," I admitted. "Save for art. All those feelings you had around Christmas? I never experienced any of that. For me, Christmas meant Mom hosting lots of grown-up parties with the town's richest assholes, and Dad handing us gift cards of outrageous amounts on Christmas morning. Mom would decorate the house, but more for the town than for us kids. And I don't believe in the 'reason for the season', as they say." I shrugged. "But, I do love how magical it all can be, and I love to illustrate it, photograph it. Honestly, I was just thinking how this is the first time I've walked this town's streets and seen anything close to beauty. I kind of wish I had my camera with me."

"You're talking about me, aren't you?"

I scoffed. "I mean the *lights* are pretty." I paused. "I just never thought that before — not here, anyway."

We were quiet again, but I felt Logan watching me, his eyes dancing over my profile as I kept my gaze on the glowing Main Street tree in the distance.

"You seemed close with your family," he commented. "Until high school. It was like something switched over the summer between eighth and ninth grade, and you were a completely different person when you came back to school."

A chill rolled over me at the thought of that summer, but I smirked to hide it. "Everyone changes before high school," I commented. "I mean, you came back with muscles the size of my head."

"First you call me beautiful, now you're commenting on my muscles?" He tsked. "Feels like some real not-safe-for-work territory we're crossing into here, Minx."

I rolled my eyes, thinking the subject would change, but Logan still watched me, waiting.

"Let's just say I had an eye-opening experience that summer, one that showed me my family's true colors."

"And you didn't like them?"

I stopped walking, and Logan followed my lead, facing me in the middle of the sidewalk at the corner of Main and Ivy.

"Your entire family hates mine," I reminded him. "Is it really so hard to believe that I share the sentiment?"

The comment came out more of a bite than I intended, and Logan softened, his eyes searching mine.

"I'm sorry, I feel like I overstepped."

"It's okay," I assured him on a long exhale and a gentle shake of my head. "It's been a long day, as you well know. I think it might be time for me to get some sleep."

He nodded. "Yeah, I think that'd probably be best for both of us." I watched the thick Adam's apple in his throat bob on a swallow, and I wondered how I never realized how hot his neck was before.

*Wait — did I just think his* neck *was sexy?*

"Let me walk you home?" he asked.

I smiled. "Alright." We took three more steps, and I stopped again. "Welp, this is me. Thank you."

Logan's brows bent together, and he looked up at the last shop in the brick building behind me. I didn't have signage up yet, and when his gaze fell to the windows — to the empty space *inside* those windows — his eyes doubled in size.

"You live *here*?"

I chuckled. "I live upstairs, above the shop." Following his gaze, I smiled at the empty building behind me — a blank canvas — before I turned back to him with a beam of pride. "This is going to be my art studio — the first one in town."

"Wait, really?" He stepped past me, framing his eyes with his hands and pressing them to the windows to see more inside before he turned to face me again. "This is *yours*?"

"Mm-hmm. Well, *technically*, it's in my father's name for now... but we have a deal and..." I shook my head. "Anyway, yes — it's mine." I swallowed, not sure why my stomach sank to my feet when the next words rolled off my lips. "Want to see it?"

"Like, go inside?"

I nodded.

Logan smiled enough to show that little dimple in his left cheek, which somehow made my stomach flip even more. "I'd love that."

It was definitely the cold Tennessee night that had my hands trembling as I unlocked the doors. It was absolutely the fact that my leather jacket was more of a fashion statement than anything that could actually keep me warm. That's what I assured myself as the bolt unlocked and I pushed inside, Logan following close behind me.

It definitely *wasn't* because I was nervous, or because I hadn't shown my studio to anyone other than my parents and my best friend, and surely it wasn't because showing someone my naked studio felt a lot like showing them my naked body.

Which meant I was stripping down bare for Logan Becker.

I kept my jacket on, hoping it would calm my tremors as I pulled off to the side once we were in the studio, Logan walking past me, his eyes wide as he looked around the space. I tucked myself into the corner, as if I could hide, as if I could disappear and not watch him dissect the space.

*Does he hate it?*

*Is it stupid?*

*Is he thinking no one will ever pay to take classes here?*

*Is he thinking art is a waste of time, just like my father?*

I shouldn't have cared. I didn't *want* to care, but thoughts like those raced through my mind as I watched Logan from the corner of the room. He traveled the space quietly, slowly, eyes roaming, hands reaching out to trace the walls, the windows, the exposed brick on the back wall. Not much had changed since Chris was there on Saturday. We'd painted the walls, cleaned the brick, swept and mopped the tile floor, and cleaned out what was left in the back storage. Where it was a dusty blank slate before, at least now it was a clean one.

But it was still blank, and I wasn't sure anyone could see the vision except for me.

"Mallory..." Logan whispered, like speaking too loud in the space would disrupt it somehow. He stopped in the middle of the room, eyes scanning the ceiling before his gaze found me. "This is incredible."

I blew out a breath. "Really?"

"Are you kidding?" He smirked. "You have your own *art studio,* your own business. I'm so impressed." Logan shook his head, looking around again. "I can't wait to see what you do with it."

"Right?" I said, excitement bubbling over the anxiety as I pushed out of my corner and flew across the room. "I want it to be a multi-channel visual arts studio, with more than just one thing to offer. Like, over here, we'll have painting classes, with live models and still life and scenery inspiration, with all mediums — watercolor, oil, pastel, maybe even spray painting to jazz it up from time to time. And over here, sketch classes." I pointed to the far corner. "I want to transform that little office back there into a dark room to develop photographs, and do some walking tours around town where I can teach the photography essentials, help those who are interested in the art. Oh!" I skipped to the other side of the room. "And, over here, I thought I could put in an electric kiln, offer some pottery and ceramic classes. I think it'd be great for kids, and I could have more advanced classes for the adults — like vases and other things they'd love to decorate their homes with. And of course, I could host parties, do a sort of paint-by-numbers fun class like they do at those little drink and paint places in Nashville."

I whipped back around, smile nearly splitting my face — because though we were standing in an empty studio, it wasn't empty to me anymore. I could see it — *all* of it — every little picture I'd just painted verbally coming alive as if I'd dreamed it into reality in that dark space.

When my eyes found Logan again, he was watching me in a way I'd never been watched before. One brow was slightly quirked, his eyes wide and curious, the corner or his mouth lifted. It was like I was a street performer he'd just stumbled upon, like he was trying to figure out what I was doing, where the act was going, how much he should leave in my tip jar.

"What?" I asked, breathless.

His smile climbed. "I just love seeing people talk about what they're most passionate about," he said simply. "And I'm excited. For you, for this place. It's going to be great, Mallory."

I blushed, and as soon as I realized that was what was happening, that the heat in my cheeks was a visible sign of being a mixture of embarrassed and flattered, I wanted to slap myself — I probably *would* have, if that wouldn't have made me look like even more of a weirdo.

Suddenly, a dark figure scurried out from the back office, little legs carrying it straight toward me. But before I could bend to scratch behind Dalí's ear, Logan wrapped his arms around my waist, swinging me behind him and standing like a brick wall between me and the ball of fluff like it was a bear instead of a cat. One hand held me in place behind him as the other splayed in front of him, like a shield or a weapon.

If it wasn't somehow so fucking endearing that he was trying to protect me from something, I would have laughed.

"Wait!" I said, grabbing his shoulders to hold him back from killing my furry friend. "It's just Dalí."

Logan relaxed — though only marginally, and he still stood in front of me. "Who?"

I chuckled, releasing my grip on his shoulders as I made my way around him and bent to pick up the cat. "Dalí," I repeated. "He was a stray, and I adopted him. Thought he'd make a pretty cute shop cat."

Dalí croaked out an old meow when he was in my arms, his signature motorboat purr sparking to life. He was warm, like he'd been wrapped in a ball sleeping somewhere in the back, but I couldn't shake the fact that I missed another warmth I'd had just moments before.

Logan's body against mine, his hand on my waist...

"He is pretty cute," Logan said, relaxing even more now. He took a step toward us, reaching one finger under Dalí's chin to rub the patch of white there. Dalí leaned into the touch, which earned a chuckle from Logan and a smile from me.

When Dalí had enough petting for his liking, he wormed around in my arms until I lowered him back to the ground. He meowed once more before skipping off somewhere in the back, and then it was just Logan and me again.

His eyes bounced between mine. "Sorry I grabbed you," he said, reaching for the back of his neck with an embarrassed shrug. "Acting like a big bad knight in shining armor, protecting you from a *cat*."

I let out a soft laugh, folding my hands in front of me. "I appreciate the gesture. Glad to know I'd have some help if small, furry animals tried to overrun the shop."

Logan smirked.

"Anyway, thanks for indulging me," I said on an awkward laugh, covering my face when I remembered how I'd pranced around the empty shop like an idiot as

I explained my vision for what it would become. I let my hands fall to my thighs with a slap, letting out a long breath. "It really has been a long day."

He straightened at that, his face leveling. "Yeah, let me get out of your hair, let you get some sleep," he said, his feet moving toward the door — toward me. He stopped with just a foot between us, and I felt that distance like it was a live wire, buzzing and sparking and warning of danger. "But, thank you for showing me... and for the apology for today."

I flushed again.

*Stupid traitorous cheeks.*

"Thank you for forgiving me," I replied. "And for letting us start over, so I can show you I'm not a *complete* brat."

"Just a somewhat brat."

"Right."

He smiled. "I'm looking forward to the new beginning."

"Me, too."

Logan stood there a moment longer, eyes flicking back and forth between mine, and if it wasn't so dark in the shop, I would have sworn I saw those hazel wells fall to my lips before he finally stepped away.

"Goodnight, Mallory Scooter."

And with that, he was gone — as was the man I thought he was before that night.

# Chapter Seven

## LOGAN

When I wasn't having dinner at Mom's or going out to the bar with my brothers, my normal night routine went like this:

Make a protein shake. Read the newspaper while I drank said protein shake, followed by a thirty-minute, high-intensity workout that mostly involved calisthenics in my back yard, and thirty minutes of yoga and meditation. Then, I'd shower, shave, and cook dinner — which was the same thing every night — chicken breast, baby carrots, zucchini, and squash — all baked in the same seasoning in the oven at three-hundred-and-fifty degrees for one hour. I ate at my small dining table alone, without the television on and without looking at a screen of any kind. After dinner, I either picked up the book I was currently reading — which almost always was a historical biography or a psychological thriller of some kind — or, on the nights I was feeling lazy, I'd plop down on the couch and indulge in a documentary.

Tonight, I wasn't necessarily in the *lazy* category, but I was very firmly in the *distracted* one — therefore, reading had proven nearly impossible and I was on the couch, trying (and failing) to watch the space documentary I'd been wanting to watch for weeks. Still, even though I was very interested in Apollo 11 and the countless people and thousands of hours that went into getting the first man on the moon, I couldn't focus long enough to actually learn anything. Instead, I watched the television as if from a distance, with the words jumbling together, the images blurred.

My workout — which usually got me out of my head for a while — seemed more difficult than usual tonight because I couldn't clear my head, couldn't submit to my body and just let it do the work for a while. I couldn't relax enough to successfully meditate, couldn't shower or cook or eat or do *anything* without all my thoughts drifting back to one thing.

To one *person*.

Mallory Scooter.

It'd been more than a week since our walk down Main Street, the Christmas lights glowing around us as the girl I'd always been curious about showed me a little more of who she was. I could still close my eyes and see the excitement on her face as she bounced around her empty art studio, showing me where things would be, illustrating her vision so clearly that I could see it, too.

It was a new beginning, a restart — and I'd found that it also might have been a mistake.

The next day at the distillery, we'd established a new sort of friendship. She was more serious about her training, and insisted on starting over — including getting another solo tour with me where I described all the points of interest on the tour we gave to guests before she even agreed to shadow me again. The rest of the week, she'd followed all my tours, bringing up the back and taking notes as we went along. By Friday, she was chiming in from time to time, telling our guests little stories about her grandfather or dad that I didn't know.

And we were getting along.

Gone was the combative girl who seemed hell bent on making my job training her miserable. She was replaced with someone determined to learn, determined to get along with everyone, determined to succeed in her role. I wasn't sure if it was Mac chewing us out that had changed her mind, or if her father had come down on her, or if maybe — just maybe — it was that she really did feel bad for what happened and she wanted to make it up to me. Whatever the reason, Mallory Scooter and I were finally getting along, and falling into a groove I never would have guessed we could find.

The problem was that the more time I spent with her, the more she drifted from hating me to tolerating me — the more I wanted to be around her.

I found myself making excuses to have lunch with her — even though I'd assigned her a different lunch buddy each day to help her get to know more people at the distillery. I'd somehow always be there, at the same table, inserting myself in their conversation so I could hang out with her. She always shadowed *my* tours — even though I could have easily assigned her to other tour guides — and after the last tour was done, I was always finding some reason to keep her around in my office a little longer.

And now, she'd invaded my thoughts *after* I clocked out, too.

I couldn't stop thinking about her studio, about the fact that she'd struck up some deal with her father that she didn't seem too keen to talk about. I wondered if *that* was why she was at the distillery — if he'd agreed to buy the studio for her in exchange for her working at the distillery. It seemed contradictory, but at the same time, I knew Patrick had wanted Mallory to be a part of the family legacy for years, and she'd always been absent.

Maybe this was his way of exerting power over her.

I wanted to know more, wanted to know what she'd decided not to tell me that night. I also wanted to see her art — her drawings, her photographs, the pottery brought to life by her hands. Sometimes, she'd walk into the distillery with paint on her jeans or a smatter of clay on her cheek, and I was so desperate to know what she created, what inspired her, what she brought to life.

I wanted to hate her. And if I'd left things alone after that day she'd gotten us in trouble — I think I could have. But no, she had to apologize, and she had to take me on that walk, and she had to remind me why I had always felt some magnetic attraction toward her.

Mallory Scooter was unlike any woman I knew, and I couldn't shake her from my thoughts.

I sighed when I realized I'd zoned out — again — thus missing the part of the documentary I'd rewinded to twice now because I couldn't focus. I clicked the television off with a huff, resting my elbows on my knees as I looked around my small living room.

My house wasn't much, but it was perfect for me. I'd embraced the minimalist life as soon as I'd moved out of Mom's, opting for an old farm house built in the late eighteen-hundreds on the northeast side of town. I was about five minutes farther out than Mom, which made it easy to get to her and yet still far enough away from town that I had peace and quiet.

I'd done my best to fix up what I could when I moved in, keep the original wood and structure alive and well.

Everything that existed in that little home had a purpose, and there wasn't anything unnecessary — no décor, no expensive rugs or plants or pieces of art, no furniture that served more than a person or two. My home wasn't made to entertain, it was made to live in.

My books had a home on the two shelves I'd built against the wall where the largest window was, the one that gave me a great view into my front yard and a way to see any cars coming down my long, dirt driveway. There was a television, a two-seat love sofa — where I sat now, and a coffee table that Dad and I had built at my camp's father-son day when I was younger. There were a few family photos on the wall near the front door, and between the kitchen and the living room was a small dining table that sat four people max. The kitchen was small, too — with older appliances that barely got the job done anymore. I knew I'd have to upgrade them soon, but fought against it as long as I could. And in the bedroom was a simple bed frame, box spring, and mattress — plus one bedside table that was home to whatever book I was reading each night before I turned out the lights to sleep.

There were no curtains, no embellishments, no frills. It was a home, a place to live.

And it was *always* clean.

I'd been accused of being a neat freak my entire life — mostly by my brothers. Still, I didn't realize the full extent of my need to have everything in order and tidy until I moved out on my own. At Mom's, I'd had no say in décor or organization other than what lived inside the four walls of my bedroom.

But here, everything was mine.

And it was always, *always* clean.

Another minute or two passed with me looking around, and my eyes caught on my bookshelf, remembering how

Mallory had teased me about the organization of the one in my office. The one at home was the same — organized by book height, color, and author last name.

I wondered if she'd started reading the book I'd loaned her.

*You could always text her to find out...*

I shook the thought off, leaning back into the couch on a sigh. But the longer I sat there, the more the idea sounded like a good one.

It wouldn't be *weird* to text her, I convinced myself. We were friends.

Ish.

We worked together, and we were friend-*ly*. There was nothing that said I couldn't text her, ask her about the book, see if she was ready for her first tour tomorrow.

Well, her first tour since the disaster one she'd had last week.

She was actually ready this time, and I'd be shadowing her first thing in the morning. Hell, I kind of owed it to her as her supervisor, didn't I? To check in and make sure she was ready?

I chewed my lip, considering it for all of two seconds before my phone was in my hands, fingers flying over the screen.

Me: *So, are you ready for your first tour tomorrow?*

Me: *Don't forget to wear an actual shirt this time.*

I smirked at the second text I sent, and before I could lock my screen and go do something to fill my time until she answered, I saw the bouncing dots that told me she was typing back.

> Mallory: *Ha, ha. I have my outfit planned out —*
> *full shirt and all, thank you very much.*

> Mallory: *Are YOU ready to lose your job after*
> *they realize what a kick ass tour guide I am?*

My smile fell, along with the food still digesting in my stomach. She'd meant it as a joke, I knew that, but the sickening reality that it could actually happen made it impossible to laugh.

> Me: *We'll see. You might be so distracted by the*
> *hot guy in the back that you forget your lines.*

> Mallory: *Ooooh, who's the guy? Do I know him?*
> *;)*

> Me: *You know his favorite book. Have you*
> *started reading that, by the way?*

> Mallory: *I have. So far, no crying. You better*
> *pray it stays that way, or else.*

I smiled, laying my phone back down on the coffee table before I decided to try the documentary again. Maybe now that I'd talked to her, I could focus a little more.

Before I hit play, my phone lit up again.

> Mallory: *By the way, if you want to text me, you*
> *don't have to make up a work excuse to do so.*

A jolt of anxiety danced with one of excitement low in my gut at her words, and I read them over and over, fingers hovering over the keys as I tried to think of what to say. I toyed with something close to a joke, trying to feign innocence and pure professionalism, but she texted again before I had the chance.

Mallory: *Goodnight, Logan Becker. ;)*

I smiled, shaking my head as I leaned back on the couch.

*She really is a little minx.*

I sent a goodnight text of my own, avoiding the fact that she'd called me out on my lame attempt at finding an excuse to text her. Then, I started the documentary again.

So I could not watch it for the third time as I tried to decipher what that winky face emoji meant, instead.

## MALLORY

"And just like that, the title of Best Scooter Whiskey Tour Guide has officially been stolen," I said, peeling my jacket off and laying it over the back of the chair in Logan's office before I plopped down into it. "Boom."

I was still making the bomb explosion gesture of awesomeness with my hands when Logan closed his office door and rounded his desk, shrugging his own coat off. "I have to admit, that was a pretty great tour."

"*Great*?" I asked, incredulous. "That was *fan-fucking-tastic*. I wouldn't be surprised if Mac doesn't burst through that door soon and tell us we got twenty-five new Yelp reviews — all five stars."

*neat*

"I'm sure that group of young bucks from the University of Michigan would give you ten stars."

I snorted. "Still wouldn't give them a chance in hell — although the tall one did sneak me his number when he gave me his tip at the end."

"I'm sure that's not the *only* tip he'd like to give you."

Logan waggled his brows as my jaw flopped open, and I reached across the desk, smacking his arm.

"Pig!" I laughed, leaning back in my chair and folding my hands behind my head like a boss. "But see, they loved me because I have tits. The rest of the group loved me because I was charming, and witty, and I had stories galore." I quirked a brow. "Admit it — that wasn't bad for a rookie."

Logan watched me with the left side of his lips quirked, that dimple making a brief appearance before it was gone again. "You killed it. Although, I was impressed as soon as you introduced yourself. I knew it was going to be a good tour."

"Really? How?"

"Because you actually wore a shirt, and you didn't have any gum."

I stuck my tongue out at him, which earned me a chuckle.

"What *is* it with you and that gum, anyway?" Logan asked, cringing. "I swear, I was two seconds away from holding my hand out like a mom and demanding you spit it into my palm the first day you came into this office."

I laughed. "Well, let's just say I traded in one bad habit for another." I held up both hands like a scale. "Quit smoking, start chewing gum like a sixteen-year-old asshole."

"At least you *admit* the asshole part."

"Say what you want, Becker. Nothing can bring me down." I fished inside the pocket of my jacket hanging on the chair, pulling out a wad of cash. "*Especially* not after getting this much in tips."

"Just wait until you get assigned to a tour of rich businessmen from some tech company in California or some brokerage in New York. The other female tour guides get five-hundred bucks *easy* on those ones."

I blanched. "Maybe I should forget my shirt for that one."

We broke out in a fit of laughter, but the noise died quickly when Logan's office door flew open, the handle hitting the wall so hard it rattled the room and surely left a dent. I jumped — out of my chair, nearly out of my *skin* — as Mac steamrolled his way into the office, face red and blotchy, breathing like a dragon again.

*Uh-oh...*

"Please, tell me what is so goddamn funny, because I could use a laugh after the shit storm you two just dropped on my desk."

Logan and I were both shocked silent, and we exchanged a glance before Logan cleared his throat. "Sir?"

"*Sir?*" Mac mocked him, slamming his phone down on the desk in front of Logan. "Thirty years. Thirty years we've been giving tours, and not once has a video been leaked. Not *once* has our most precious process been exploited to the public. Until today."

Logan's face was sheet white as he watched whatever was on that phone screen, and he swallowed a lump, not even looking at me before he slid the phone across the desk so I could see.

It was a video — one taken in the warehouse where the boys were raising barrels. What was worse, you could hear me in the background, explaining the entire process as whoever it was that snapped the video got a close up of the machinery we used, of the way Noah was arranging the staves, of *everything*.

"Mac, I—"

"It's my fault," Logan said before I could get another word out. He stood, meeting Mac's eyes. "I wasn't paying attention, I didn't realize the phone was out."

"Nor did you explain to *anyone* in that tour that there was no photography allowed in that part of the tour — as this little shit has repeatedly told me since he tagged us in the video and I've been private messaging him trying to get it taken down." Mac turned his glare on me next. "I knew it was a bad idea when your father told me you were going to work here. If you don't want any part of this company, fine — but don't try to take it down in a fire while you're here."

I narrowed my eyes, standing so I could look my uncle in the eyes, too. "I didn't do this on purpose," I defended. "And, besides — it's on our fucking *website* that we make our own barrels. And anyone who takes the tour can easily write up what we tell them about the process. It's not like it's a secret, or like we gave away any information that they couldn't find on Google."

"The reason we don't allow photos or videos is because they may know that we make our own barrels, but they don't know *how*. They don't know the products we use, the methods, the charring. This barrel process and our natural spring are the only things setting our whiskey apart from the competition — and you just gave one piece of that secret recipe away."

I had to clench my jaw to keep my mouth shut — mostly because Logan was giving me a warning look from behind Mac.

"It won't happen again, sir," Logan said, drawing Mac's attention back to him. "I'll make sure of it."

"Your damn straight it won't happen again, because until further notice, you're both suspended from giving tours."

"What?!" we both exclaimed, Logan taking a step toward Mac with the word.

Mac put his hand up, both as a note to Logan to stop where he stood and to signal that he was done with the conversation.

"I don't want to hear another word," he said, still fuming as he eyed us both down. "Now, I'm going to go do as much damage control as I can do and try to get this little fucker's video down before someone who actually matters sees it. In the meantime, you two are excused." He turned toward the office door, pausing at the frame. "And tomorrow, I'll have a new assignment for you."

"*Assignment?*" I asked.

"We're cleaning out the big storage closet, archiving what we need to keep and trashing the rest so we can make room for this year's files once the New Year passes." He gave us both a condescending grin. "I'm sure a little time in that dusty closet will be punishment enough for the two of you while I clean up your mess."

He turned and left at that, leaving Logan and me alone again, and I closed my eyes on a sigh.

*Fuck.*

It was *my* fault that video had been taken. Mac was right — I'd forgotten to tell them no photos or videos were allowed in that room, and I hadn't *seen* anyone filming — but they had. And now, I'd gotten Logan in trouble.

*Again.*

*heat*

Here he was trying to get promoted, and was doing a fine job of getting himself there before I showed up and ruined it all. I'd landed him at the top of Mac's shit list.

And worse, I'd gotten him suspended from giving tours.

I turned, opening my eyes but keeping my gaze on my shoes. "Logan, I am so—"

But before I could get the words out, Logan zipped past me, shoving one arm in the sleeve of his coat before the other.

"Where are you going?"

"You heard Mac," he said, not looking at me. "We're excused for the day."

"So, where are you going?"

"Buck's."

He was already out the door, but I chased after him, offering awkward smiles to the other tour guides who watched us like hawks on our way out. When we were in the hallway, I grabbed his sleeve, forcing him to stop.

"Logan, I'm sorry. I'm so sorry. I'll talk to him, I'll—"

"It's *fine*, Mallory," he bit out, his gaze hard. "Please, just leave it alone. Mac isn't going to change his mind."

I swallowed, nodding as I released his sleeve.

"I really am sorry," I whispered.

Logan nodded, but didn't say a word before he turned, making his way toward the door at the end of the hall that led to the employee parking lot. I watched him go, feet glued to the floor, knowing that a glass of whiskey and a game of pool wouldn't fix what I'd done this time.

When the metal door slammed behind him, I let out a long sigh.

*So much for starting over.*

# Chapter Eight

## LOGAN

The hot coffee in my left hand did little to sooth the pounding of my head as I walked through the distillery halls the next morning. I sipped it anyway, hoping it could somehow erase the absurd amount of whiskey I'd consumed the night before. Going to Buck's to drown out what had happened with Mac seemed logical when I'd decided to do it, but hindsight reminded me that a Thursday night was *not* a Friday night, and reporting for work the day after drinking wasn't as easy as it had been when I was twenty-two.

The hot coffee in my *right* hand was for Mallory, but just like the one in my left, it did little to soothe my anxiety as I made my way toward the office. I knew she'd be there — even though I was early and she wasn't expected to be in for another hour. I knew, because I saw it on her face when I'd stormed out the day before.

She was sorry, and she felt bad for what had happened.

Which in turn made *me* feel like a bag of shit, because it wasn't her fault. What happened could have happened to any new tour guide, and in reality, it was more a reflection of *me* than it was of her. I'd been giving tours for years. I was the Lead Tour Guide. If anyone should have realized we didn't tell that group that there were no photos allowed, it should have been me.

And I didn't.

Because I was distracted.

I sighed, shaking my head at my own stupidity as I pushed through the door that led to the guide lobby. No one was in yet, not even Mac, so the lobby was empty.

But there was a blonde mess of hair in my office.

Her back was to me as she waited in the same chair she'd been in yesterday when Mac rushed into the office, her attention fixed on the swinging Newton's Cradle on my desk. I wondered if she'd left at all, if she'd slept, if she'd let go of what happened or if she'd simmered on it all night like I did.

When I rounded my desk and saw the bags under her eyes, I got my answer.

Mallory looked up at me like a little girl who got caught eating a cookie before dinner. She sat on her hands, her brows furrowed, eyes watching mine as I took a seat in my chair across from her. I could tell she wanted to speak, she wanted to apologize again, but I spoke before she had the chance.

"Mallory, I'm sorry for how I acted yesterday."

"No," she said, immediately shaking her head. "It was my fault. And you had every right to be pissed — to *still* be pissed. I am so sorry I fucked up... *again*."

I smirked. "You didn't fuck up. It could have happened to any new guide, and truthfully, it was on *me* to point that out if you missed it. I knew better — you didn't."

"But I *did*," she argued, shaking her head. "I asked you to start over last week, and then the first chance I get to show you that I'm serious now, that I care, I go and make the worst mistake I possibly could have."

I chuckled at that. "Mallory, it was a video of some stupid barrels being made — not a terrorist attack."

She smiled as much as she could, but it fell quickly, her eyes on my desk.

"It's okay — really. Mac made a bigger deal out of it than necessary. The video is down, and nothing proprietary was leaked. If it was really *that* top secret, they wouldn't let us take tours through there at all. Right?"

She tilted her head a bit at that. "I guess that's a good point."

I nodded, sliding the coffee I'd brought for her across the desk. "Here. A peace offering. So we can stop arguing about who was wrong and whose fault it is and focus on today's tasks. Deal?"

Mallory sighed, like she wanted to keep arguing and apologizing rather than accept my offer. It was kind of adorable, seeing the woman who'd given me so much hell look so upset that she'd let me down. And truthfully — *she* hadn't. It'd been my own damn self that had let me down.

Regardless of whose fault it was, the whole thing was in our past — and that's where I wanted to keep it. The sooner we got the storage closet cleaned out, the sooner we could both get back to tours.

I edged the coffee a little closer, waggling my brows. "It's mochaaa," I sang.

After a long pause, she reached forward for the cup with a long sigh, wrapping her hands around it. She nodded once, smiling a little more genuinely now, her shoulders visibly relaxing.

"Okay," she finally said. "Deal."

*neat*

"Where do we even start?" Mallory asked, squinting through the dusty fluorescent light of the oversized storage closet. She hung her hands on her hips, surveying the mountainous stacks of file boxes and plastic storage containers that lined every single wall and filled three rows in the middle.

I followed her gaze with my own sigh. "I guess we pick a corner and go from there."

"And we're supposed to decide what's worth keeping and archiving, and what we can pitch?" She wrinkled her nose. "I feel like this is a job for a secretary who's been here for a long time and knows more about this stuff."

I tapped the printed list on top of my clipboard. "Lucy gave us a guide to go by, with a list of what to keep and what to pitch," I said, referencing the closest thing to a secretary the distillery had. Lucy sat in the front lobby, greeting guests and getting them ready for their tours, as well as handling all the admin tasks for our officers in her down time. "She said if we had any questions to call her or stop by the front desk."

Mallory shook her head, still not convinced, before pulling the highest box she could reach from the corner stack. "This sucks."

I chuckled. "It does, but hey," I offered, pulling my Bluetooth speaker from my backpack and propping it on one of the middle rows of boxes. "At least we have music."

I hit play on one of my go-to playlists on my phone, the familiar sound of "Fever" by The Black Keys filling the closet. Mallory paused where she was opening the first box, brows popping up into her hairline as she assessed me.

"*You* listen to The Black Keys?" she asked.

I shrugged. "Why is that hard to believe?"

"I don't know, I just took you for more of a country boy... you know, George Strait and the like."

"George Strait is the fucking man," I said, grabbing a box of my own off the stack she'd started on. "But so is Dan Auerbach."

She smirked, amusement dancing in her eyes as she assessed me. She took a step toward me, then another, and I hadn't noticed how small that closet felt until her chest was nearly touching mine.

"I couldn't agree more," she said, reaching behind me and turning up the volume on the speaker.

She backed away then, mouthing the words and moving her hips to the beat. My gaze fell to those hips, watching them sway like a hypnotizing pendulum. With her arms up over her head, a sliver of her toned stomach peeked out from under the Scooter Whiskey polo she wore, and I couldn't tear my eyes away from that stripe of bronze skin.

Not until her arms dropped, the sliver disappearing, and when I looked up, she was watching me with an even more amused smile.

"Let's get started, shall we?"

I swallowed, murmuring something close to a *yeah* before I turned and opened the box I'd pulled down from the stack. Mallory chuckled from behind me, but I didn't dare look back — not with my cheeks as hot as they were. I just bobbed my head along to the music, pulling the first file from the box.

And then we got to work.

As the morning stretched between us, it became overtly clear to me just how different Mallory and I were.

Where she was huffing with each new box she opened, and sighing with each file she slapped down on the archive pile, and groaning when she came across something she couldn't decipher easily whether to keep or toss — I was in my own version of organizational heaven. The music helped me zone out, and I hummed or sang along to each new song as I filtered through the boxes, making neat piles, labeling anything that didn't already have an identifier, organizing by color and size so I could figure out the exact best way to re-pack it all in the end.

It was definitely a punishment for her, but as much as I wanted to be outside giving a tour, our task was something close to therapy for me.

I was still in the zone, flipping through some photographs from the Scooter Whiskey Single Barrel Soirée of 2004 when Mallory let out a larger sigh than usual, turning the music down a little and flopping down on the floor. She leaned her back against a stack of boxes, looking up at me with a pout.

"Can we take a break?"

I chuckled. "You can. I'm in a rhythm."

I wrote on a lime green label with Sharpie, sticking it to the folder of photos and placing it on top of the other files of photos I'd found that morning. I glanced at Mallory before I grabbed the next file in the box, and she smiled.

"God, you *love* this, don't you?" She shook her head. "I'm over here watching the minutes tick by like years and you're geeking out over putting everything in its place."

I smiled, peeking down at her before I flipped the new file open in my hands. "I can't help it. I've always been this way," I said. "There's just something so satisfying about putting things in order, giving them a place."

"You'd freak out if you saw the shop right now," she said, crossing one leg over the other. "There's not a corner of that previously empty space that's not covered with shit right now. I'm trying to set everything up, separate the room like I told you I envisioned. And Chris tried to help, but..."

"Chris has a different vision, I'd wager?"

She made a noise. "That's one way to put it. I mean, you know Chris — he'd have that place covered in glitter if I let him have his way."

I chuckled, because I *did* know Chris — at least, I knew him back when we were younger. He was the first person I'd ever known to come out, and the only one in our high school at the time. I didn't hang out with him, and didn't know him personally, but I remembered talking to Dad about it the day Chris told everyone he was gay.

I was confused, mostly because all the other guys in our school were being dicks to him suddenly — although he was the same guy he'd been the day before, when everyone adored him. Chris was the captain of the JV soccer team. He was on student council. He was hilarious, and was always surrounded by a huge group of friends who loved to watch him, to let him entertain them.

And it all changed overnight.

I could still remember Dad's furrowed brows as he listened to me, the calmness in his voice as he explained to me that people didn't understand people who weren't like them, and so they lashed out, afraid of the unknown. He told me not to be like them, not to run from what I don't understand, but to embrace it, instead.

And the last, most important thing, he told me was that I needed to be ready to stand up to those guys at school should they pull any shit with Chris.

Luckily, Chris proved that he could hold his own over the years, but he had a silent ally who watched his back from a far — just in case.

"It's my own fault," Mallory continued on a sigh. "I shouldn't have ordered everything at once. I don't even know where to start."

"Maybe I could help you," I offered — a little too quickly. My eyes darted to hers before I turned my attention back to the file in my hands, aiming for nonchalant as I shrugged. "I mean, if you want an extra hand. I could come by sometime this weekend, help you sort through it all."

"You'd give up your weekend to sort through the pile of crap in my art studio?" she questioned. "Come on now, I can't take you away from your hot dates."

I scoffed. "The only hot date I have this weekend is with a Nat Geo documentary on Sunday night."

She hummed a soft laugh. "That so? I've been wondering what you do outside of this place," she said, motioning to the closet around us. Her eyes skated over the mountain of boxes we had yet to get to before they found mine. "What's the documentary about?"

I scratched the back of my neck, murmuring a reply into my chest before tossing the file in my hand in the trash box and picking up the next.

"What was that?"

I sighed. "It's called *Creatures of Light Underwater*," I said, loud enough that she could actually hear this time. "And I know what you're thinking, but it actually looks really cool. It's all this new footage put together by deep sea scientists who are finally able to get deep enough to capture some of the wildest displays of light from species that live in pitch black water. No external light reaches that far down, yet they *create* light — to mate, to capture their prey, whatever."

Mallory bit back a smirk, shrugging and putting her hands up. "Hey, I didn't say a word."

"You were thinking of some, I'm sure."

"No, seriously. Zero judgment. If anything, I'm excited to see *you* so excited about something." She tilted her head. "So, you get off on biology, huh?"

I shrugged. "I guess. I just love learning, in general. That's why I like to read — to learn something new that I didn't know before. And I love watching documentaries, mostly because there's no acting or anything fake about it. There are so many fascinating stories that are *true*, that have real footage. It's incredible." I laughed through my nose. "Plus, I've lived in the same town my entire life and never traveled out of the state. It's nice to go places — to learn about other people, other cultures, other ways of life."

Mallory watched me for a long time without saying anything — so long that I peered down at her, and another shade of embarrassment tinged my cheeks when I found curiosity dancing in those blue eyes of hers.

"What?"

She shook her head. "Nothing. You just surprise me, that's all."

"Because I'm a nerd who listens to rock music?"

"No," she said easily. "Because you're smarter than you let on. And you're cool."

I snorted, deciding to make a joke rather than admit what her words did to my stomach. "If me geeking out over glowing fish is cool, don't get me started about my love for space."

Mallory laughed, tucking her feet closer and balancing her chin on her knees as she hummed along to the new song that had just come on. I eyed her from my peripheral, still flipping through the old training documents in the box I was working on, even though my attention was on her. I traced the black lines shaping her eyes, the long wisps of her lashes, the platinum strands of hair that had fallen from her ponytail and lined the edges of her jaw. I had the sudden urge to see her without makeup, to study the curves of her cheeks without them being covered with blush, or to look into her eyes without the tips of them being painted black, or to see the color of her nude lips, to feel them without smudging a line of lipstick...

To taste them.

That last thought zapped me out of my trance, and I cleared my throat, moving on to the next box in the stack. It was the one that had been buried on the bottom in the very back corner of the room, and it was extra dusty as I plopped it on the table in front of me.

I waved away the cloud, squinting. "Did it hurt?"

"When I fell from heaven?" Mallory snickered. "Come on, Logan. You've got better lines than that."

I chuckled. "No, I meant *that*," I said, motioning to the ring hanging from her nose. I pinched the septum of mine to illustrate. "I feel like that had to be painful."

Mallory reached up, fingering the diamonds that lined the bottom of the ring and shaped her too-perfect nose. It was ridiculous, really, that I noticed her fucking nose — but I did. It was perfectly sized for her face, the tip of it rounded like a little button, and that ring she wore only called my attention to it more.

"A little," she admitted. "But then again, I was eighteen and on a mission to piss off my parents. It could have felt like childbirth and I still wouldn't have backed down."

I cocked a brow. "You got that pierced to prove a point to your parents?"

"No, I did it because I liked it and I wanted to," she said, but the corner of her mouth lifted. "Driving my father insane was just a perk."

"I'm sure he loved the tattoos, too."

"Oh, the one on my lower back is his *favorite*."

I laughed, peeling the top off the dusty box. "Why were you so hell bent on pissing them off?"

A long sigh left her lips. "That's a very long story, and one that would require libations. Maybe—" Her words died mid-sentence. "Logan? What's wrong?"

I wanted to say *nothing*.

I wanted to shake my head, laugh it off, tell her to continue with her story.

I wanted to put the lid back on the box in front of me and pretend I'd never opened it and seen what was inside.

But I couldn't.

All I could do was stand there, gaping at the charred remnants of the most horrible day in all my life.

The box had been unlabeled — and now that I saw what was inside it, I knew why. It was a box not meant to be found, one not meant to be dug through. Black soot lined the edges of it, and the items that filled it looked like someone had cleaned out their desk after being fired, ready to make the walk of shame through the halls to their car with everything that had decorated their office loaded into a box.

The photo frame that sat on top was busted — the glass broken, the silver frame mostly black now, and the photo seared and water damaged. Only one little inch of it remained clear enough to make out.

It was my oldest brother's face — his smile, one sparked by the joke Dad had told us just before the photo was snapped.

I swallowed, gripping the edges of the folding table the box was on to keep myself from stumbling backward or passing out. All the blood drained from my face, from my neck, from every vein in my body.

"It's my Dad's stuff."

The words were barely out of my mouth before Mallory scrambled up from where she was sitting on the floor, peering into the box with me. "What?!"

I nodded numbly. "That... that's Jordan," I said, swallowing the lump in my throat as I pointed to what was left of the photo. "He had this picture on his desk. It was from our fishing trip the summer before he died."

"Jesus..." she murmured, reaching inside the box to retrieve the frame. She held it as delicately as she could, but already, her fingers were covered in black. She pulled the frame close to her eyes, studying it, and I watched her eyes trace the photo before they found mine again. "Logan, wasn't there an investigation done that day?"

I nodded, every movement slow and distant, like I was submerged under icy water just seconds from passing out.

"Wouldn't this have been evidence?" she asked, pulling the next charred item out of the box. Bits of ashes fell off the once-gold paperweight, now mostly black. It was one my mom gave him for Christmas, engraved with his favorite Colin Powell quote.

*There are no secrets to success. It is the result of preparation, hard work, and learning from failure.*

I couldn't speak. I just stared at the weight in her hands as Mallory stared at me.

"Logan?"

I blinked. "I don't know. Maybe they didn't think it was relevant."

"Maybe," she agreed, thumbing the small part of the quote that peeked through the grime. "But, if it wasn't relevant to the fire department or the police... then why did someone keep it?"

We shared a look then, and my heart kicked back to life in my chest, thundering hard in my ears as my hands dug into the box. One by one, I pulled out each item in that box — what was *left* of each item, anyway — until I got to the very bottom and retrieved a thick, heavy, dated and familiar rectangle that I never thought I'd see again.

Mallory gasped. "Is that..."

"His laptop," I finished for her, swallowing as I carefully sat it on the table. "Yes."

For a while, we both just stared at it, but then Mallory rounded the table to stand on the same side as me. She reached forward, carefully flipping the monitor of the laptop up to reveal the damage inside.

The screen was shattered and covered with a thick, black gunk, and what was left of the keyboard was melted and warped, revealing the plates and wires that made everything work underneath.

Mallory peered inside the box again. "Is there a power cord? Do you think it would turn on?"

"Look at it," I told her, waving a hand over the damage.

She sighed, nodding.

We both stared for a while again — me because I couldn't believe the ghosts we had found, Mallory likely because she didn't know what to do or say. But after a moment, her hand dipped into her pocket, and she pulled out her phone, typing something into a search browser.

"We may be able to recover the hard drive," she said, showing me an article she'd found. "And if we can get that, then maybe..."

*heat*

"We can get answers."

The words sounded like they'd come from someone else's mouth, in someone else's voice. They shook and croaked out of my throat, and I swallowed, trying not to let the hope I felt building in my chest get enough air to surface. The longer I stared at that burnt hunk of computer, the heavier I breathed, and the more my pulse raced.

Little black dots invaded my vision, encroaching from every angle until I could only see through a lens the size of a pin hole.

I felt hands on my chest, on my neck, on my face, pulling me. Mallory's voice was somewhere in the distance, pleading with me to look at her, to breathe.

"Logan," she repeated, this time her voice clearing the fog in my head. "Look. At. Me."

I blinked, over and over, trying to find her through the darkness. It was her cerulean blue eyes I saw first, just an inch from mine. I felt her forehead against mine, her cool fingers framing my jaw, and the next thing I knew, my hands were reaching for her, wrapping around her waist, pulling her closer.

"Breathe," she said, and I sucked in the first breath in minutes, my lungs burning with the inhale before I let the air out again, slow and long through my mouth. "That's it."

I repeated the process, keeping my eyes open and locked on hers, but the more my body approached awareness, the more it buzzed to life at our proximity.

My cheeks heated under her fingers, breaths shallowing out again as I swallowed past the sticky knot in my throat. My gaze fell to her lips — dusty rose, plump and full, and now, parted just a centimeter, letting sweet breath through that met mine between us.

My eyes snapped to hers, but her gaze was on my lips now.

She let out a shaky breath.

Her tongue glided over her bottom lip, wetting it.

She leaned into me — just a fraction of an inch, the movement so subtle I couldn't be sure it happened at all.

All it took was the tilt of my chin, and our lips brushed, the slick heat of hers meeting the shaky coolness of mine. Mallory sucked in a breath at the contact, her fingers curling where they held my face.

"Logan..."

It was a warning, a whisper of desperation for me to stop — or maybe to *never* stop. I couldn't be sure, but I pulled away, wrapping my hands around her wrist as I pinched my eyes shut and took a real breath now that we had some distance between us.

"I'm sorry," I rasped out, shaking my head. "I... I think I was having a panic attack."

"It's okay," she assured me. "It's fine."

I released my grip on her wrists, breathing deep again before I let my eyes flutter open. My hands found balance on the flat of the table, and I stared at the computer, shaking my head.

"What do we do?" I asked — and I wasn't sure if I was asking Mallory, or my deceased father.

But it was her who answered, and her voice was steady and sure.

"We find a way to get that laptop home with you."

My eyes met hers, and the determination I found there lit a fire in my chest.

"Tonight."

# Chapter Nine

## MALLORY

Later that Friday night, Chris sipped from his wine, commenting on the bogus drama happening on the reality TV show he was watching while I read the same sentence in *All the Light We Cannot See* ten times in a row.

I was actually enjoying the book — which was a new feeling, since I hadn't read for pleasure in as long as I could remember. College textbooks had turned me off to reading, especially since I preferred to make art in my spare time rather than read it. But this book was intoxicating, drawing me into another country, another time, another perspective. I loved reading it at night before I went to sleep, and since Chris knew how much I hated reality TV, he wasn't offended that I had the hardback splayed open in my lap while we hung out.

The problem was I couldn't read tonight any more than I could stomach watching two housewives fight over who had the best birthday party for their kids. As much as I wanted to escape into another world, I couldn't stop thinking about what was happening in my own.

Logan Becker had nearly kissed me.

Or was it *me* who had nearly kissed him?

It didn't matter, I'd decided, because either way — our lips had touched.

I shivered again at the memory, eyes glossing over that same damn sentence with my thoughts somewhere else entirely. I could still feel the coolness of his lips against mine, the warmth of his breath, the strong grip of his hands around my waist. I could see his eyes, honey gold and dilated as they searched mine before they fell to my lips. My fingers had curled where they held his face when that first bit of contact was made, and just a dip of his chin or a tip of my own would have sealed the deal, would have closed the final distance between us.

But he'd pulled away.

My stomach dropped, just like it did every time I replayed what happened in that storage closet. Logan pulling away felt like the most painful mix of relief and rejection — and I couldn't figure out how to decipher which feeling was more prominent.

I sighed, readjusting the book in my lap and trying again to focus on what I was reading. It didn't take longer than sixty seconds for my thoughts to float back to Logan — this time, to the box of his father's belongings that we'd found.

We'd stashed that box away where we'd originally found it, stacking the boxes of items the distillery would keep and archive around it to hide its presence. Everything stayed in the box — except for the laptop, which I hid in my messenger bag as Logan and I walked to his truck after work. We checked to make sure no one was looking before I pulled it out, and Logan quickly placed it inside his truck and covered it with an old ratty towel.

"This is stealing," he reminded me, his eyes darting around the employee parking lot. "If someone catches us..."

"They won't," I was quick to assure him.

He still looked a little worried, a little numb, a little like he was going to throw up or pass out or both when he nodded, climbing into his truck. I'd stood there like a statue when he drove away, my fingers tracing the flesh of my bottom lip as I watched him go.

I could still taste him.

I let out another huff of frustration just as my phone lit up on the coffee table. I slapped the book closed, feet hitting the floor and heart hitting the ceiling when I saw Logan's name in a text notification.

Chris eyed me, one brow climbing. "I've never seen you move so fast for a text in your life," he commented. "Who is it?"

"No one," I murmured, but my eyes were glued to my phone now, reading and re-reading the text Logan had sent.

**Logan: I got the hard drive out. It doesn't look damaged, but after some research, I think I'll need a USB hard drive enclosure to plug it in to my own computer and see if any of the files survived.**

My fingers flew over the keys, and Chris hummed, sipping his wine with a knowing grin. "Mm-hmm. *No one* my ass."

**Me: Okay. This is a good thing, yes?**

**Logan: I guess we'll see.**

**Logan: Thank you, Mallory. For helping me get the laptop out. For everything.**

My stomach lurched.

**Me: Of course.**

I stared at the screen, waiting, hoping — for what, I had no idea. But after a moment, the little bubbles that told me he was typing something popped up. I held my breath as I watched them, but then they disappeared again. I was just about to start typing something else when they reappeared, and just as quickly, they were gone.

He didn't know what to say any more than I did.

I wondered if he wanted to ask about the almost-kiss, if it was replaying in his mind as much as it was my own. Did he *want* to kiss me? Or did he want to make sure I didn't read too much into something that was nothing?

Maybe he wanted to clear the air, to let me know that he was having an anxiety attack and didn't actually want to hold me, or brush his lips against mine, or suck in the breath that I'd just let out.

Maybe he wanted a redo, and this time, he wanted to pull me into him instead of push me away.

Something close to a growl came from my throat when the bubbles disappeared again, and Chris paused the TV, turning where he sat on the opposite end of the couch until he faced me completely.

"Okay, enough with the animal noises. I can't focus with all the barking and growling you've been doing for the past hour." He snapped his fingers twice as he took a long sip of his red wine. "Spill."

"There's nothing to spill."

Chris flattened his lips, and then before I could react, he snatched my phone from me and read the screen as I wailed on him to give it back to me.

"Logan Becker," he mused with a smirk, handing my phone back.

I huffed, pulling it into my chest like I could protect what had already been seen. "It's just work stuff."

"Right. And I only cross dress during Pride Week." He rolled his eyes. "What happened? Did you get him in trouble again? Or is his grumpiness rubbing off on you?"

"I'm not grumpy," I defended. "And neither is he."

Chris cocked a brow. "That man has been a broody, keep-to-himself piece of eye-candy since we were teenagers. Who else do you know who sits at Buck's alone with a scowl and a glass of whiskey."

I opened my mouth to retort, but Chris held up his finger.

"*Besides* his brothers, because that will only prove my point further."

I shut my mouth again.

Chris chuckled. "Come on. Tell me what's going on so I can stop bugging you and get back to my show."

I covered my face with my hands, blowing a hot breath through the fingers. "I don't know," I groaned out. Then, I peeked through my fingers at Chris. "There may or may not have been lip contact."

"*Lip contact*? As in, *kissing?!*"

"No." I bit my lip. "Well... maybe kind of?"

Chris filled his glass of wine before topping off mine, and then he kicked back, making himself comfortable on the couch. "Tell me *everything.*"

So, I did. I told him how Logan and I had started getting along, how I'd brought him into my studio that night after our walk, how we'd found a rhythm at work. I told him about my first *real* tour, how it had felt so good before we realized we'd forgotten the no photos allowed speech. I told him about Mac, about our punishment, about Logan's surprising taste in music and how his nerdiness somehow made me like him more. I told him about the box we found, the laptop, the hard drive.

And finally, the almost-kiss.

Chris was giddy the entire time, smiling like a loon and completely unable to keep still the longer I talked. By the time I finished, I thought he was going to squeal or giggle or jump up and down.

"This is *bad*, Chris," I pointed out. "We almost kissed. Or... at least... I *think* we almost kissed."

"Oh, you definitely almost kissed," Chris agreed. "Honestly, I'd say lip contact classifies, but since there was lack of embrace or tongue, we can file it as an almost."

I sighed.

"Why are you acting like he kicked your cat?"

Dalí croaked out a meow from where he was curled up under the coffee table.

"Lip-locking is *fun*, Mallory — especially with a Becker boy." Chris waggled his brows.

"Did you hear what you just said? He's a *Becker*. His entire family hates *my* entire family — and honestly, if you ask me, it's for good reason. Plus, we work together. Plus, my father would *murder* me."

Chris scoffed. "And? Like pissing off your dad isn't your favorite pastime."

"It's different this time. He has me by the balls with this building being in his name," I said, gesturing to the studio apartment we were sitting in above the shop.

"Fine," Chris conceded. "But, does he even need to know? I mean, it's not like it has to be anything serious.

It sounds like you like him, and from what you've told me, he likes you, too. Why not have a little fun?" He tipped his glass toward me before taking a sip. "From what I know of the guy, he could use it." Chris grimaced. "Who watches *space documentaries* for joy?"

I chuckled, flying through the list of reasons why entertaining any kind of feelings for Logan Becker — whether *just for fun* or otherwise — was a terrible idea. Still, just a centimeter of his skin on mine had sent me into this spiral, and now that I'd had a taste, I couldn't stop wondering what it would be like to dip the whole spoon in and take a full bite.

My phone vibrated, and Chris eyed me with a smirk. Before I could even think to reach for the phone, it was in his hands, unlocked with Logan's newest text pulled up — since I shared everything with my best friend.

*Mistake*.

"Still need help with the shop tomorrow?" Chris read, mimicking a deep voice that I presumed was supposed to be Logan's. He quirked a brow at me. "Help with what?"

"He likes to organize and clean and put things in their place," I explained with a shrug. "I told him he could help me put the shop together this weekend, if he wanted to."

Chris smiled triumphantly, tossing me the phone before kicking back and pushing play on the remote. "Sounds like *fun* to me."

I sighed, looking at the text with every quiet voice inside me saying I should decline. Logan Becker and I should have had a relationship that existed only within the walls of the Scooter Whiskey Distillery. He as the Lead Tour Guide, me as the guide in training. He'd show me the ropes, and I'd try not to get him into any more trouble.

Because he was a Becker, and I was a Scooter.

That was where all the lines should be drawn.

But the louder voices inside me wanted more of the Logan I got that night we walked Main Street, wanted to know what other music lived on his playlist, wanted to crack his shell, loosen him up, add a little color to his life.

*Maybe it really couldn't hurt*, I thought. *Maybe we could be friends, hang out, have a little fun…*

It was a stupid idea. Obtuse, really.

But it didn't stop me from sending the next text.

**Me: Tomorrow at noon. Wear something you can get dirty in.**

I was obsessed with the little wrinkle between Logan's eyebrows.

I stared at it all afternoon as he worked in my shop, opening up boxes and building furniture, hanging up signs and unpacking paint, organizing easels and brushes and sponges and cups. I loved how concentrated he was, how the same fire that fueled me when I envisioned the shop seemed to live inside him. It was like it was *his*, like he had something to fight for with me — something to lose.

We'd worked tirelessly all afternoon, and made a substantial dent in what was previously complete chaos. The studio was actually beginning to *look* like a studio, like a business, like what I'd always dreamed it could be. I could finally see the little sections I'd imagined, the division of the wide space, the different themes of each that helped them stand out while still bringing a cohesive feel to the shop.

My chest was light, wings fluttering against my rib cage.

*It's happening. It's really happening.*

The 1975 played on Logan's speaker — which he'd brought with him at my insistence. I'd offered a suggestion from time to time, but for the most part, it'd been his music, his favorite bands and artists, and I loved getting a sneak peek inside his soul. He listened to everything from yacht rock and country to folk and classical — and he knew the words to every single song that came on. My favorite songs were the ones he couldn't help but belt out rather than just quietly singing along.

Right now, he was bobbing his head along to "Sincerity is Scary," one hand holding a slice of the pizza I ordered us for dinner and the other making more notes as he looked around the room at what we'd done and what was still left to do. I sipped on the sweet tea I'd made, watching him.

I'd told him to wear something he could get dirty in, so I guess I had myself to blame for the traveler sweat pants hanging off his hips, leaving practically nothing to the imagination when it came to how round and firm his ass was — as well as what he was packing in the front. And if those pants weren't already a distraction, the old, ripped, slightly stained Stratford High t-shirt he wore with the sleeves ripped off in such a haphazard way that the muscles that lined his ribs were visible, would have done the trick. When he'd first taken his jacket off, I'd had to turn away, clearing my throat and commenting on something about the mess of boxes to keep from staring.

Now, after a long day of working, his hair was disheveled, curling out from under the edge of his ball cap.

And that little wrinkle was present, his brows furrowed in concentration.

I bit my lip, watching him balance that slice of pizza in one hand as he made notes with the other. I swear, I *tried* talking myself out of what my fingers ached to do most, but instinct won out.

I slipped off the little bar stool I was on — one that would be used in the painting corner of the studio — and crept to the back office. My camera was on the desk there, and I strapped it around my neck, fussing with the lens and settings before I made my way back into the shop.

I stood off to his left, the setting sun casting his strong profile in an orange glow through the large shop windows. Shadows stretched out behind him, and I lifted the camera, looking through the viewfinder at my subject just as he furrowed his brows even more, jotting something down on the notepad.

*Click.*

The sound was soft and quiet, but still audible over the music, and Logan's head popped up, searching for the source. When he saw me still looking at him through the camera lens, he grinned.

"Did you just take a picture of me?"

I shrugged, lowering the camera. "Just testing some of the settings," I lied. "It's the golden hour, great time for shooting. I wanted to see how the light came through the windows."

He nodded, the corner of his mouth still quirked as he watched me from across the studio. "You're really into photography, huh?"

"It's one of my favorite mediums," I said, making my way back to the bar stool across from him. I pressed the button on the back of the camera that would show me the images I'd taken, and when I saw the one I'd just snapped of Logan, my heart squeezed. "Although, I still haven't managed how to capture the beauty of something you see with your eyes through the lens. Seems like, for some things, it's impossible to accomplish."

Logan was completely oblivious to the compliment, and he started in on his notes again. "I bet you do better than you think. Why don't you have any of your art down here yet? Your paintings, photographs..." He glanced at me before pulling his attention back to the pad. "I'm sure you have thousands."

"Most of them are upstairs," I said. "And I do have thousands, but probably only a dozen that are good enough to display."

Logan stopped writing, meeting my gaze. "I doubt that. I'd love to see what you've created."

His eyes were intense where they watched me, the air thick and heavy in the shop. He swallowed, taking to his notes again as I fiddled with the settings on the camera to keep myself busy.

"You'll have to show me some of your shots sometime," he said after a moment.

I nodded, watching his face level out as he got back to work, wondering why my lungs were being so weird with breath all of a sudden. It was like I was under water, or like I'd completely forgotten the simple, natural body functions of *inhale, exhale.*

It wasn't just me who was feeling it. I could tell Logan was off, too — and I was determined to change that.

Pulling the strap from around my neck, I set my camera down, circling the table we sat at and placing my hand over the notepad he was writing in.

He quirked a brow up at me. "Hard to write with your hand in the way."

"So take a break," I told him. "We've been working all day, and if I'm being honest, the stress rolling off you has been stressing *me* out."

I plucked the pen from his hands, shoving it and the notebook too far away from him for him to reach for them. He looked at them longingly for a moment before he let out a deep sigh.

"I'm sorry," he said, scrubbing his hands over his face. "Honestly, you giving me so much to do today has been a blessing for me. I can't stop thinking about the box we found, about my dad..." He swallowed, the thick Adam's apple in his throat bobbing. "Working on stuff like this helps me get out of my head for a while."

I frowned, crossing my arms to keep myself from reaching for him. I knew that feeling all too well, the need to escape, to move my hands in an effort to stop thinking — even if just for a while.

"I just... I can't figure out why that stuff was in there," he continued. "You know? Why was *that* stuff saved, tucked away? How did it survive as well as it did? Why didn't the fire department take it, or the police? Why wasn't it given to my mom, to my family, if it wasn't needed for evidence?"

I blew out a sigh of my own. "I don't know, none of it makes sense to me either."

Logan's frown deepened, his eyes falling to where he folded his hands in his lap.

I nudged his shoulder with my elbow. "Hey, you got the hard drive out, right? And you got the necessary equipment to see the files that are on it. That has to be comforting, at least."

"Yes," he agreed, lifting his gaze to mine. "But the hard drive is password protected. I can't access anything until I crack that code."

"And you will," I assured him. "But, until then, there's no sense in stressing yourself out over answers you can't find — no matter how many times you ask the questions."

His brows folded together again, and I chuckled, uncrossing my arms and taking a tentative step toward him. Before I could think better of it, I reached out, smoothing my thumb over the wrinkle I'd been marveling at all day.

"Have you ever painted before?" I asked, eyes on the skin that was smooth now that I'd run my thumb over it.

Logan's breath was shallow, his eyes locked on my face as I stared at where that wrinkle had been. "Not since elementary school."

I laughed, letting my hand drop from where I touched his face. "I think it's time we changed that." I held out that hand for his. "Come on, let's have some fun."

He grimaced. "I don't think I can. Not right now."

"Well," I insisted, wiggling my fingers and nodding toward his hand. "We're at least going to try."

Reluctantly, Logan took my hand, and I tried not to feel the warmth of his hand in mine as more than a friendly gesture as I guided him over to the corner of the room we'd started setting up for the painting workshops. A circle of easels faced the middle of that section, each station loaded with paint and brushes and palettes. I instructed him to sit, and then I moved to the corner, pulling out two large, blank canvases.

I placed one in the easel in front of him, the other in the one next to him where I would sit. As I poured paint for us and got rinse cups ready, Logan was quiet, not even singing along to the music anymore. He was staring at the blank canvas like it was a threat rather than a release.

"You'll like this," I promised him when I took the seat to his left. "Just try to relax and let go."

Logan nodded, another sigh leaving his lips as he picked up the first brush. "I don't really know what to do."

"That's the whole point," I said. "You don't have to know anything. You just... feel. Do. Whatever you want."

I turned my attention to my own canvas, hoping it would help release some of the pressure Logan felt to produce something. I let the music fill in the space between us, and after a few minutes of me working on my piece, Logan finally dipped his brush in the salamander orange paint and began.

We worked in a comfortable silence for a while, and the more time stretched on, the more Logan seemed to relax. He started singing again, and I just hummed along beside him until he surprised me when he belted out every word to "Man of Constant Sorrow."

"He's a bluegrass fan, too," I mused, keeping my eyes on my canvas. "Is there any kind of music you *don't* listen to?"

"Death core," he said easily. "And really, *all* metal music. Although, not because I didn't try to love it."

"I'm trying to picture you head banging and screaming with the rock on sign." I held my index and pinky finger up to illustrate, sticking out my tongue like Gene Simmons.

Logan chuckled. "I even went to a show in Nashville once, wondering if I'd appreciate it more live. And I did, but... not enough to listen to it on my own." He pointed the tip of his brush at me. "Did you know there are literally *hundreds* of sub-genres of metal music? It all depends on the vocal style, instruments used, what era or region or bands they draw inspiration from. I mean, there's literally a genre called Celtic Metal that's inspired by Celtic mythology."

It was the most enthusiastic I'd seen him all day, the excited grin on his face too contagious for me to fight.

"You're like a walking encyclopedia," I commented. "Like, you know a little something about *everything* it seems."

He shrugged, turning his attention back to his canvas. "It's all useless, except for maybe a trivia night. But like I said, I love to learn, so I usually find myself deep in the rabbit hole of the Internet reading about some subject I didn't even know existed before I stumbled upon it."

"You make me feel lazy, I never do anything productive like that — not now that I'm out of school. If anything, I avoid anything that looks suspiciously educational."

Logan gestured to the shop around us, to the canvas in front of me. "Are you kidding? Look at what you can create, at the art you can bring to life. And you're sharing that with your hometown, giving kids here the options that you never had to explore their creativity." He lowered his brush, pausing to look me in the eyes. "That's incredible, Mallory."

I wanted to hold his gaze forever, to lose myself in the specks of brown that dotted the gold irises of the man next to me. But I couldn't bare it, couldn't look at him any longer without wanting to shrink away from the parts of me he saw that no one else did.

I cleared my throat. "You know, it means a lot to me that you see it that way," I said, dipping my brush in the rinse water. "The studio, I mean. For a while, it's felt like this pipe dream, and even now that I'm making it a reality..." I shrugged. "I don't know. It just seems like I'm the only one who takes it seriously, who sees what it can be." I looked at him again then. "Except for you."

Logan smiled, his eyes searching mine for the briefest moment before he turned back to his work. I did the same, and for a while it was just brushes over canvas, a soft rock ballad in the background.

"Mallory," he said after a moment, still painting. "The night we walked Main Street, you sort of mentioned that you had a deal with your dad. A deal regarding the studio." He didn't look at me, not even when my hand froze where I was painting a snowman in the yard of the Christmassy cabin scene on my canvas. "What does that mean?"

I blinked. "It's complicated, but long story short — he bought the studio in exchange for me finally working at the distillery. For at least five years, I have to be there Monday through Friday, and I'm free to use my evenings and weekends here."

My voice was low, tone short, my brush strokes on the canvas a little more violent.

Logan nodded. "I guess he's always been a little desperate for you to be a part of the family legacy, huh?"

I scoffed. "That's putting it lightly."

"What happened?" Logan asked, and this time, he stopped what he was painting to look at me. "The summer before high school, you said something happened that changed everything with your family."

I shook my head, the blood draining from my face as I recalled the memory. I thought about avoiding it, telling a lie, saying it was nothing and I was just a dramatic teen. But even now, even twelve years later, I still felt the same way about what happened as I did that hot summer night.

And for some reason, for the first time since I'd told my best friend Chris, I *wanted* to share it with someone.

"Something not a lot of people know about me is I have a very sharp sense of what's right and what's wrong," I said, continuing work on my canvas. "I've always had this moral compass, and a desire to be just, and to seek justice for others. I even thought about being a lawyer once," I confessed on a sarcastic laugh. "Until I realized how corrupt our judicial system is."

Logan was quiet, just listening, watching me.

"Anyway, one night that summer before high school, Dad had a big party at the house. It was catered, giant tents everywhere in our yard, a band and — of course — a casino. I'm sure you've heard of how he likes to offer the residents of Stratford a place to gamble since they have to drive out of state otherwise."

He gave me a face at that, because we both were well aware that my father's "underground" casino was nowhere near a secret — at least, not in this town. He was protected by the local police, and no one had ever reported him to any higher authorities — mostly because nearly everyone in town had participated at one point or another.

Logan and his family had an even more in-depth knowledge of it all, thanks to his older brother, Noah. Noah had started dating the mayor's daughter, Ruby Grace, and the mayor was now famous for his debt owed to my father from nights at the casino — a debt made public at what was supposed to be Ruby Grace's wedding to another man. It was the biggest scandal Stratford had seen in some time, and even now, six months later, it was whispered about.

"The casino part of the night was in our basement, and I went down there a little after midnight to get a soda. I also wanted to sketch, since I couldn't sleep with all the noise, and my favorite set of drawing pencils were down there with the rest of my art supplies — which I'd *begged* Mom to let me keep in my room, but she'd refused, saying the mess of paint brushes and pencils were eye sores."

I swallowed, still keeping my eyes on my canvas as I told the story.

"When I went down there, there was a group of guys playing blackjack. One of them was Randy Kelly."

"As in, *Chief* Kelly?"

I nodded. "Yep, the very one. He had just been appointed police chief, like two days before that. He was definitely celebrating that night, too, because he was so drunk he could barely keep upright in his chair." I pursed my lips, dunking my brush in the paint harder than necessary. "Not that it stopped him from groping me in front of everyone in that room and insinuating that when I was old enough for it to be legal, I should find my way to his bed."

"What the fuck?" Logan snapped. "You're joking, right?"

"Nope," I said, the word leaving my lips with a pop. I finally looked at Logan then, and even though it was cliché and made me want to roll my eyes at myself, I loved that his hands were curled into fists at his side, that his eyes looked murderous as it all sank in. "He even pulled me into his lap, refusing to let go of me until I punched him in the groin and high-tailed it out of there."

Logan's mouth fell open, his eyes flicking back and forth between mine in a look of horror. "What did you do?"

"I told my dad," I said. "Obviously. Because that's what any fourteen-year-old girl would do. I told my dad." I swallowed. "And I thought he would fly in like the superhero I thought he was, kick Randy's ass, save the day." My lip twitched, something between a smile and the beginning of a sob finding me. "But he didn't. He said it was nothing, that Randy was drunk, that he was sure Randy didn't mean any harm, that I was being *dramatic*," I spat the word. "And that I should let it go."

"How could he say any of that?" Logan asked, that wrinkle between his brows again. "You're his *daughter*. That man practically molested you."

"Yeah, well, pissing off the police chief wouldn't bode well with my father's underground casino staying in operation, would it?"

Logan shook his head. "And your mom?"

I scoffed. "She's soft, weak, and does whatever Dad tells her to. She had nothing for me other than a hug and an offer to run me a hot bath."

"Jesus..."

I nodded, but as soon as the last words were said, I drew in a deep breath, picking up my brush like nothing had happened. "Anyway, I decided then that I didn't want anything to do with my family or their *legacy*. And that I was going to be my own person, and I didn't give two shits what they had to say about it."

Logan was quiet for so long that I paused where I was painting to make sure he was still breathing. He was, and in fact, it was about all he was doing — just looking at me, and breathing.

"What?"

"It's just that I've been trying to keep my father's legacy alive, to be everything he'd ever wanted me to be and more. I would give anything to have another moment with him, and meanwhile, you've been trying to escape *your* father for over a decade." He swallowed. "I can't imagine being in your shoes when that happened, or what you must have gone through ever since. You're really strong, Mallory. Really fucking strong."

My heart squeezed painfully in my chest, but I played off the emotion with a scoff. "Yeah, so strong that I had to come crawling back home to Daddy and take his money to make my dream come true."

"Hey," Logan said, reaching over to place his hand on my forearm. He squeezed until I looked at him, and I hated the sincerity I found there.

That The 1975 song was right — sincerity *was* scary.

"That's not what you did, okay? You're making your dream a reality, and doing whatever it takes to get there — that's a strong entrepreneur. That's a warrior."

The way Logan watched me in that moment, I knew he meant every word he said — and he wanted me to believe them as much as he did.

Suddenly, the air around us was too thick, too dense with emotions that I didn't want to feel. I blew a breath out loudly through my lips, pulling my hand from where it had been paused in front of my canvas. "Alright," I said, shaking my head. "That's enough of that. I brought you over here to paint to *relieve* stress, not make more of it."

"I'm not stressed."

"Well, you're not having fun, either," I argued. Then, my eyes flicked to the brush in my hand, to the paint on the palette between us, and I grinned. "But I think I know how to change that."

Logan quirked a brow, watching as I dipped the brush in the mahogany paint on my palette. I lifted the brush, made it look like I was going back to painting, and waited until Logan had turned back toward his own canvas.

Then, I flicked my brush and sent paint splattering all over him.

Specks of the orangish-brown color hit his biceps, the muscles of his rib cage peeking through his shirt, his neck, his eyebrow, the corner of his mouth — now popped open in surprise. He turned his head slowly, blinking several times before he wiped his thumb over the corner of his mouth where the paint had splattered. Logan looked at his thumb, at my challenging smile, and then he dipped his own brush.

"Oh, you're going to pay for that."

I squealed, jumping up from my bar stool and running away before he could even dip his brush. I took my palette with me, reloading my weapon before I turned back around. But Logan was there, and as soon as I was facing him, I saw paint flying my way in slow motion.

I closed my eyes just in time to feel the cool liquid splatter all over my face.

Logan laughed as I blinked my eyes open again, charging after him with my brush. He ran behind his canvas, and when I flung another attack, it landed all over the painting he'd been working on.

"Hey!" he said, peeking over the top at the new addition to his work. "You ruined it!"

"I made it better."

"Oh, yeah?" Logan swiped his brush over my painting, making a haphazard smiley face right over my snow man. "There. I returned the favor."

I laughed, walking over to marvel at the new addition. "Huh. You kind of did."

Logan peered over to look at the painting with me, like he wondered if it actually *did* look better with that smiley face, and it was just the distraction I needed to reach out and run my brush in a line from his ear to his collarbone.

I ran out of his reach before he could react, but he was on my heels quick, chasing me until I was hiding behind one of the chairs in the new pottery section. He hid behind his own barricade, and when I stood and slung another brush full of paint at him, it went everywhere — on the chair he hid behind, the new firing oven, the anvils and bevel cutters and other tools we'd arranged neatly in bins on the shelf.

Logan's mouth popped open as he stood. "Wait, stop," he said, putting his hands up before I could fire off another round. "You're messing everything up."

I laughed, ditching the brush all together and dipping

my hands in the palette. A rainbow of colors stained my fingers and palms as I ran over to him and planted them right in the middle of his chest.

"Who cares! It's paint," I reminded him. "It'll come off."

"This is one of my favorite workout shirts!"

I shrugged. "Shouldn't have worn it to an art shop."

Logan narrowed his eyes, but then he dropped his own brush, hands on a path for the paint on his palette.

I took off screaming, looking for my next shield. Logan rounded the stack of boxes we had yet to unpack before I could hide behind them, catching me in his wet, paint-covered hands just as I slid around them. He wiped them down my arms, leaving multicolored streaks from my shoulders to my wrists.

"This shirt looks better with sleeves," he said with a grin.

I wiggled out of his grasp, panting and laughing as I sprinted across the shop to get more ammo. But I hit a wet spot, my shoe sliding over the gob of paint left by one of our attacks, and before I knew how to stop it, I was windmilling, the world tilting.

"Oh, shit!"

I tried to steady myself, but it was useless, and I wrapped my hands around my head to try to protect it from the fall.

But it never came.

Logan slid in like a baseball runner stealing home, catching me in his lap as I tumbled to the floor. It was a loud and awkward contact — me hitting him, him hitting the hard tile, both of us a mess of limbs and paint as we tried to figure out what had just happened.

"Are you okay?" Logan asked, hands framing my arms first, then my face, his eyes searching me for bruises or bleeding. He still had paint all over those hands, but I couldn't find it in me to care that he was getting it in my hair and all over my cheeks.

"I'm okay," I said on a laugh, giggling more when the worry didn't erase from his face as he continued his search.

I reached forward, running my own paint-covered thumb over that line between his brows again. It was like that touch pulled Logan into another room, another time, another world where it was just me and him and the warmth of my thumb on his forehead.

The music faded, the only sound now the steady thumping of his heart and mine.

Logan's next breath was a shallow rasp, a hard swallow rocking his Adam's apple as I continued dragging my thumb down, over the bridge of his nose, the tip, slipping down to catch his bottom lip before I dragged it off his chin. I watched my thumb making its descent, and when it fell from his face, my hand rested on his chest, fingers twisting in the fabric of his t-shirt.

I flicked my eyes back to his, but his were locked on my mouth now.

I smirked. "You want to kiss me, don't you, Logan Becker?" I whispered.

His eyes fluttered a bit, but otherwise, there was no response. There was no effort to deny or confirm, just his golden eyes locked on my lips, his hands still framing my face, my fist in his shirt, tugging him closer.

"Do it," I whispered, fingers curling more into his cotton t-shirt. I tilted my chin up, seeking him, heart pounding in my ears so loud I couldn't be sure I'd actually said the words.

A pained sound rumbled somewhere deep within Logan — his chest, maybe, or his soul. Those strong hands slipped farther into my hair, cradling my neck, pulling me closer, his eyes still locked on my lips.

But he stopped himself.

With less than an inch between us, Logan stopped, his lips parting, a shaky breath slipping from the new space. His fingers curled in my hair, and I closed my eyes, pulling his shirt once more until the man wearing it followed.

"I said *kiss me*," I urged, the words whispered against his mouth, our lips brushing now, eliciting that same electric charge I'd felt in the storage closet.

Logan took one last trembling breath.

And then he answered my plea.

# Chapter Ten

**LOGAN**

I'd fantasized about it for years, what it would be like if I ever got the chance to kiss Mallory Scooter. In each and every scenario, I was timid and nervous, overwhelmed with a mix of fear and excitement. The possibility that I could ever actually taste her seemed so preposterous to me that all my dreams consisted mostly of disbelief.

So, when my lips crashed down on hers, capturing her next breath and a moan inside my mouth, I waited for those thoughts to hit.

*Oh, my God.*

*This can't be happening.*

*Holy shit, it's happening.*

*I'm kissing Mallory Scooter.*

*I can't* believe *I'm kissing Mallory Scooter.*

But none of those thoughts came.

Not when our lips met. Not when her hands slid up my chest, wrapping around my neck. Not when I tightened my grip in her hair, pulling her in, kissing her with such force I was sure I'd bruise both our lips.

There was no disbelief, no uncertainty, no nerves or timidness to be found.

I kept my lips pressed to hers as I waited for the *other* voices I expected to hear, the ones that would whisper *no, stop, you can't, you shouldn't.*

But again, they never came.

All I felt was a profound sense of *right*, and the most powerful wave of possession I'd ever experienced in my life.

*Yes.*

*Finally.*

*Take.*

*Mine.*

Those were the thoughts on repeat in my mind as I left one hand in her hair, the other sliding down to grab her by the hip and move her fully into my lap. Her legs straddled me, the warmth of her thighs surrounding my hips, the heat of her center calling to the growing bulge between my legs.

She gasped for air when I finally broke the kiss, only long enough for each of us to take a breath before my lips captured hers again, hard and urgent. My tongue broke the barrier of her lips this time, seeking hers, the taste of paint and sweet tea mixing on my taste buds.

Mallory didn't seem to have a single voice in her head warning her to stop, either. Her hands were in my hair, knocking the ball cap I'd been wearing to the ground as she tangled her fingertips in the strands and tugged, owning me in the same way I was owning her. She bucked her hips, rubbing the seam of her leggings over my erection, a lustful moan rolling through her at the contact.

My hands found her hips then, squeezing, locking her in place to keep myself from coming before anything even started. My body was reacting to hers in a way it'd never reacted to any other woman's in my life. It was like two magnets being held away from each other for years, finally being released and clashing together in the middle, touching for the first time, feeling what it's like to be whole.

I broke the kiss, biting and sucking my way over her jaw, her neck, up to capture her earlobe between my teeth. I sucked it gently, breathing a hot, wanting breath there that made her shiver, her thighs clenching around me.

"Take me upstairs," she breathed, and the words were barely out of her mouth before I was kissing her again, lifting us both up from the floor with her still wrapped around my waist.

I stumbled a bit, sneakers sliding over the mess of paint we'd stained the floor with as I blindly made my way to the staircase in the back that led up to her studio apartment. One hand gripped the rail to keep us from falling while the other held her against me, her arms tight around my neck, our mouths bruising each other in an effort to get closer, to taste more, to feel *everything*.

We crashed through her door at the top of the stairs, the handle swinging back and hitting the wall so hard I was certain it'd left a hole. Dalí jumped from where he'd been on her couch with a hiss, tail poofed as his nails skittered across the hardwood floor. He bolted between my legs and down the stairs into the shop, and I reached back for the door, slinging it shut before I dropped Mallory's feet to the floor.

As soon as she was standing, I twisted us until we'd traded spots, whipping her around to face the door and pressing her hard into it.

"This is bad," I warned, running my tongue up the back of her neck until my lips were next to her ear. "You know it. I know it."

Mallory whimpered, rolling her ass against my erection, her hands planted on the door, lips kissing the wood when she gave her reply.

"So stop, then."

Her words said one thing, but her body elicited another plea, chills racing from where my breath met her neck all the way to where her fingers intertwined with mine on the door frame. I lifted those hands above her head, leaning my body into hers more, not sure if I wanted to get closer or somehow put so much pressure on her that she'd push back, push me away, tell me to stop — and mean it.

"Stop what?" I whispered, leaving her hands above her head as I trailed mine down her arms, her rib cage, her waist. I slipped one arm between her and the door, holding her to me, as the other hand rounded over her ass, fingertips slipping between her thighs.

She gasped, arching her back, head falling back as she leaned into the touch.

"Touching you?" I asked, sucking the skin on her neck. "Kissing you?"

"No," she breathed, rolling her hips again, ass up, begging for me to slide my hand between her thighs just a little more. "Stop *thinking*."

Her request might as well have been a spell for how quickly it knocked every negative thought out of my mind in that moment. All the stress I'd felt the last twenty-four hours, all the worry, all the pain — *gone* with those two words and the roll of her body against mine.

It was only her now, my seductive little witch casting her charm, pulling me in.

And I dived willingly into her incantation.

My hand slipped farther between her thighs, the side of my thumb brushing her seam as she arched into the touch. Her hands flew down from where they were held above her head, reaching behind her, seeking me, but I clamped my hands around her wrists, forcing them up the door again.

"Keep these here," I demanded, my whisper a soft-spoken command that she whimpered in response to as if I'd whipped her, instead.

I kissed the back of her neck, her jaw, capturing the side of her lips as my hands trailed down again. One slid between her and the door again, holding her to me, but this time, the other dived under the hem of her leggings, fingertips dipping between the sweet swells of her perfect ass.

And my suspicion that she wasn't wearing panties under them was confirmed.

Her head fell back, lips no longer able to kiss me as they parted. Her neck was elongated, eyes closed, a desperate, shaky breath finding her as my fingers made their descent. I felt her asshole tighten when the pads of my fingers brushed it, and though I never would have even *approached* that topic the first time with any other woman, I realized quickly that Mallory Scooter was *far* from any other woman I'd ever known.

I paused my downward climb, circling the tip of my index finger over that sensitive opening, feeling it pucker beneath the touch.

Her entire body froze, but just when I thought she'd pull away, or open her eyes, warning me not to even think about it... she arched, instead. Her lips parted even more, the paint from my own staining those rose-colored swells, and I sucked her bottom lip between my teeth, releasing it with a hard pop as I applied just the slightest bit of pressure with my finger.

"You want it here, don't you?" I asked, voice rasping against the chills on her neck as I pressed a little more. It wasn't enough to penetrate, just enough to make her writhe between me and the door.

Mallory didn't answer, but she didn't have to. The way her ass poked up higher, her back arching so deep I wondered if she'd break told me more than her words could what she wanted.

I shook my head, kissing her neck as I pulled back on the pressure a bit. "I'll give it to you. But not tonight. Tonight," I said, slipping my fingers down farther until they slid between her drenched lips. "I'm taking *this*."

I dipped two fingers inside her at once, hips thrusting into the back of my hand to assist as she cried out, head falling back on my chest, eyes shooting open to watch me as I withdrew my fingers and repeated the motion, over and over, stretching her wider each time, reaching new depths.

Her eyes were an icy tundra, so blue they were somehow almost white as she watched me. Her eyes searched mine, lips parted, eyelids fluttering just slightly each time I pressed my fingers inside her again.

I let her watch me while I fucked her with my fingers, our breaths coming in short pants, mixing in the air between us. When it was too much not to kiss her any longer, I crushed my mouth to hers, keeping my fingers deep inside her and curling the tips on a search for that magic spot that would make her come undone.

Mallory's legs shook so violently I thought she'd fall if it weren't for me pinning her to the door. So, I gripped her tighter around the waist, taking her weight, my fingers continuing their assault as I sipped every breath of air she was finished with.

"Logan," she half-whispered, half cried into my mouth.

I waited for more, for her to tell me to stop, to keep going, to fuck her, to get on my knees and suck her clit. But all she said was my name, a longing, sigh of syllables, and then her legs seized, along with every other muscle in her body.

She came with a moan in my mouth, and I gobbled up that noise like my first meal in years, curling my fingers the same way I had been to keep her orgasm going as long as I could. Wetness sprayed from where I fucked her, soaking through her leggings and my sweat pants, too.

"Oh my *God*," she cried, finally pulling back from my kiss to ride out the rest of her climax. She screamed and moaned, back arching, legs shaking again as she surrendered to the feeling.

When she was done, she fell limp, and I really did carry her full weight as I slowly, carefully, withdrew my fingers.

Mallory panted, letting her hands fall from where I'd told her to keep them above her head. She turned in my grasp, pulling at my shirt, my hair, my pants, like she needed me closer — and I obliged in every way possible, holding her to the door, my lips trailing over her slick neck.

"Holy fuck," she breathed, pressing a hand to her forehead. I pulled back, locking eyes with her as she shook her head. "I've never... I didn't know I..."

I chuckled, kissing her nose. "That was fucking hot."

Mallory laughed, but as soon as the sound found her, it was gone again, her eyes heated, tongue rolling over her bottom lip. She fisted her hands in my shirt, pulling me to her for a long, hard kiss before she tugged on the fabric.

I leaned back, letting her pull the shirt over my head before I was kissing her again. She pushed us away from the door, her legs shaking as she backed me up to the couch. My legs hit the edge of it, but before I could sit, Mallory yanked at the hem of my sweatpants.

"Take these off."

I smirked, eyeing her as she stepped away from me, stripping her own shirt over her head and flinging it somewhere across the room. "Yes, ma'am."

We watched each other like animals about to fight rather than fuck as we stripped — me pulling my sweatpants and boxer briefs down my legs, her peeling her damp leggings to her ankles, kicking them the rest of the way off. Only a simple, black sports bra hid her breasts, and with one quick tug and maneuver of arms, it was over her head and on the floor, too.

I let my eyes devour her like she really was my prey, gaze sliding over the mountains and valleys of her goddess-like body. Her breasts were modest but round and plump, the peaks puckered and begging for my tongue. Her stomach was flat and toned, a dipped line running from the bottom of her rib cage down to just above her belly button — another trail begging to be licked. Tattoos that merely peeked out from the edges of her clothing before were now on full display — a phoenix starting at her hip and wrapping up her rib cage, a half-sleeve of flowers stretching from her elbow to her shoulder, a line of script highlighting the curve of her hip. Those lips I'd stared at for years were swollen, parted, her own eyes feasting on what she saw between my legs before they flicked up to mine.

She didn't say a word, just pressed one hand hard into my chest and shoved. I fell back, bare ass hitting the couch cushions, and as soon as I was sitting, she was on top of me, her mouth hard on mine.

And *that's* when it all hit me.

Maybe it was her being on top, me submitting, her taking control. Maybe it was her slim waist between my hands, her lips on mine before they kissed a trail over my jaw, down my neck, and back up again. Maybe it was her paint-matted hair falling in a curtain over my face, or the slick heat of her sliding over my shaft, eliciting a guttural groan from me that sounded like something off National Geographic.

Whatever it was, it finally hit me.

I was kissing Mallory Scooter.

I was touching her. She was touching *me*. It was bad. It was wrong. I needed to stop, to push her away, to rewind time and go back to when I would never even entertain that she could want me like this.

But it was too late.

My next breath was a shaky one, and now it was *my* hands that trembled as I held her, as she rocked her hips, coating me in her climax. She moaned when the tip of my cock brushed her sensitive clit, her eyes fluttering closed before they shot open again. In seconds, she was off me, digging in a drawer somewhere near where her bed was set up in the corner opposite the living room.

There were no walls in her studio apartment, just one giant, open space. Still, that distance between us was too far, and I found myself crossing it to meet her again, sliding my erection between the gap of her thighs just to feel her warmth again.

She sighed, falling back into me, and I flexed my hips again, fucking her thighs and somehow knowing just from that that fucking her pussy would be the end of me.

Mallory spun in my arms, holding up a shiny gold packet. "Condom," she rasped, and then she pushed me back again — this time, into her bed.

Items Checked Out
*****************

Daniel, Avery Luke
23446001530649
Daniel, Tiffany L.

Title:          Fetch-22 /
Item ID:        33446008399517
Call Number:    X PIL
Out:            02/08/2020
                9:23 AM
Due:            03/21/2020
                11:59 PM
Renewals        1
Remaining:

Current fine    $0.00
balance:

I fell into the sheets, her bed unmade from when she'd climbed out of it that morning. I smelled her all around me — in the sheets, on the pillows, in her hair that fell over me as she straddled my lap again. This time, she rolled that condom down over my shaft, and then she placed her hands on my shoulders, her eyes wide and locked on mine as she lowered down onto my tip.

I hissed, inhaling a breath so hot it felt like smoke in my lungs.

Mallory dropped a little lower, the tip of me stretching her open again, and with each centimeter that she dropped, I swore the fire spread. I felt it in my lungs, my veins, every muscle and joint and organ burning alive with one all-encompassing thought.

*Mine.*

I was fucked.

I knew it when she took me in completely, when she paused there with me inside her, our eyes locked, her lips parted and my bleeding heart in her fucking hands. She'd taken a part of me, and given me a part of *her*, and now — without the other — neither of us would be the same again.

Mallory's breaths worked in time with her movements — an inhale each time she lifted, a shaky exhale each time she lowered — over and over, again and again, her hands braced on my shoulders, her eyes locked on mine. My grip was so tight on her hips I knew I'd leave a mark, but I couldn't move them, couldn't release for fear she'd disappear like a fantasy I'd had so many times.

Her pace was so slow, so torturous. I felt every centimeter of her walls pulsing around me, and the climax was right there, waiting to release, but never quite reached.

I rolled us, maneuvering until I was on top, and I pushed up onto my knees with my hands braced on her thighs. With each pump of my hips, I pulled her toward me, reaching a new depth that made her eyes roll shut. Her fists twisted in the sheets, yanking until one corner popped off the mattress.

She moaned and writhed under my pulses, her beautiful breasts bouncing with each new thrust. I fell down over her so I could suck each mound into my mouth, tongue circling her nipples, hands kneading the flesh. She was everywhere — her nails on my back, her ankles locked behind my ass, her breasts in my mouth, my hands, her pussy tightening around my cock.

I sucked in a breath when she pulled my mouth to hers again, kissing me hard, and I pumped once, twice, a third time before I pressed so deep into her I saw stars.

She cried out, her moans living and dying in my mouth as I found my release inside her. Everything was still except for where I pulsed between her legs, and for that moment in time, I'd found the kind of ecstasy I thought only drugs could produce.

Maybe I blacked out.

Maybe I traveled through time, to another universe, another dimension.

I couldn't be sure, but when I came to, I was on my back, panting, my fingers tangled in Mallory's hair. Her leg was draped over my stomach, her arm over my chest, both of us riddled with such a fierce exhaustion that we couldn't open our eyes.

For a while, it was just us breathing, fingers gently moving — mine in her hair, hers trailing a path from my pecs to my abdomen and back again. When our breathing smoothed out, I could hear the distant sound of the music still playing on the speaker downstairs, and the soft whiz of a car driving by on Main Street.

Mallory lifted her head, balancing her chin on my chest as her eyes searched mine. She quirked one brow. "I think you ruined my pants."

I barked out a laugh, and I wasn't sure if it was because of what she'd said or because I'd just realized that it was real. What had only happened in my dreams before tonight had just happened in reality.

I had a naked Mallory Scooter sprawled across me, and it was so much sweeter than anything I'd ever dreamed.

"Well, paybacks are a bitch," I said, nodding toward my paint-stained shirt on the floor. "Told you that was one of my favorite shirts."

Mallory smiled, her eyes heavy and sated. She climbed up my chest, pressing her lips to mine, and when she pulled away, she watched me with questions and concerns dancing in those blue irises of hers.

But she didn't speak any of them out loud.

Instead, she rested her head again, wrapping herself around me even tighter as I pressed a kiss to her forehead.

And in the arms of denial, we both fell fast asleep.

I didn't know what time it was when I finally woke the next morning, only that the weight of Mallory's head was still resting on my chest.

It was warm, even with the comforter kicked down to my feet and the sheets covering only half of my naked torso. My body ached as I stretched my toes, flexing my calves, feeling the muscles in my quads protest at the movement after last night.

Sometime in the middle of the night, I'd woken up to Mallory's ass pressed against my groin. I didn't remember what time, or how long we'd been out. If anything, it felt almost like a drunken dream, like something I'd imagined — spooning her, kissing her neck, feeling her nipples harden under my touch, her back arch as I pressed my erection between the gap of her thighs.

Neither one of us had rested again until we were both spent, and then we'd curled back up easily, like we'd been together for years, like me being in her bed was the most natural thing in the world.

I ran my fingers through Mallory's hair, ready to gently wake her, but when the silky strands ended abruptly, I peeked one eye open.

Dalí flicked his tail from where he was curled up on my chest, croaking out something between a meow and a yawn as he watched me with lazy yellow eyes.

"Well, hello there," I murmured, scratching behind his ear.

I looked around the rest of the studio apartment for some sign of Mallory, but found nothing. It was just a series of messes everywhere I gazed — the wad of paint-stained sheets on the bed, our clothes littering the floor. I couldn't help but let my eyes wander over her own mess that had existed before I'd even been there, too — the dishes in the sink, the half-empty glasses and mugs on the coffee table, the wires from her curling irons and straighteners falling over the cabinet of the bathroom sink, the dozens of paintings and sketches and framed photographs leaning against the base of nearly every wall.

I smiled, feeling completely surrounded by her.

And in the next instant, my stomach dropped so violently I nearly puked.

I shot up in bed, causing Dalí to scamper off much the way he did the night before. He hid under the couch as

I had my heart attack, and I pressed a hand to my chest, feeling the hard pumping of the frantic organ beneath.

*Holy fuck.*

*I slept with Mallory Scooter.*

I ran a hand back through my disheveled hair, cursing under my breath when I couldn't get my fingers through the matted paint. All the thoughts swirling around in my head now felt just as sticky and complicated.

Thoughts that were *nowhere* to be found last night.

I couldn't grasp onto one worry before another bounced in, like a set of ping pong balls let loose inside a rotating box. I thought about my mom, my brothers, about the fact that Mallory had been off-limits to me my entire life due to the last name she bore. My job was the next thought in my mind — the title I had, the one I wanted, the years of effort I'd put in to be the best at what I did.

I thought about the laptop, the hard drive, the password I wasn't sure I'd ever be able to decode to see if there was anything my father left behind. I'd been so fixated on that yesterday, and maybe that's why I'd had the lapse in judgment.

I wasn't in the right frame of mind.

But perhaps the biggest worry of all was that the number-one thought in my head *wasn't* that it was wrong, that I had fucked everything up by giving in, that I'd finally had Mallory Scooter in the way I'd always desired.

It was that I still wanted her, even *more* so now, and she was nowhere to be found.

Anxiety was still rippling through me as I let out a sigh, trying to calm my breathing and looking around the room as if it would have some sort of answer for me. When I looked past the pillow Mallory had slept on last night, I saw a sketch pad near her phone charger. It was propped open to a page somewhere in the middle, with chicken-scratch scrawling across it.

I reached over, pulling the pad into my lap, and when I saw the doodle next to the words, I smirked.

It was us — her mid-slingshot with her paint brush, sending paint flying across the page at me. And I had a brush in my hand, though my arms were crossed, shielding my face. We were both laughing, our features large and cartoonish.

And my awe for Mallory grew even more at the fact that she could bring that image to life, that she could bring *any* memory back with just a pencil, a sheet of paper, and those magic hands of hers.

*Had to leave early for church — you know, princess of Stratford, and all. ;) Help yourself to some coffee. - M*

I was still smiling, but my stomach dipped and flattened at her words. Other than the half-hearted joke and a winking face scrawled after it, there was no indication of how she was feeling, of what she was thinking about what had transpired between us the night before.

Then again, I couldn't exactly blame her — since I had no fucking idea what to think about it all, either.

Another sigh left my chest as I crawled out of bed, tugging on my sweat pants before I tore out the note and the doodle, folding it into a square and tucking it in my pocket. I pulled on my t-shirt next, and then I padded my way over to the still-hot coffee pot, pouring what was left into a mug I'd plucked from the clean dish rack.

I sipped carefully on the hot liquid, leaning against her kitchen cabinet and looking around at the mess again.

I couldn't de-tangle any of my thoughts, so I decided to put them to rest for now. I needed to talk to her — that much was fairly clear — and I couldn't talk to her right now. Until I could, I needed to calm down, to not let anxiety convince me I needed to break through the doors of that church and demand answers in front of God and the whole town.

I *did* need to get through those church doors, though — not to interrogate Mallory Scooter, but to show face and make Momma happy. I'd already missed the first service, but I could make it to the second one, and knowing Momma, she'd wait to make sure I showed up since I hadn't made it for the early one.

And though I was able to put *most* of my worries to bed, at least for the moment, I wasn't able to leave that apartment in the disarray it was in.

So, I finished my coffee, coaxing Dalí out from under the couch and loving on him while I made a plan. Then, I did the best thing I could do for my anxiety.

I cleaned.

And left a note of my own before slipping out the back door.

# Chapter Eleven

## MALLORY

It felt like someone else sitting at the country club brunch with my parents.

It must have been someone else's hand reaching for that mimosa, someone else's mouth moving, answering my parents' questions. It absolutely had to be someone else's legs crossing in the sun dress under the table.

Because in my mind, I was still in bed with Logan Becker.

I was across town, at the opposite end of Main Street, stretched out under the sheets in the morning sun with my bare chest pressed against his ribs. My arms were wrapped around him, his around me, my head on his chest, his breath on my ear.

Or maybe I was still stuck in a memory of last night. I could still feel his hands running gently over my spine, could hear the tender way he moaned my name in the middle of the night, could feel his lips pressing to the back of my neck before his hands slipped between my legs...

I bit my lip against a blush and a smile, sipping the delicious mixture of champagne and orange juice from the flute in my hand.

"I'll take that as a yes?" Mom asked.

I blinked, blotting my lips with the linen napkin in my lap. "Hmm?"

She chuckled. "You're so cheery today, but I swear, you're a million miles away," she commented. "I asked if you'd started unpacking at the shop yet, if things were coming together?"

A flash of last night hit me — paint and lips, music and eyes, a sigh and a kiss and a...

"Yes," I said, unable to hide my smile this time. My cheeks flushed as I traced the tip of my finger around the lip of the flute glass. "Things are coming together quite nicely."

My parents likely thought I was high, for how much I'd smiled at church that morning and now at brunch with them and my brother, Malcolm. I hated spending time with them — they knew it, I knew it — but every Sunday, our family was forced together.

At least, that's the way it was when I was in town.

I'd been able to escape the Stratford way of life when I was in college, but now that I was back — and, even though not living with them, *technically* living under a roof that they owned — I had to play by their rules again.

Dad beamed proudly, glancing at me over his menu. "That's my girl. I can't wait for the grand opening. We're going to throw the biggest party this town has seen." He cleared his throat, looking back at his menu — even though we all knew he'd order the same thing he always did and order it for Mom, too. "As long as it's in proper order, of course."

That was his nice way of saying that if he was going to show face and endorse my little *project*, it would have to be something bright and shiny and perfect. God forbid anyone with the Scooter blood in their veins make even the slightest mistake. He was still trying to fight off the rumors circling around town after the mayor of Stratford was called out for owing him a hefty debt from his nights in our underground casino.

Daddy didn't like stains on the family name, and he'd do anything to avoid them.

My brother, Malcolm, seemed bored at the table that morning. He was the spitting image of my father, only about a foot shorter and fifty pounds lighter. He was drinking champagne *without* the orange juice chaser, and constantly looking at his watch — no doubt counting down the minutes until he and Dad would go golfing.

When the waiter came, Dad ordered two eggs over easy, three slices of bacon, cheesy grits and one single pancake — for both him and Mom, of course. She hadn't ordered a meal for herself in the time I'd been alive, and I wondered if she even knew what food she liked anymore or if she just ate whatever her husband decided was fit for her.

Mom was the perfect southern belle that morning, her short hair freshly dyed brunette again — like no one in this town knew she was old enough to have grays — an Easter-egg-yellow sundress covering her shoulders and knees, and a classic string of pearls around her neck. She smiled and nodded and spoke when spoken to, chiming in when it was classy and helpful but keeping her mouth shut otherwise. She'd had years of training, and I knew part of it was that she grew up in a different time than I did.

Still, I wondered what went on in her head, what she would say if somehow I could rip that filter she wore to shreds. I had been around my mother for more than eighteen years of my life, and I still had no idea who she really was.

"So, things are all set up, then?" Dad asked when the waiter was gone.

"Pretty close. The different areas of the shop are in order for the most part. I need to work on the schedule, on what classes I want to offer consistently and brainstorm the first few special workshops. I'm waiting on some additional supplies and a few furniture items, too, and I'd like to get some art and décor on the walls before I consider announcing the opening. But, I think we're getting close."

My heart squeezed, because I couldn't believe I'd turned it around in such short notice, that everything I'd imagined coming to life was within my grasp.

It wouldn't have been possible without a certain man whom I couldn't stop thinking about.

My brother seemed to have read my mind, because he harrumphed a laugh, chugging what was left in his champagne flute before refilling it to the top. "I heard you had some help yesterday."

I narrowed my eyes at him, but he just smirked. I loved my brother — truly, I did — but he was a kiss up, and always liked to be on Dad's good side. Not that it was hard for him to be the favorite child, since he stayed out of trouble for the most part and did any and everything Dad asked of him.

I, on the other hand, would do the exact opposite of what my father expected on principle alone.

He'd told me one time in high school when we were in a fight that *I* was the favorite child, that I was all our parents ever talked about. I realized then that maybe part of him resented me for it. But what he didn't understand was that they talked about me because they wanted to *change* me, to stop my embarrassment on the family.

He was their pride and joy, and I was not after that title.

"Oh?" Mom asked, polite as ever. "Was it one of your girlfriends?"

I snorted, because my entire family knew there wasn't a single girl in Stratford whom I got along with.

Dad gave a disapproving grunt of his own. "Let me guess, it was that gay friend of yours, right? What's his name?" He waved his hand with a wrinkled nose. "*Christoph* or something?"

"Chris," I corrected, rolling my eyes. "His name doesn't morph into something more flamboyant just because he'd rather love a man than a woman. Also, there's no need to refer to him as my gay friend. He's my friend. No adjectives needed."

Dad waved me off again. "I'm sure he was helpful in the décor department."

I ground my teeth, but as much as his comments about my best friend perturbed me, I preferred that frustration to what I experienced when my brother spoke again.

"Nope. I heard Logan *Becker* was there. All. Day. Long."

My parents both snapped their eyes to me then, Dad's brows furrowing and Mom's mouth popping open in a shocked *O* as they waited for an explanation.

"Calm down," I said, holding up both hands like I'd just been accused of doing meth. I ignored the way my heart pounded hard inside my chest, hoping they couldn't see right through the lie I was about to tell. "He's good at organizing things, which I learned from our *punishment* this week." I gave Dad a pointed look. "Thanks for that, by the way. I'm sure you and Uncle Mac loved thinking that one up."

"I have no idea what you're talking about," Dad lied. I *knew* it was a lie, but I didn't press him on it. "And don't turn this on me. Why was Logan Becker at your shop?"

"Unpacking boxes, building furniture, hanging art, setting up and organizing supplies in a way that would make sense for classes. He was *helping*," I emphasized. "Which is more than any of you three have done, and you're my family. So, back off."

Mom seemed to relax a bit, reaching for her mimosa for a sip, but Dad narrowed his eyes in suspicion.

"I don't think it's a good idea for you to be hanging out with him outside of what's necessary during your training at the distillery."

"Yeah, well, you also didn't think it was a good idea for me to pierce my nose, but, here we are."

"Do not get smart with me, young lady," he barked, and Malcolm snickered, which earned him a swift kick to the shin under the table.

"Relax," I said as my brother rubbed his leg. "I'm not hooking up with Logan Becker, Dad."

Mom gasped. "Mallory Loraine!"

"What?" I shrugged. "That's what he's thinking. That's why he's all freaked out."

"That's enough, Mallory," Dad warned under his breath, and it was just as our appetizer of cinnamon bread was brought to the table. He smiled at the waiter, thanking him, and glared at me one last time before he unraveled his napkin. "I just want to remind you to keep your distance and remember the deal we have in place. I wouldn't want you to lose everything you've worked so hard for over something stupid." His eyes hardened, but

*neat*

then he pulled his gaze away, smiling at Mom and reaching over to squeeze her hand. "Now, I think we've had enough of this talk at the table. Malcolm, tell us how things are going in the marketing department."

That launched the conversation back into Scooter Whiskey territory — the most comfortable subject for my father — and launched *me* back into my own thoughts. I let myself tune out, hearing my father's warning as I envisioned Logan's smile, his honey gold eyes, his ridiculous arms that I'd felt up close and personal last night.

My chest tightened, because I never considered all the things that would come *after* a night like last night. And now that I was sitting at the table with three reminders of why I never should have even *thought* of kissing Logan, let alone going through with it, I realized how careless I'd been.

Normally, I wouldn't have cared. Normally, I would have freaking *married* Logan Becker, if it meant giving my father an ulcer and distancing myself more from the family name.

But normally, I didn't have an art studio on the line, and not a prayer of making it happen without my father's help.

My thoughts were a hurricane as I sat mute through the rest of brunch, and by the time I got home, all I wanted to do was take a hot shower and sleep the afternoon away. I walked straight upstairs, slung my keys and purse on the coffee table, and started stripping.

But I stopped right in the middle of the room.

Nothing in my apartment was how I'd left it. The dirty dishes were washed and laid in the rack to dry, my bathroom counter was wiped down, my hair product all put away on the shelf, flat irons and curling irons tucked away into a basket on the counter that I forgot I even owned. The bed was made, the tables cleared, and if I didn't know better, I'd say the floors were swept and mopped, too.

And every single wall was decorated with my paintings, sketches, photographs, and awards.

They were everywhere — the sunset photo I'd captured on the white, sandy beach in Alabama, the self-portrait sketch I'd been assigned to do my second year in school, the shockingly bright and vivid painting I'd done of a trio of jazz musicians on the street in New Orleans. Even my diploma — which, before, had been curled up and tossed into a box of other worthless things — was flattened and framed, the wrinkles of my treatment of it barely visible.

I covered my smile, shaking my head as I looked around the room. "Oh, Logan Becker," I whispered to myself. "What kind of strange creature are you?"

In the middle of the bed was a note, scrawled on the same sketch paper I'd left him one on that morning. When I picked it up, I laughed again at the stick-figure drawing — a girl and a boy in a very promiscuous position, her bent at the waist, him behind her, both of them smiling.

*Thanks for the coffee, and for a great night. Made the bed, but fair warning — there's still paint on the sheets. I thought about washing them, but decided I wanted you to go to bed with a reminder of me. Try not to get too turned on without me here. See you at work. — L*

My cheeks shaded, and I pressed my hand to the heat there, shaking my head at the note.

I was in a special kind of trouble now.

## LOGAN

Later that Sunday evening, all my brothers and I were gathered around the fire pit in Mom's backyard, kicked back, each with a drink in our hand. The night was quiet, save for the sounds of us sipping and the soft music coming from inside the house. Mom was in there making dinner, singing and bopping along to her favorite Fleetwood Mac album. Something about the quietness made me miss the summer, when the katydids chirped loud throughout the night, and the fireflies flickered on and off in the yard.

I'd tried my best to get my mind off Mallory, but had mostly failed. Church had been a small distraction, and I'd gotten in a good workout afterward, using my own bodyweight as torture until my muscles were aching and sweat was rolling off every inch of me. But now that I was quiet again, my hand wrapped around a glass of whiskey and my eyes watching the fire dance, all thoughts bounced back to her.

I hadn't heard from her.

I expected a text when she got home and seen that I'd cleaned up her place, but nothing came. Neither of us had initiated talking about last night, and the longer the silence stretched between us, the more my stomach turned.

I wondered if she regretted it.

I wondered if she was across town right now, cursing herself and thinking through excuses to blow off work tomorrow to avoid seeing me.

I wondered if I'd ever be the same again, now that I'd had her.

I knew the answer to that last musing, though I chose not to admit it. Instead, I lifted my glass, taking a sip of the amber liquid inside it and glancing at my older brother across the fire.

Noah could barely sit still, and every two seconds, he was pulling his phone from his pocket to spout off a text before tucking it back in. Tomorrow morning, he was getting on a plane to Salt Lake City to go see his girlfriend, Ruby Grace, for the first time in a month.

Jordan sat next to him, possibly more drunk than I'd seen him my entire life — and that was to say, he had a slight buzz. His eyes were glossy, lids heavy, and a permanent smile was fixed on his face — which, again, was rare, considering he smiled about as much as I left my bed unmade in the morning. The high school football team had finished out their season with an epic win at the state championship game Friday night, making it the second time he'd lead them to that victory as head coach. The trophy was inside, set up as a centerpiece on the dinner table for us to celebrate around tonight.

And Mikey, who was sitting on the other side of me, was the complete opposite of his oldest brother. I couldn't remember the last time I'd seen him smile, and watching him now — his eyes on the fire, his hands empty, no longer strumming on a guitar like they normally would have been around a fire before dinner, I wondered if this was one of those moments in his life where everything changed — namely, who he was.

I'd had a few of those pivotal moments in my life, and I knew there were some things you bounced back from, and other things that permanently shifted you. I guess if the love of my young life left me to go to Nashville when I'd always thought we'd chase her dreams together, I'd be fucked up, too.

neat

Noah let out a frustrated sigh, kicking back in his chair with so much force he knocked a bit of whiskey out of the glass balancing on the arm of it. He wrapped his hand around it to steady it again, but his foot immediately started bouncing, taking his whole leg with it.

I smirked. "Nervous, bro?"

"I can't fucking sit still," he said, stating the obvious. "I should be excited to get on that plane in the morning, but instead, I feel so nervous I might actually vomit."

"Why in the world are you nervous?" I asked. "I was joking. I thought you were just so excited you couldn't wait for that six a.m. wake-up call."

"I haven't seen her in a month," he pointed out, wiping the sweat off the outside of his glass with his thumb. "What if she hasn't missed me. What if she's having the time of her life out there and not thinking about me at all. What if I get there and I'm only in her way and she can't wait for me to leave. What if she met someone who—"

"I'm going to stop you right there," Jordan said on a laugh. He held out his hands. "Ruby Grace loves you, Noah. She's probably so excited *she* can't sit still on the other side of the country. It's okay to be nervous," he added with a shrug. "It's been a while, and you guys went from living in the same town to being long distance overnight. It's going to be different. But the love you have?" He shook his head. "That's the same. If anything, it's stronger."

"But—"

"She walked out on her fucking wedding for you," Mikey said, cutting off Noah's rebuttal.

We all grew silent, turning to face our youngest brother who had said more to us in that sentence than he had in weeks.

"If that doesn't tell you that woman loves you, then I don't know what will." He tossed a rock he'd been turning

172

over in his hands somewhere behind him, standing. "I'm going for a walk. Tell Mama I'll be back in time for dinner."

He didn't say another word, and none of us tried to stop him. He disappeared down the driveway, only the moonlight guiding him past that.

Jordan's mouth turned to the side as he watched him go. "We've got to do something to help him."

"It's only been a couple months," Noah said. "I'm sure he's just grieving."

"Maybe," I chimed in. "But, we may also have to come to terms with the fact that the young, carefree Mikey we knew before is gone now. I mean, didn't we all hit a point in our lives where all that perpetual joy left? When we realized the world could be a really fucking cruel place?"

My brothers were silent then, each of them remembering a time in their life when it happened, just as I was remembering mine. I was almost positive it was the same moment for all three of us — that unforgettable summer day when we lost the man who'd raised us.

Noah turned the subject to Jordan, asking him to recount the game Friday night. Mom had gone out of town with him to watch the game, but Mikey had asked to stay behind, so Noah offered to stay back with him. And I'd been at home trying to figure out dad's laptop — which I still hadn't told my brothers about.

My stomach turned, because for some reason, I didn't feel like I could open up to my brothers about anything going on with me — not the punishment I'd received at work, not the laptop I'd found, and *definitely* not the fact that I'd slept with Mallory Scooter and liked it.

I'd been able to go to my brothers with everything in my life up until that point, but something in my gut told me I couldn't go to them and get the answer I wanted to hear.

What I *wanted* was for them to nod in understanding, to smile when I admitted I'd had a crush on her forever, and to high five me when I told them I'd had the best sex of my life last night. I wanted them to say they loved me and didn't give a fuck if I was dating a Scooter.

But the reality was that not a single one of them would say anything close to that.

And I couldn't blame them.

There was a tie between our families — Mallory's and mine — and though no one said it out loud, every single one of us thought that line was drawn in blood. In my *father's* blood, to be exact.

Something shady happened at that distillery the day my father died.

But maybe, if I cracked the hard drive open, I could find the answers we'd been looking for for years — and free Mallory of the stigma my family had for her in the process.

Still, I needed someone to talk to, and since Mallory wasn't texting me and my brothers all had their own shit going on, I turned to the other best friend in my life.

"I'm going to go see if Mom needs any help," I said, draining the last of the whiskey in my glass. "You guys need anything?"

They shook their heads, jumping right back into their conversation once I was standing. I made my way across the backyard and up the steps of the back porch, swinging inside just as Mom did a little twirl to the chorus of "Rhiannon."

She didn't hear me come in at first — not that I was surprised, with the level the music was blasting — and she bopped across the kitchen, swaying her hips and singing along on her way from checking whatever was baking in the oven to revisiting the cutting board where a parade of vegetables were in the middle of being diced.

I would have given anything in that moment to see my Dad sneak in behind her, twirling her out before pulling her back into him and kissing her nose the way he'd always do. I'd have given anything to hear her laugh, see the crinkle of her nose as she shoved him off playfully, only to watch him go back to the room where my brothers and I were, all the love in the world in those eyes of hers.

I swallowed past the knot in my throat, and I took his place as best I could. I stepped into the kitchen, slipping one of Dad's old aprons over my head and tying it behind my waist as I sang along with Mom. She smiled when she saw me, handing me the knife so I could take over where she was dicing and she moved to the bowl she was mixing the batter for dessert in.

"This is the best album in the world," she said, still bopping along to the song. She pointed a whisk at me. "And if anyone says otherwise, you tell them they'll have to fight your mama."

I chuckled, but didn't argue. The *Rumors* album was definitely one of the best albums in my mind, too.

For the rest of the song, we worked side by side just singing and swaying to the music. When it faded out, Mom crossed to the stereo in the living room and turned it down enough for us to talk over it. She gave me a knowing smile when she was back beside me in the kitchen, but then her eyes fell back to the task at hand.

"So," she said. "What's going on, Logan Daniel?"

I shrugged. "Nothing. Can't a son help his mom in the kitchen?"

Mama chuckled. "Yes, he certainly can. But, a mom can also know when her son has something on his mind."

She lifted a brow in my direction, but kept right on working, scraping the batter she'd mixed into a small pan. I realized then that she was making her famous double chocolate brownies, and when she handed me the whisk to lick the excess batter off like I'd used to as a kid, my chest ached for those simpler days.

I took the whisk, running my tongue over the bottom where the batter was about to drip. "You're too smart for your own good, woman."

"You sound like your father." She chuckled, squeezing some caramel over the top of the batter that she'd weave in with a toothpick. "Now, talk to your Mama."

I licked one whole side of the whisk, hoping the time it'd take me to eat it and lick the excess chocolate from my lips would give me the chance to find the right words.

"There's a girl," I settled on, and as soon as the words were out of my mouth, there was a smile curling on Mom's.

"Ah," she said, eyes on the toothpick she was dragging over the brownie batter, creating swirls of chocolate and caramel. "As there always is."

"She's..." I paused, licking the whisk again as I tried to figure out the right way to put it. "She's unlike any woman I've ever known, Mom. She has a mind of her own and thinks for herself, instead of falling into the town gossip or doing what everyone else does. And she's creative, and talented, and smart..." I smiled. "And funny. She's quick on her feet, and she doesn't take shit from anyone — least of all me. I don't know, I guess hanging out with her has just been... refreshing, if that makes sense."

"It does," Mom said, nodding with that same smile on her face. "You know, you're a lot like your father, in the sense that you never were entertained by the ordinary. You always craved the *extra*ordinary, even as a boy. You didn't want the same toys or video games that your brothers wanted. You wanted books, and Legos, and puzzles that challenged you." She chuckled. "If you ever fell for a run-of-the-mill girl, I'd probably croak from surprise."

"Mom," I said, frowning. "Don't even joke about that."

She waved me off. "Oh, stop it. You know what I meant." She checked the casserole in the oven, but apparently decided it wasn't done yet. She closed the door again, leaning her hip against it and folding her arms. "Are you and this girl dating, or are you just... what do the kids call it now? *Hooking up?*"

Mom made air quotes around that last part, and I barked out a laugh, shaking my head.

"We're not hooking up," I lied, because for all intents and purposes, that was probably the best way to describe what had happened between us last night. Still, it felt like more... even if we didn't have a title, or even a conversation about what had happened yet. "But, we're not dating either."

"So what are you?"

I sighed. "I guess that's part of the problem, isn't it?" I cleaned what was left of the batter on the whisk, dropping it into the sink before I turned to face Mom again, my hands braced behind me on the counter. "I think right now, we're friends."

"But you want to be more."

My stomach soured, because it was the first time I'd admitted it — to myself or otherwise.

I nodded.

Mom smiled, looking thoughtful for a long moment before she spoke. "Well, I think it's time you had a conversation with this girl. You know, your father and I always said that the reason our relationship worked as well as it did was because we were best friends first, and lovers second. We could come to each other with anything — even when it was uncomfortable to talk about. The other one was always there to listen, to understand — no matter what." Mom shrugged. "Maybe being honest with this girl about how you're feeling will be a test of sorts, to see if you have communication established, if you can go to her and make her feel comfortable to do the same with you."

I nodded, eyes on the old laminate floor between Mom and me. "Dad would have given that same advice," I mused. "He was always telling us not to shy away from our emotions, that it never made us less of a man to feel."

Mom's eyes glossed over a bit at that, but she smiled past them, shaking her head. "He was the best man," she whispered. "The best father."

I nodded, that thick knot back in my throat as silence settled over the kitchen.

"So," Mom said, swiping at a tear that had slipped free and fallen down her cheek. She forced a smile. "Do I know this girl?"

I frowned. "You do, actually... and that's partly why I haven't talked to her about how I'm feeling."

"What?" Mom shook her head, face screwing up in confusion. "Why on Earth would the fact that I know her be part of the problem?"

I didn't respond, just watched her with brows folded together, hands gripping the counter behind me. She shook her head again, waiting for me to answer, but then like a cloud passing over the sun, recognition slid over her face, slowly erasing the confusion as her mouth fell open.

Time stretched in that moment, a few seconds feeling like hours as Mom blinked, closed her mouth again, and turned her back on me.

She picked up the knife I'd abandoned for the whisk, chopping the tomatoes on the cutting board with more force than necessary as she shook her head. "No."

"Mom, hear me out."

"No!" She spun, facing me again with red cheeks and wide eyes. The knife was shaking in her hands. "Now, I'm sure Mallory Scooter is a nice girl, Logan, but it's so much bigger than that. Her family is trouble, son. You don't understand what they're capable of."

"Mom, come on..."

"I don't want to hear another word about this," she said, turning back to the cutting board with her mind made up.

She chopped away while I stood there with my hands open toward her, my jaw slack in disbelief. Mom had always been the most level-headed of the family, even when Dad was around. When he got up in arms about something, she was the one to cool him down. But now, she could barely cut a vegetable, she was so angry.

All because of me, and the feeling I'd given into after fighting it for half my life for this exact reason.

"Mom," I tried again, but she cut me off.

"Set the table and call your brothers inside." She dumped the tomatoes she'd cut into a large salad bowl, turning for a cucumber next.

She wouldn't look at me.

I swallowed, nodding numbly even though she wasn't looking at me to see my silent agreement. I set the table as she asked, called my brothers in, and crawled inside my thoughts for the rest of the night.

Dinner was lively, all of us celebrating Jordan's win at state, but the smile on my face was hollow. The questions I asked felt like they came from someone else's mouth, the jokes I made were distant and foggy, like I was playing host to a foreign entity running my body for me that night.

On the inside, I was the loneliest I'd been in my entire life.

If I couldn't even go to *Mom* about Mallory, I knew for sure I couldn't go to my brothers. And if I couldn't go to any of them, that meant I was facing what would happen next with Mallory on my own.

That cold sense of loneliness settled in like a thick fog, and by the time I was crawling back into my truck to head home for the night, I might as well have been in a one-man submarine in the middle of the Atlantic.

I stared at the Chevy emblem on my steering wheel until it blurred — hands on the wheel, mind somewhere far away that I'd never been before. When I finally blinked my way out of the daze and turned the key, bringing the engine to life, my phone lit up in the passenger seat.

And Mallory's name filled the screen.

You would have thought I was a shortstop diving for a ground ball for how fast my hand shot out, scooping the device into my grasp, fingers typing out my password until her text message popped up.

**Mallory: You bastard.**

The excitement I'd felt just moments before evaporated in a whoosh, taking my next breath with it. I watched the bouncing dots on the screen that told me she was typing more, and I ran through all the possible messages that might come next.

*You didn't call.*
*Why did you clean my house, you weirdo?*
*The sex was awful, don't ever talk to me again.*

But instead, an entire paragraph of text mixed with emojis came through.

**Mallory: I told you I'm not good with emotions, and you recommend this book??? Are you an emotional serial killer? Frederick just got beat up, and Werner went home with him, but now they're saying he's been lying and that he's 18 when he's actually 16 and all because they want him in Berlin to build technology for the Nazis. And then poor Marie-Laure is growing up and losing her innocence because she knows her dad isn't coming back and Etienne won't let Madame Blanchard run her rebellion out of his house anymore and... and...**

There was a pause, and then a single crying face emoji came through.

I chuckled, relief washing over me at the same time that a powerful ache rolled through my chest again. I remembered those feelings when I'd read *All the Light We Cannot See*, and the way the story unfolded, the incredible writing, the powerful emotions — they were all part of the reason it was my favorite book.

She was reading my favorite book.

And somehow, that string of emotions she was feeling while reading it was better than anything else she could have said in that moment.

**Me: You're reading.**

*neat*

**Mallory: I'm reading.**

**Mallory: And can barely breathe let alone put this book down, all thanks to you. Asshole.**

I smiled, chest tightening as my fingers hovered over the keyboard, wondering what to say next. I didn't know if I should bring up last night, if I should take the opportunity to ask what she was thinking. But before I could decide, another text came through.

**Mallory: And maybe it was ME looking for an excuse to text YOU this time...**

My heart leapt like a fucking leprechaun, and I couldn't bite back the smile that bloomed on my face if I tried.

**Me: I'm glad you found one.**

I waited for another text to come through, but when it didn't, I slipped my phone into the cupholder in my console, deciding to save the words I really wanted to say for when I'd see her tomorrow. Then, I put my old truck in drive, and I drove home with a twist in my stomach — the same one that had been there all night, only now, it wasn't from anxiety, but from an unbearable excitement.

I couldn't wait to see her in the morning.

# Chapter Twelve

## MALLORY

I was way too giddy to be going into work.

After the conversation I'd had with my dad, I should have been dreading walking through those distillery doors. I should have had a stomach full of knots because I'd have to tell Logan Becker that what happened Saturday night could never, *ever*, happen again, that we had to draw a line between us and stay firmly on opposite sides, that I had a lot to lose and so did he, and we should just stay away from each other.

But I realized as I bounced down the hall to the tour guide lobby that *should have* didn't matter much to me — and it'd been that way my whole life. I didn't heed the warnings I was given, and I didn't do what I was told.

I had two coffees in my hand when I slipped into Logan's office, and just like I knew he would be, he was already there, highlighting something on his clipboard when I sat the coffee down in front of him.

"Happy Monday," I said, plopping down in the seat across from him.

Logan kicked back in his chair, and for the first time since he was inside me on Saturday night, our eyes met. "Mornin'."

I drank him in like *he* was the piping hot cup of coffee then, my neck heating as his eyes trailed slowly over me, too. My fingers ached to run through his hair, to pull on it until it was as disheveled as it had been that night in my bed. I let my eyes stop at every memorable spot as they grazed his body — that wide chest I'd laid my head on half the night, the abs I now knew he hid under that polo, those strong hands that had pinned me against my front door.

I squeezed my thighs together, meeting his eyes at the same time his snapped up from my lips.

"So... Saturday happened."

He chuckled, crossing one ankle over the opposite knee and folding his hands behind his head. "Indeed, it did." He frowned then, and I watched the Adam's apple in his throat bob. "I told my mom."

My eyes shot open wide. "You told your mom that we fucked?"

"No, no, no," he said, eyes doubling as he held his hands out toward me. "I would never... no. I just, she *may* have noticed that I was distracted at dinner last night, and I *may* have told her that... well, that *you* were the distraction."

Even though I could tell by his features that the conversation with his mom hadn't gone well, I couldn't help but smirk at the fact that he'd told her about me, at all. It was a silly, foolish feeling, like the kind I'd had as a teenager when bad boy Ronny Carmichael passed me a note between classes.

I'd been on his mind.

And he'd told his mom about me.

*Why did that make me want to swoon like a fucking Disney character?*

"I'm guessing she wasn't too thrilled that her son was being seduced by Mallory Scooter, huh?"

Logan cocked a brow. "I think we could argue who did the seducing that night."

"We could, but I'd win.

He let out one bark of a laugh at that, shaking his head. But the smile slipped off his face like a mud slide on the side of the mountain, his mouth pulling to one side. "You could say she wasn't exactly receptive..." He ran a hand back through his hair, and again, my fingers ached in jealousy. "Not that I should have been surprised, I guess."

"My father was the same."

It was his turn to blanch. "You told your *dad*?"

I laughed, folding my arms over my chest. "Relax. I didn't tell him you had my wrists pinned above my head and your hands under my yoga pants."

He smirked at that, the dimple flashing an appearance on his left cheek before it disappeared again.

"But," I continued. "My loud mouth brother dropped the bomb that you'd been at the studio helping me, and my dad drew his own conclusions." I lowered my voice and frowned, mimicking my father's voice. "*I don't think it's a good idea for you to be hanging out with him outside of what's necessary during your training at the distillery.*"

I waggled my finger with every word, and Logan chuckled, shaking his head.

"It's silly, isn't it?" he asked. "To let some old family feud define what we can and can't do."

"It is," I agreed, and though it sounded like we'd both just admitted that we didn't give a fuck about what our parents thought, we both knew it wasn't true. Logan loved his mother and his brothers more than anyone in the world, and I knew it killed him to disappoint them in any way, to let them down. As for me, I had an art studio on the line — one my father would rip away in the blink of an eye if he ever found out what happened between me and Logan.

"So... I guess we should just be..." Logan swallowed. "Friends?"

The way he asked it, the way his eyebrows bent together, his lips flattening — I knew it was a hollow offer.

I nodded. "Sure. Of course." A smile that felt like a wave of nausea found my lips. "Friends."

Logan watched me, and I watched him, both of us waiting for something more. It seemed like there were a million unborn words between us, floating in the air, waiting for us to reach out and grab them and bring them to life. When a long moment of silence had passed, Logan bit the inside of his cheek, picking up his highlighter he'd abandoned on the desk when I'd walked in like he was ready to get back to work.

"But," I said, and his eyes snapped to mine, the highlighter frozen over the page. "I mean... there's another option, isn't there?"

Logan dropped the highlighter, leaning back again. "There is?"

"I'm just saying," I said, voice shakier than I wanted it to be in that moment. I took a sip of my coffee, shrugging. "What if we kept things low key... casual... just between us?" My eyes found his again. "It is what it is, and it's not what it's not. Right? No need for anyone to know."

"Low key," Logan repeated, like he was tasting the words, checking them for poison with his tongue. "So, friends... with benefits."

I snorted. "If you want to be twenty-one about it, sure."

Logan nodded, over and over, just a slight movement of his chin up and down as he considered it. I watched him as he stood, and I expected him to start pacing the office, but instead, he crossed it, closing his door and turning to face me.

His eyes swept over me, sparking a fire low in my stomach.

He wet his lips.

He took a step.

And then I was out of my chair, meeting him in the middle, the two of us crashing together like magnets.

His hands weaved into my hair when he captured my mouth with his own, both of us sighing on an inhale, moaning on the exhale, leaning into each other like we could somehow melt together completely. All the electricity I'd felt that night came back like a tidal wave, and I surrendered to the waves, letting them drown me. I wanted him to fill my lungs, to conquer every breath, to imprison me.

It was a kiss that told me we were both lying. We both wanted more.

But if it was a choice between this, or nothing at all?

There wasn't a decision to make — not where I was concerned. It had already been made *for* us, without either of us having a say, without either of us having an ounce of control to throw this story in another direction.

We were inevitable, me and him.

And maybe we knew it from the start.

Logan backed me up to the desk, and when my ass hit it, I hiked both legs up, wrapping them around his waist and squeezing. He hissed, sucking my bottom lip between his teeth and releasing it with a pop, his hips rolling against mine. I broke the kiss to let out a gasp, and his mouth was on my neck in an instant, sucking and biting, my eyes rolling back at the contact.

He paused with his lips by my ear, breathing heavy. "I think this could work for me," he whispered, running his tongue over my ear lobe. "This... *friends* agreement." His hands squeezed where they held my hips, and the familiar pressure sent flashes of Saturday night barreling through my memory. I gasped, mouth still hanging open when he kissed my neck over to the opposite ear to whisper again. "What do you think?"

Against the voice inside me warning me not to, I ran my fingers through his hair, gripping those dark strands and pulling his lips back to mine.

That kiss was an answer.

That kiss was a lie.

And distantly, I realized that kiss might be the biggest mistake of my life.

**LOGAN**

For the first time in my life, I had a new routine, and it went like this:

Wake up early, so I could get in the workout I *usually* did in the evenings before I walked out the door for work. Then, I'd practically skip through those distillery doors, and wait as patiently as I could for Mallory to slip into my office and into my arms. It was easy to sneak time together under the guise of our "training" — especially when we finished up the storage closet and got back to tours. We ate lunch together, took break together, walked out together after work... and kept all the touching for behind closed doors.

After work, I went straight to the shop with Mallory. She sprung it on me that she wanted to have the grand opening on Friday — less than a week after we'd unpacked that first set of boxes. And though I thought she was crazy and that she needed at least another two months to be fully ready, I didn't argue — mostly because it gave me an excuse to spend every waking hour after work with her.

We'd paint, and build, and catalog and arrange. We'd test out equipment, and do calculations on the prices each class would have to cost to make a profit, and make plans for how to allocate supplies to each class so that we didn't overspend what we were making. We got the necessary permits and insurance — expedited, of course, thanks to her last name — and with every evening we spent together, working until after midnight, that dream of hers slowly came together.

And somehow, it felt like mine, too.

Mallory asked my opinion on everything, and I had a hand in every single corner of that space. It almost felt like building a home together, and I blamed that for the insane way I was feeling. It had to be that we were spending every day at work together, every night together, only separating long enough for me to shower and crash at my place just to wake up and do it all again. I brought food and toys for her cat and she cooked us dinner. I rubbed her shoulders after a long day and she straddled me at the end of a very long night.

I hadn't thought about the hard drive, or the password that protected it, or anything remotely negative since we'd made our agreement.

Because it was *easy*, playing house with Mallory —
hell, playing *life* with Mallory.

And I found myself in extreme danger of falling faster
than an anvil in an old *Looney Tunes* episode.

I was watching her read next to me on her couch
Wednesday night when I realized it. It'd been another long
night, and she was wearing only the t-shirt she'd ripped
off me when the work was done. I was sated from her
touch, smiling at the way she tucked her feet under her on
the cushion, the way her wide eyes scanned each page, the
way she nervously chewed her thumbnail as she read. Her
platinum hair was grown out a bit, the darker, brunette
shade showing at the roots, and she had all of it pulled
back in the tiniest little ponytail, with loose strands falling
all around her face and down the back of her neck.

In that moment — that quiet, seemingly average
moment — she was the most beautiful woman I'd ever
seen.

I'd never fallen for a woman, or for a girl — not in all
the years I'd "dated." Women had mostly been a pastime
for me, as ashamed as I was to admit it. I warmed a bed
from time to time, let them give me a fun distraction from
my routine, provide me company to combat the loneliness.

But, falling in love? I'd never been even *close* to that.
If anything, dating those other girls was like walking in
the plains of Oklahoma. There wasn't a cliff in sight, not
an edge nearby to accidentally trip over and tumble down
into an unknown territory of emotions. It'd been safe, level
ground, and I'd walked it easily — and left it just the same.

With Mallory, it was a tight wire.

I knew I was balancing on that thinly stretched,
wobbling wire the moment I met her. Even when she
frustrated me, even when I wanted to throttle her more

than I wanted to kiss her — I still somehow sensed it. I'd been walking that wire since she walked into my office that Monday after Thanksgiving, and now, I was balancing on one foot, with a stack of plates on my head and a glorious fall calling my name from below.

But I couldn't surrender to it — *that* was the kicker. Where we were now, this little hidden secret that we lived in — that was our world. That was where we could exist, and we'd drawn that line so we knew where we *couldn't* exist. Her father would rip this shop out from under her faster than she could say *wait* if he ever found out she'd slept with a Becker. And my own *mother* nearly had a heart attack when I'd told her I was interested in Mallory. She'd disown me if I told her I was falling for her, and if *she* couldn't even understand, there wasn't a prayer that my brothers would.

Everyone in my family had a sick feeling in their gut that Patrick Scooter was hiding something when it came to my father's death.

And here I was, pretending there was absolutely nothing wrong with the fact that I was falling for his daughter.

Still, there was a part of me — the larger part of me — that wondered what she'd say if I told her what I was feeling. If I told her *everything* I was feeling. Would she run, tell me I'm crazy, cut off what we have now because it's apparent that I can't handle it? Would she shake her head and tell me she wished I could be casual and low key like she suggested, that now I'd ruined everything?

Or would she fall into me, too?

I closed my book, setting it on her coffee table before I reached over and grabbed the one from her hands, too.

"Hey," she pouted, reaching for it even after I'd set it down next to mine. "Come on, Becker. You get me into heat

reading and then you take my book away just when things are getting crazy? What sick kind of cruel are you?"

I didn't laugh, didn't make a joke back. I just pulled her into my lap, framing her face with my hands, and slowly, I pulled her lips to mine.

There was no roll of my hips — or hers. There was no quick rush of air on an inhale, or slick coat of desire pooling deep in my gut. With that kiss, I whispered things I couldn't say out loud against her lips, nipping at each one, my tongue seeking hers, hands sliding back until I cradled her neck, holding her to me.

She melted into the touch, but pulled away with a giggle, shaking her head and kissing my nose as she settled on my lap. "Nice distraction, but I'm still mad at you for taking me away from Marie-Laure and her fight against the Nazis."

"Come to my place tomorrow night."

I was stone-cold serious, and when she saw my expression, hers leveled out, too. "It's the night before the grand opening."

"I know, and we've done everything that needs to be done. You need a break before the madness takes over. Let me cook for you."

She smirked. "Macaroni and cheese, I'd imagine?"

"Let me cook a *real* meal for you," I said, still serious. My eyes searched hers, and I swallowed past the sinking in my gut that told me I was coming on too strong, that I was freaking her out.

I'd never felt this way in my entire life, and I refused to keep silent about it.

"I've never been to your place," she said — and I wasn't sure if it was an argument, or just a statement.

"Let's change that."

She bit her lip, considering, but then a smile bloomed over those rosy lips of hers, and she kissed my nose. "Okay, Chef Logan. But I expect a four-course dinner."

"And you'll get it," I said, kissing the corners of her lips before I pulled her mouth to mine again. My hands slipped over her arms, down her back, gripping her hips briefly before I smacked her ass. "Dessert, too."

She giggled, swatting at me with absolutely zero intention of actually getting me away from her before she wrapped her arms around my neck. The kiss deepened, all jokes gone, and I ignored the clock on the wall that told me it was late and I needed to go.

Maybe if I didn't point it out, if I didn't say a word, I could just stay there.

Stay the night.

Stay forever.

And maybe, if I played my cards right, I could get her to stay, too.

# Chapter Thirteen

**LOGAN**

My place was the cleanest it had ever been — and that was saying something.

I'd rushed home from work to scrub down every corner, dusting and sweeping and mopping and tidying until it was time to run to the grocery store. And even now, with dinner cooking in the oven and my hands busy chopping veggies for the appetizer, I was looking around the space, making mental notes of things I wanted to tidy up or rearrange before Mallory got there.

It was the first time I'd ever invited a woman into my home.

It sounded crazy, because I'd *slept* with enough women that it should have been hard to believe that statement. But, regardless of what the town liked to think or gossip about, it was always me going to *their* place, not bringing them to mine. To me, there was something personal about the space I lived in — the photos on the walls, the books on the shelves, the magnets on the fridge. There were little pieces of me everywhere, and I had never wanted to share those pieces with anyone before.

Until now.

My stomach was a wreck the entire evening, and I wondered if I'd even be able to eat the dinner I was cooking. I'd gone all out, remembering from a brief conversation we'd had while cleaning out the storage closet that Mallory loved Greek food but rarely had it, since there wasn't a Greek restaurant within fifty miles of Stratford and her family was a steak and potatoes kind of family. So, I'd made homemade tzatziki, with fresh vegetables and hot pita bread brushed with seasoning to dip. I'd also made a classic Greek salad, and a creamy, feta-smothered chicken bake with artichoke hearts and olives and tomatoes and Mediterranean seasoning. And, even though it'd been a giant pain in my ass, I had baklava made and waiting to go in the oven as soon as I pulled dinner out — complete with the honey sauce in the fridge that I'd pour over top of it when it was done.

The meal and the way my house looked were the only things I could control that night. Maybe that's why I had obsessed, teaching myself more than I really even needed to know about the Greek culture and their diet before choosing a perfectly balanced menu. And maybe that was why I'd cleaned every corner of my already-spotless house, as if even one photo frame being out of place would be the difference between Mallory feeling the same way I was or thinking I was a crazy person.

I sighed, shaking my head at myself as I arranged the freshly cut cucumber slices around the bowl of tzatziki. "Pull it together, man."

There was a knock at my door, and my heart thundered to life, kicking so violently in my chest I had to grip the edge of the counter to keep from toppling over. I ran my hands under the faucet, drying them on the towel hanging from my oven before I made my way to the door, checking each spot in my house one last time on the way over. I touched a few things — not really moving them, but feeling like I was doing *something* — and then I stood in front of the door, blew out a long breath, put on my best, easy-going,     nothing-is-wrong-and-everything-is-casual smile, and turned the handle.

When the wooden door was open and only the screen door stood between us, I stood there like an idiot, not moving to open it and invite Mallory inside because I'd been stunned stupid by how incredible she looked.

Her hair was down and riddled with beach-like waves, the edges still framing her chin in the most perfect way. Her eyes were lined, a dark wing giving them an exotic look, the golden eye shadow making her ocean-blue eyes pop against her olive skin. She wore a jean skirt with dark leggings underneath, the thighs of them shredded to show little slivers of her skin between each black piece of fabric. That skirt was paired with an oversized white sweater that hung off her shoulder, and for some reason, that sweater made her look so adorable, so small and sweet and delectable that I considered forgoing dinner altogether and pulling her inside for the full, in-depth tour of my bedroom.

Those lips I loved to taste were painted my favorite shade of dusty rose, and they curled into a soft smile as she watched me gawk at her. "You going to invite me in, or should I grab a blanket from my car and throw a picnic out here on the porch?"

I shook my head, pushing the screen door open and clearing my throat.

I still couldn't speak just yet, and Mallory chuckled, slipping between me and the door and standing in my foyer as I shut the door behind us. I took her scarf and purse, hung them on my coat rack, and then stood there like an idiot again with my hands in my pockets, eyes trailing over her again.

"You look beautiful," I managed to murmur, and Mallory grinned wider, stepping into me.

"You look pretty handsome, yourself," she teased, tugging on the apron fastened around my waist. "Can I see you in *only* this later?"

That earned her a laugh, and like the first breath after being submerged under water, I relaxed, every muscle easing as I pulled her into me for a hug. "Only if you're a good girl."

She pulled back on a pout. "But, I thought you liked it best when I'm bad?"

Her hands slipped down, down, into the back pockets of my jeans, where she squeezed and pulled me closer. Her teeth grazed her bottom lip, eyes dancing over my neck, my jaw, my mouth.

A zip of electricity shot fast and hot down my spine, and I groaned, kissing her mouth hard and quick before I smacked her ass and ushered her toward the kitchen. "Stop distracting the cook."

She giggled again, but let me guide her deeper inside, and I ran back to check on dinner in the oven as she looked around.

"There's fresh tzatziki here," I said, motioning to the plate I'd set up on the kitchen island as I pulled the oven door open. The cheese was melting nicely, the chicken sizzling, the aroma making my stomach growl. "Fresh pita, cucumbers, carrots, tomatoes and such." I stood again, turning to face her, and she was watching me like I was some mystical creature she'd never seen before. "What?"

"You made me Greek food."

I grabbed the back of my neck. "You said it's your favorite."

"Once," she reminded me. "Like... in a passing comment. I can't believe you remembered that."

"I listen to you," I said on a shrug. "And I have a pretty good memory."

"Explains how you can recite some sort of knowledge about practically every event that's ever happened in history." She laughed, reaching for the bottle of wine I'd set out next to the appetizer and pouring us each a glass. She dipped a hot piece of pita in the dip next, shoving it in her mouth and letting her eyes roll back on a groan. "*Homgahgawd*, dis ish amazing."

I grinned, picking up my glass and cheersing it to hers. "Thank you for coming over."

She swallowed, sipping her wine to wash down the pita before doing a little twirl and giving herself a tour through the living room. "Thank *you* for reminding my taste buds why pita bread is the best thing to ever exist."

I watched her from behind the kitchen island as she swept through my home, running her fingertips over the top of my couch, the book-lined shelves, the photo frames that held memories made with my family. She paused in front of one of me and my mom, taken at my high school graduation. She was wearing my graduation cap, one arm around my waist and the other squishing my cheeks together while I pretended to be annoyed, rolling my eyes. The grin I wore gave me away, though — and it was one of my favorite pictures of us together.

Mallory smiled, tracing the glass over my face before she moved on, lifting her wine to her lips and letting her eyes wander the books on my shelf. "You have even more here than you do in your office," she mused.

"I've read all of them except the ones on the top shelf," I said, walking over to join her. "That's my *to-be-read* shelf."

Mallory lifted a brow, trailing her fingers over the spines of the books on the second shelf. "You've read *all* of these other ones?"

"I told you I'm a nerd."

She laughed. "I think reading is sexy." She folded one arm over her middle, balancing the elbow of the one holding her wine glass over it as she looked around more. Her diamond eyes danced in the low light of my living room, and she shook her head, still smiling. "Your place is so... *neat*. Not that I should be surprised, I guess." She looked at me then, poking me in the chest with one of the fingers wrapped around her glass. "You need a little color in here. And maybe a little mess, too."

"You volunteering to be that mess?" I asked, reaching out to hook my finger in the belt loop on her skirt. I tugged her into me, sweeping her hair behind one ear.

"I'd be honored," she whispered, and then her lips were on mine.

I pulled her into me as much as I could with one hand, each of us balancing our wine glasses while we drank each other in. The kiss was soft and sweet, and far too short when the oven timer went off.

"Mmm," I said, kissing her nose when I pulled back before I released her. "You better get over there and eat more of that tzatziki. Main course has got about ten more minutes after I add this last bit of cheese."

"Feta?"

"You know it."

She pressed a hand to her chest, closing her eyes. "My hero."

I finished up dinner with Mallory sitting at one of the bar stools at my kitchen island, sipping on her wine and snacking on the dippers and tzatziki as we talked. She asked me about every single picture in sight, begging for stories when I offered short explanations, and I asked her about her childhood and family, too. It was crazy to me that we grew up in the same town, with nearly the same tie to the same whiskey distillery, and yet, we'd had drastically different upbringings. Where my home was filled with laughter and love, with memories being made, hers was filled with business and agenda, with parties and reputation. She had so much expected of her at such a young age, whereas I was free to be a kid.

We ate the salad and main course at my small dining room table — the table that had only served me before that night. Mallory marveled at my skills in the kitchen with every bite she took, making unnecessary moans and asking for seconds, and I watched her laugh and sip her wine with my heart pounding in my rib cage, with words I was still too afraid to say dancing in my head.

The baklava came out of the oven right as I was putting our dishes from dinner in the sink, and Mallory poured the last of the bottle of wine in each of our glasses as I poured the honey over the fresh pastry. I knew it was best to leave that honey to set for hours before eating, so that it soaked down into the flaky dough, but I served it hot, anyway, and Mallory devoured every single bite. She even ran her finger over the plate to get the last bit of crumbs and honey.

"You're a god," she said on a final moan, dabbing her lips with her napkin and kicking back in her chair like a king would after a feast. "Seriously. You should open a Greek restaurant so I can have this type of food more often."

I chuckled, taking a long sip of my wine before I swirled what was left of it around the glass, watching the red liquid splash up the sides.

*I could cook for you,* I wanted to offer. *Every night. If we were together.*

"You've been so quiet tonight," Mallory observed, kicking those thoughts out of my head before they could materialize.

I peered up at her, offering a smile and a half-hearted shrug. "Just listening to you, enjoying the evening."

"Mm-hmm," she said, lips pursed. "You've got something on your mind. Spill, Chef."

I spun my glass again, eyes on the wine, before I abandoned the glass altogether and gathered my napkin off my lap, depositing it on the table. I stood, heart in my throat and voice a little shaky as I extended my hand for hers. "Dance with me."

One eyebrow arched high into her hair line. "Uh... I don't... I *can't* dance."

I beckoned her with my hand, smirking. "I'll lead. Come on."

Mallory looked at my hand like it was a spider that I'd swore wouldn't bite her, her face screwing up in a mixture of uneasiness and fear. But, to her credit, she took one last sip of her wine, and then she slipped her small hand into mine and stood.

I led her a few feet away from the table, in the space between my small dining area and the kitchen, and then I pulled her into me — one hand at her waist, the other still holding her hand — and to the soft, melodic voice of Leon Bridges, we began to sway.

She was nervous, at first, looking down at her feet and cringing, apologizing when she misstepped. But I guided

*neat*

her with my hand at the small of her back, encouraging her to keep her eyes on mine, and by the first chorus, we'd found a rhythm.

"My mom and dad used to dance after dinner," I said, spinning her out gently before I spun her back into my arms. "Every single night. My brothers and I would clear the table, do the dishes, and Dad would pull Mom into the living room, turn up the music, and dance with her."

Mallory's eyes sparkled, a smile tugging at the right side of her mouth. "That's so romantic."

"Dad always was," I said, laughing a little. "He always taught us to be vulnerable, to be emotional, to share what we were feeling even if we felt ashamed or embarrassed. And he taught us how to respect a woman, how to care for her, make her feel good." I swallowed, searching her eyes. "Make her feel loved."

Mallory swallowed then, too, and she pulled her eyes from mine, resting her head against my chest, instead. "My family was the exact opposite," she said, voice low. "We didn't talk about anything, least of all how we were feeling. I have no idea who my parents are, outside of the entertainer and business owner façade they present to everyone in town. And my brother?" She shook her head against my chest. "I don't know a single thing about him, other than that he likes to golf. And I don't even know if he really *likes* it, or if he just does it to do business with Dad."

"And they know nothing about you, either, do they?"

A soft laugh left her lips. "Not a thing."

I sighed, swaying to the music, holding her close. "That's a shame. Because if they knew you the way I do, if they could see what I see, they'd be the proudest family in this whole town."

She smirked, lifting her head from my chest and reaching up to thread her arms around my neck. We

202

slowed to a two-step sway, back and forth. "Oh, yeah? And what is it that you see, exactly?"

It was my shot.

And I was taking it.

"I see a woman who isn't afraid of anything," I said, searching her eyes with my own. "I see an artist with heart and passion, and talent that she's so modest about that it somehow makes it even more impressive. I see a business owner with hustle and drive, with a dream that has no other option *but* to come true with her in the driver seat."

I swallowed, watching her eyes widen, her lips soften until they parted slightly.

"I see an intelligent woman, who had to grow up faster than she should have, but who handled it with grace. I see strength, and thoughtfulness, and care. I see someone who doesn't stand for being walked on, who refuses to follow the stream just because someone tells her it's what she's expected to do. I see a voyageur, someone who makes her *own* path, her own journey, and who gives off a light that draws everyone around her in like moths to a flame."

"Logan..."

"And I see someone who fights for justice, and who learns before she judges." I stopped swaying, sliding my hands up her back, over her arms, eliciting a wave of chills in my wake before my hands framed her face. I swept her hair back, looking into those almost-violet pools of her eyes as I spoke my next words. "I see the first woman to steal my heart, and the only woman I ever want to keep it."

Mallory's bottoms lip quivered, eyes glossing as they flicked between mine. For a long moment, we watched each other, those last words hanging between us, the air so thick I felt it pressing in on every side of me. Then, she took a breath, stepped back, away, my hands dropping

neat

from where they held her as she pressed a hand to her head.

"Gosh, I'm sorry," she said, swallowing and offering half a smile as she shook her head. "I'm feeling a little dizzy, I think. I should probably go lie down and get some rest." She was already walking toward the door, swiping her scarf off the coat rack and wrapping it around her neck. "We both have to work tomorrow, and the grand opening, it's going to be a long day." She laughed. "Need to be sharp, you know?"

"Mallory..." I tried, reaching for her and pulling her into me again. "I..."

She watched me, waiting, but I found I didn't have anything else to say. I didn't want to apologize, though by the way she was reacting, I felt like maybe I should have.

But I wasn't sorry. I'd said what I'd meant, and I'd said it because I wanted her to know.

What she did with it now was up to her.

I swallowed. "I can drive you home," I finished. "If you're feeling dizzy."

She shook her head. "No, no, I'm okay. It's not too far." Her eyes glanced at the table, where our dessert plates and half-empty glasses of wine still sat. "Thank you," she said, looking up at me again. The gloss in her eyes was gone, but her voice trembled slightly. "For the dinner, and the wine." She smiled. "And the dance."

I nodded, swallowing, unsure of if I was allowed to kiss her, to pull her into me even more than I already had.

"With the grand opening tomorrow, will you..." She reached for the back of her neck. "I mean, I know everyone will be there, and with our families... I just... I understand, if you can't come. If you don't want to."

I shook my head, sliding my hands back into her hair and bending to look straight into her eyes. "Mallory, I wouldn't miss it for anything."

She nodded, but her eyes slipped to my chest. She couldn't hold eye contact, and she avoided it even more when she pulled away, grabbed her purse, and opened the front door.

Mallory zipped out, leaving me inside with the warmth of our embrace battling against the cool wind whipping in now. But she paused on my porch, turning to face me.

"Goodnight, Logan," she spoke softly.

"Goodnight, Mallory."

Her eyes flicked between mine one last time, then she was gone.

And I was there, on the wrong side of the line she'd drawn between us, wondering if I'd ruined everything, wondering if she'd call it all off tomorrow, wondering if I'd have to live without her — all because I couldn't live within the terms she'd set for us.

Knowing I wouldn't be able to move on — not now that I'd known what it was like to have her.

With nothing left to do, and the ball firmly in her court, I swallowed, closed the door, and started cleaning.

# Chapter Fourteen

## MALLORY

Twenty minutes before the grand opening of my very own, very first art studio, I stood upstairs in my loft apartment, staring at myself in the mirror, and hating everything I saw.

I hated that my hair was pinned up instead of straightened and framing my face. I hated that it was blonde instead of the bright violet I'd loved so much. I hated that I was wearing a white dress that was cut under my knees in the front but fell down to the floor in the back, like a goddamn bride, instead of my raggedy old jeans and a t-shirt and Chucks. I hated that I was a picture-perfect vision of what my parents wanted me to be that night, instead of who I really was.

"It's just for tonight," Chris reminded me gently from where he stood behind me. He fixed the strap of my dress, touching up a piece of my hair that had fallen before he handed me a tube of nude lipstick.

Nude, instead of the red or rose or burgundy I preferred.

"I look ridiculous."

"You actually look quite beautiful," he argued, but it was hard for me to believe him, considering he was wearing a fitted, fuchsia tuxedo. He did somehow manage to pull it off, though, and he looked — as he would have called it — *gay boy chic*. "And I know you hate hearing that, since this is the last thing you'd ever pick for yourself to wear. But, you do. And, regardless of what you're wearing, this is a night of celebration." He framed my arms, turning me to face him instead of the mirror. Then, he unscrewed the liquid lipstick tube, tapping my bottom lip until I parted my lips enough to let him paint them. "Tonight is the opening of *your* business, Mallory. Your art studio. And no one can take that away from you."

I mumbled, not really able to speak with him doing my lipstick, and he rolled his eyes.

"Yes, okay, except for your father. BUT, he won't. Because you're holding up your part of the deal. So, just relax, and try to find a way to not hate the world long enough that you can enjoy this?" He gave me a pointed look, and a smile, but my stomach was sinking as he turned away.

My father *wouldn't* take it away, what I'd worked for, as long as I held up my end of the deal.

But he would, if he knew about me and Logan.

I realized, very distantly, that the bigger reason why I was feeling agitated and shaky was because of last night more so than tonight. It was because I'd fled from the first man to ever confess he saw me for who I was, to confess he *liked* what he saw, to confess that he was into me — and more than just casually, like we'd agreed upon.

I'd ran out of there so fast you would have thought someone told me the studio was on fire.

But how could I *not* run? How could I not feel every nerve in my body warning of danger with Logan Becker that close to me, telling me in not so many words that he wanted more? It was impossible. His family would disown him, which would absolutely crush him. Everyone in that town knew how tightly bound that family was, and I couldn't stand to be the one to ruin that.

*My* family wouldn't just disown me, they'd make my life a living hell in this town until I had no choice but to leave it. And my studio? It would be gone before it even had the chance to get started. Everything I'd worked for, everything I'd sacrificed up until this point — my dignity, my pride, my weekdays, my fucking sanity — it would all be for nothing.

My father would rip it all away in a heartbeat.

I thought when I saw Logan at work today, we would be back to normal. I thought it'd be jokes and laughs and sneaking makeout sessions in his office.

But it was more like prison.

I'd barely seen him, and when I had, it'd been awkward, forced conversation — with both of us avoiding what he'd said last night while holding me in his arms.

I closed my eyes, pinching the bridge of my nose as a headache started, and Chris hurried over to me, framing my arms again. "Hey, are you okay?"

I let my hand fall to my thigh with a slap, sighing. "I'm nervous."

Chris narrowed his eyes. He didn't believe me, and if anything, now he *knew* there was something more on my mind than just the fact that I was in a dress and heels.

To his credit — *bless him* — he didn't push.

"It's normal to be nervous," he said, and his eyes searched mine, his hands rubbing my arms encouragingly.

"But, ready or not, in about fifteen minutes, those doors are opening." He paused, mumbling the next words with a flick of his imaginary hair. "Of course, *not* with a blast of glitter, like there would have been had *I* been the one to throw this shindig, but still."

I tried to smile.

"Your family is downstairs waiting," he continued with a sympathetic smile. "I think it's time we join them."

I nodded, numbly, in lieu of an answer, and let my best friend guide me downstairs to where my father, mother, brother, uncle, aunt, and cousins waited.

It was all a blur from there.

The studio that Logan and I had brought to life shone like a new penny under the string lights Mom had installed. They hung from the rafters above, giving the shop a hip, industrial look. There was a jazz band playing softly in the corner of the room, right next to where the bar was. Servers waited at the ready, silver platters loaded with hors d'oeuvres in their hands. Each section of the studio was pristine — tidied, cleaned, decorated, and ready to be shown off. Tables near the front entrance held class and event schedules for the next few months, along with a pamphlet about me, my education, the shop and how it came to be.

If it were up to me, I would have just opened the doors. I would have just hosted the first class tonight, and maybe gotten drunk on a six pack by myself later tonight when it was all over with.

Still, I tried to find it in me to be thankful, to recognize that this was how my parents showed their love. They didn't know much when it came to parenting, but they *did* know how to throw a party.

Mom already had a glass of champagne in her hand when she scurried over to me, eyes watering as she took in my appearance. She went on and on about how beautiful I looked (though how I would have looked better had I taken the nose ring out), how stunning the shop was, how proud she was of me. Dad chimed in with his own prideful speech, saying he knew I had it in me. They both kissed my cheek, and my brother gave me a stiff hug, and my uncles and aunts and all the cousins bearing the Scooter surname shook my hand and congratulated me.

And all the while, I stood there, numbly smiling, responding to their questions in a way that felt like it was someone else speaking entirely. Someone handed me a glass of champagne — Chris, I presumed — and my father gave a speech. Some people laughed during that speech. Some people cheered. Mom dabbed at the tears leaking from her eyes.

Then, glasses clinked, bubbly was sipped, and the doors opened.

The first thing I felt was a suffocating kind of overwhelmed. My parents' friends were all the first to pile in, each of them pulling me into a hug or shaking my hand and marveling at how pretty I looked and how nice the studio was before they wandered off to find champagne and talk business with my dad. It felt like *everyone* was there — the mayor and his wife, all of Mom's stuck-up debutante friends, all the officers and board members from the distillery, the police chief and his wife, though he was smart enough to stay away from me. It made my stomach churn that he was there at all, but I knew my father, and if there was a chance to invite his high-roller friends and remind them how powerful he was, he'd take it.

Chris stood by my side with each person I greeted, smiling and taking over the conversation when I could no longer hold it. Of course, not many people stood to talk to him for very long. He was one of only a handful of openly gay people in our town, and let's just say that the first wave of people in attendance were very *old-fashioned* folks.

I thought I was living in my own personal hell, in a nightmare I wouldn't be able to escape for hours. I couldn't believe the grand opening of a studio I'd dreamed of for so long had turned into a social function for my fucking parents.

But then, slowly, people who had no ties to my family other than the fact that they lived in Stratford began to arrive. Families wandered in, with kids bright eyed and excited to play with the paint and the ceramic knick-knacks I'd laid out for anyone to bring to life with color and heat. I found myself flitting around the room, talking to young high school students who were interested in art but unsure of where to start, chatting with parents about after-school opportunities and summer programs, visiting with the secretary of the nursing home in town about field-trip opportunities for senior citizens. I was showing children how to paint, showing adults how to mold a pottery vase with their hands, showing a group of young adults pretending they were too cool to be there a brochure on a midnight photography tour where they could learn how to shoot the stars in the sky with long exposure.

So, the *second* thing I felt was that same pride my parents had. I felt joy, and accomplishment, and like I might actually be able to make a difference, to make art possible — even if it was just in the small town of Stratford, Tennessee. I watched so many eyes light up when I showed them something new, when they made the first stroke of color with their brush, when they lit up with the possibility that they could create something beautiful.

*neat*

An hour ticked by, and then another, with people coming and going, and me floating around the room to do my best to talk to every single person who stopped in.

The third thing I felt was longing for the one person who had yet to show.

Logan assured me last night when I was mid-flee from his place that he would be here. He said he wouldn't miss it. Still, I didn't know why I was surprised that he hadn't come — especially after how I'd acted, how things had been at work. Why would he come? Why would he show up for *me* when I had run out on him?

I tried to ignore that hollowness in my stomach, filling it with champagne and what hors d'oeuvres I could keep down, and keeping busy with my guests. I convinced myself it was okay that he wasn't there, that I understood, that I didn't blame him and I didn't have a right to be a precious little baby about it.

But when Chris pulled me away from a family I was working on painting rocks with — rocks that I hoped would be little surprise Easter eggs throughout our town — and told me a special guest had just arrived, the way my heart stopped called me out on my bullshit lies.

Chris grinned at my dumbfounded expression, nodding to the door behind me before he sipped his champagne and twirled away to make himself busy. I closed my eyes, took a breath, and slowly — *very* slowly — turned around.

Logan was just inside the door, searching the room, with that damn wrinkle between his brows on full display. He shifted uncomfortably, holding a bouquet of flowers in one hand and a small white box in the other. His chestnut hair, which was normally ruffled and hidden under a baseball cap, was parted to one side, gelled, every strand in its place. He'd shaved, giving his scruff a clean line that somehow made his jaw and neck even sexier than before. He wore a light-blue button up, cuffed at the elbows, the top two buttons left unfastened. It was covered by a russet vest, one that showed off his broad shoulders and chest, accenting the narrow waist that drew my eyes down to his dark jeans. I smiled when I noted the rugged leather boots under those jeans — boots that matched his vest. He was so devastatingly handsome, my throat tightened, a knot forming that I couldn't swallow past.

His eyes were a fierce honey gold, even from across the room under the hanging string lights, and when they stopped on me, and a smirk crept up on the left side of his face, that damn dimple popping under his cheek — I knew he'd found what he'd been searching for.

My heart slowed as he walked toward me, as did the blood in my veins, and the breath filling my lungs. The people around me seemed to morph and fade until it was quiet altogether, until only the soft jazz music the band was playing and his footsteps walking toward me existed. He stopped with just a foot between us, and his eyes crawled over me, searing every inch, before he found my gaze once more.

"Hi."

I let out a long laugh of a breath. "Hi."

"You look..."

"Like a bride from the nineties?"

"Took the words right out of my mouth." Logan shook his head, brows folding together as he tugged on a piece of lace dangling from one of my wrists. "I mean, don't get me wrong. You're beautiful no matter what you wear. But... you just... you don't look like *you*."

"What does *me* look like?"

*neat*

His eyes danced back up to mine, an uneasy smile finding his lips. "Effortlessly gorgeous in a pair of jeans, a t-shirt, and off-white sneakers. Hair down." His eyes fell to my lips. "Lips painted my new favorite color of dusty rose." When his eyes met mine again, I found I could barely breathe, and when he leaned in a little closer, I couldn't breathe at all. "Although, I prefer you in just my t-shirt and a messy ponytail."

Every inch of my skin heated when his breath touched my lips, but just as soon as the contact was made, he pulled back, handing me the bouquet of flowers.

He looked sheepishly at the pile of other flowers on the table next to the bar behind me. "I feel super original now."

I laughed, tucking the bouquet into my arms. "Most of those are for my mom, I assure you." I glanced around the room. "If you haven't been able to tell yet, this is more a party for *them* than for me."

"Explains your dress."

I smiled.

"I'm sorry I didn't come earlier," he said, grabbing the back of his neck with his now-free hand. "I was thinking maybe if I waited a while, it'd give your parents a chance to get busy with other things and not even notice when I arrived."

My eyes fell behind him, where my father was talking to the mayor, but looking directly past him at where we stood.

"I think you could have dressed up in a cat mascot costume, complete with the head piece, and my dad's radar would still go off when you walked in the room."

"He's looking at us, huh?"

"*Oh,* yeah," I said, but I brought my eyes back to him with an assuring smile. "But whatever, let him look. I'm glad you're here." I swallowed then, as the truth of that statement really sank in. "Really, I am."

Logan nodded, and a silence fell between us — with him looking at me, me looking at him. There were so many words left unsaid between us last night, so many things I knew I needed to tell him. I needed to put us back in the casual zone — *fast* — or perhaps, push us all the way back into the friend zone we'd existed in before.

But I couldn't.

The longer he stood there, the more I wanted to fall into him, to pull him into me and kiss him right there in front of God and my family and everyone else.

It was insane. I was absolutely certifiable to even consider it.

And yet, it was all I wanted.

"Speaking of the cat," he said. "Where is Dalí? It's not *Dalí and Mal's Art Studio* if Dalí isn't here, is it?"

"He's upstairs. God knows he'd probably shit himself and hide in the corner shaking being around all these people."

"Or he'd just walk under their feet and eat the crumbs they drop, flicking his tail in a bored fashion as he frolicked from person to person."

"And he'd whisper *peasants* under his breath."

"Of course, because it's his kingdom, after all."

I chuckled. The name of the studio had been the one thing I hadn't been able to figure out, and when we started filing the necessary paperwork to open the doors, we had to pick one. It'd been Logan who had suggested Dalí and Mal's, and when he'd said it, I could have kissed him for how perfect it was.

Okay, I maybe *did* kiss him.

My parents hated it, of course. Even Chris wrinkled his nose at the name when I'd told him. But it was perfect, for more reasons than just the fact that we had a shop cat. Salvador Dalí was one of the most unconventional artists of his time, and one of my biggest inspirations. Honoring his name with the name of my studio was perfect.

And, of course, Logan knew that.

Because Logan knew *me*.

"I... uh..." Logan held up the square, one-inch thick box in his hand, bringing me back to the moment with him. "I got you something else."

"Anal beads?"

Logan barked out a laugh, shaking off the tension that had been hanging over us like a cloud. "Not exactly, although now I kind of wish I had."

"Next time," I teased, and then I took the box from him, giving it a little shake like a kid at Christmas before I carefully pulled off the top. Inside was a simple gold frame around an all-glass, thin shadow box. There was a white rectangle in the center, and above it, written in black script, were the words *Dalí and Mal's First Dollar.*

I frowned, tracing the words with my fingertips before I looked up at Logan, confused.

"It's... you know, it's for your first sale," he said, shrugging and reaching for the back of his neck again. He pointed to the rectangle inside the frame. "You put your first dollar there, and then you can hang it up behind the register. I mean, I know it's a Square register now, and everything is digital, and your first class will probably be paid for with card. But, you could take a dollar out of the register, anyway. And pretend. You know? Just, as a symbol."

I smiled.

"It's a thing, a lot of old businesses used to do it. I think new ones still do. I don't know." He let his hand drop, reaching for the frame. "It's stupid. I'm sorry."

I yanked the frame out of his reach. "No! I love it."

"Are you sure?"

I chuckled, touching his arm. "Logan, I love it. It's thoughtful. It... it means you believe this place will be around for a while, that it will have history."

"It will," he said immediately, effortlessly, as if he'd never believed anything to be more true in his life. "It will, Mallory. Because it's you."

His hand covered the one I'd placed on his arm, squeezing it, holding it for a moment before he let it go and cleared his throat, taking a sizable step back from me.

"I'm going to go make myself scarce," he said. "Talk to the other tour guides who are here from the distillery, keep busy, stay out of the way. You know, just so I don't give your father an aneurysm, or anyone else in this town ammo for Sunday morning church gossip."

I laughed, looking around the room at the eyes that were on us. "Might be too late for that, but yes, good idea."

"I'll see you around."

"Wait," I said before he could turn away. "Can you stay after?" I swallowed. "There's something I want to show you."

He cocked a brow. "I'd love to stay after, but I think your dad might actually murder me if I'm here when everyone else is gone tonight."

"Sneak upstairs in an hour. If anyone asks, I told you to check on Dalí. And just wait there until I call you down."

Logan shook his head. "Sneaking around like teenagers. Why do I like it?"

"Because you're a troublemaker." I shoved him playfully. "Now go, be invisible."

We both laughed like it was a joke, and it might as well have been. I wasn't the only one who watched Logan for the next hour as he talked with families and couples and kids, showing them the different stations of the studio just like I would have if it were *me* talking to them. He handed out brochures, event schedules, showed pieces of my art on the walls and spoke of my education like he'd been the one to give it to me.

Logan treated that grand opening like it was his own.

And I wasn't the only one who noticed.

Mom's friends were tittering around the cocktail tables, eyeing Logan with suspicious glares. Dad hardly ever took his eyes off him, and even the other tour guides from Scooter were leaning in close, whispering conspiracies as they watched him.

I managed to call a toast near the end of the night, holding my champagne high as I thanked everyone for a memorable evening. It was the only way I could get the attention off Logan, and I watched out of the peripheral of my eyes as he slipped away and up the stairs while I talked. When the glasses were clinked and a hearty *hear, hear!* rang out, one by one, people began to leave, the band died down and started to pack up, and though everyone seemed to be looking around for Logan again, he was nowhere to be found.

"Proud of you, young lady," my dad said at the end of the night, when everyone was gone other than me, him, and Mom. Malcolm had ditched after an hour, and even Chris had finally left, at my insistence that I could clean up on my own. Dad pulled me into a stiff hug, one that felt foreign and awkward. "It was a great night."

"It was," I said. I gave Mom a hug, too, and kissed her cheek. "Thank you both for coming, and for doing all this," I said, gesturing to the lights, the tables of leftover food, the corner where the band had been. "I never would have made it so special."

"We're just so happy you've found your place in this town," Mom said, eyes welling again.

Dad looked around me, as if he was sure Logan was hiding in a corner somewhere. "That Becker boy was sure here a long time."

I shrugged, pretending like I didn't notice. "Was he? I was so busy making the rounds, I guess I didn't realize."

Dad narrowed his eyes at me, and I knew without him saying so that he didn't believe me for a second. Thankfully, he didn't press, just patted my arm. "Well, we're going to head home. Don't forget, Monday is Christmas Eve, and we have the annual Christmas Party at the distillery with all the employees and their families. I'd like you to be presentable," he said, waving a hand over my dress. "Wear something nice like this again."

"This is literally the only dress I own, Dad. Other than the one I wore to brunch on Sunday."

"It doesn't have to be a dress," he said. "Just... I want you to make a good impression. Okay? Can you please do that for me?"

I sighed — and I'll admit, it was a bit of a dramatic sigh, even for me. "Yes, yes, got it. I won't show up in jeans."

"Thank you." He leaned in, kissing my forehead before he placed his hand on the small of Mom's back and led her toward the door. They gave me one last wave after their coats were on, and then they were gone, and the door was locked, the lights were out, and the studio was finally empty again.

Well.

*Almost* empty.

# Chapter Fifteen

## LOGAN

Dalí was curled up in his favorite place — directly in the middle of my chest — when Mallory called for me to come downstairs.

I lifted a brow, scratching behind his ear as he closed his eyes and purred, leaning into the touch. "You're going to hate this, but I gotta go."

The cat creaked one eye open, as if he was telling me our relationship was *over* if I left that spot.

I chuckled. "I know, I know. But, there's a pretty lady calling me downstairs, and I can't make her wait."

"Are you talking to my cat?"

Mallory leaned against the frame of her front door, smirking at where I lay on her couch with Dalí. As if he sensed there was no use in trying to keep me in my spot, Dalí stretched on my chest, his claws kneading my skin, then he hopped down and trotted over to his food bowl.

"He's been the best conversation of the night," I said, sitting up.

Mallory shook her head. "Let me get out of this fucking dress, and then I want to show you something."

She disappeared into the bathroom with a handful of clothes, and moments later, emerged as the Mallory I found impossible not to fall for. Her hair was up in a messy ponytail, the tendrils that fell around her neck and face curled a bit from how it had been pinned back before. She wore an oversized Nirvana t-shirt and sleep shorts that were practically invisible beneath it, and I watched her legs with desire building like a storm inside me.

"Ready?" she asked, dropping the dress into her laundry basket before smiling up at me. Her face was makeup-free now, blue eyes tired, but shining, and I thought back to a passing thought I'd had, how I'd wished to see her without her eyes lined, her lips painted, her lashes slicked with mascara.

She was somehow even more beautiful, and I wasn't even slightly surprised.

I think I'd always known.

I swallowed, heart sinking and reminding me how quickly she'd left the night before. So, rather than tell her how devastatingly gorgeous she was, I just tucked my hands in my pockets and smiled. "Lead the way."

I followed Mallory downstairs, the shop quiet now that the band and guests had cleared out. The place was a mess, though, and I grabbed the trash can near the bar, tossing empty plates and napkins into it as I passed by the various cocktail tables.

"What are you going to do with all these champagne glasses?" I asked, piling them up on one of the empty tables.

Mallory shook her head, stealing the trashcan from me and putting it back by the bar. "I'll do a special event where basic bitches can paint a set to take home for when they host brunch," she answered, then she turned, pointing her finger straight at me. "Now, stop cleaning and follow me."

She looked so adorable, her little ponytail swinging, feet shuffling in her slippers as she led me over to the photography section of the shop. It was just a small corner, right next to the office she'd converted to a dark room, with shelves of lenses and tripods and photography books. There was something hanging on the wall above the shelf, but it was covered with a gray sheet, and she stood in front of it, waiting.

"I was going to uncover this tonight, but when you see what it is, you'll understand why I wanted to wait," she said when I took my place next to her. She stared at the sheet like it was a bed hiding a monster, like if she pulled it down, there was a chance she'd be screaming and running for her life.

I cocked a brow. "It's a beautiful sheet... thanks for showing me?"

She poked my rib, which earned her a yelp and a laugh. "Don't be a smart ass."

"Well, what exactly am I supposed to be looking at?" I rubbed the spot where she'd poked me.

"It's what's *under* the sheet."

"And are you going to show me?"

She pulled her mouth to the side. "I was... but now I'm nervous."

I laughed. "Why?"

Mallory turned, watching me with worried eyes before she shook her head, and let out a long, meditative breath. "Just... don't laugh, okay?"

I frowned, confused, but when she stepped forward, took another deep inhale, and tugged the sheet free from the wall — I understood.

And laughing was the last thing on my mind.

It was, perhaps, the most stunning photograph I'd ever laid eyes on. The colors were so rich, it was hard to believe they were real, that it was a moment captured in real life instead of one painted, one imagined. It was pensive, while somehow still being romantic — the decadent hues of orange and yellow bursting across the large photograph, playing with the deeper, darker shadows present there, too. It almost looked black and white, except for where those sun beams stretched, creating an illusion that made you look twice, three times, forever.

And it was me.

I sat on bar stool, back bent, brows furrowed and eyes focused on the notes I was making in a legal pad. It was the pad I'd jotted down all my thoughts for the shop in, from what furniture I still needed to build to how to lay out each section in order to bring Mallory's vision to life. I balanced a slice of pizza in the opposite hand, one bite taken from the tip, and I had one foot on the floor, the other on the second rung of the bar stool, knee propped up. My hair was wild and unruly, peeking out from under the edge of my old baseball cap, and the muscles that lined my rib cage were visible through the rips in my old Stratford High t-shirt that I'd cut into a muscle tee when I was eighteen.

It was just me. It was just a man eating pizza and writing down his thoughts.

And she'd somehow turned it to art.

The shadow from the window pane stretched over the left half of my face and body, up the wall behind me, cutting the image into four invisible window panes. Those shadows contrasted the soft glow from the sun setting over Main Street, casting me in its warmth. And the way she'd focused in on my face, somehow bringing the viewer's eye straight to where I was frowning in concentration, it brought a troubling feeling that sat deep within me, like the man I was looking at was going through more than anyone could know — that even though he was just eating pizza and jotting down a few notes, he was in turmoil.

And yet, he was at peace, too.

I stepped closer, eyes scanning the photo over and over, taking in every corner, catching more beauty with every round I made. I didn't realize how long it'd been, how long I'd remained silent, until Mallory stepped up, trying to throw the sheet over the photo again.

"It's stupid," she said, tucking the edge of the sheet behind the top corner of the frame.

My hand jutted out, catching her wrist, the sheet falling to the floor in a puddle at our feet. I was still staring at the photo, unable to take my eyes away until I pulled Mallory into me. I tilted my chin down then, looking into the eyes of an artist. "It's incredible."

"Really?" she whispered.

I shook my head, swallowing, not knowing what the right thing was to say in that moment. Instead, I tucked a strand of hair behind her ear, and then bent ever so slowly to kiss her cheek. She sighed at the contact, hands reaching for the edge of my vest, and she pulled me in, not letting me back away.

"It's the most amazing thing I've ever seen," I said, searching her eyes. "I don't have the right words to tell you what it means to me. Thank you."

She closed her eyes, leaning her forehead against mine with a relieved sigh. "I wished I could have revealed it tonight, shown it to everyone, you know? I wish..." She swallowed, hands tightening into fists around the fabric of my vest. "I wish so many things."

"What do you wish for most?"

"You."

She answered quickly and effortlessly, sending my heart into a spiraling rhythm. My hands trailed up her arms, sliding to hold her neck gently, her forehead still pressed to mine.

"You can have me, Mallory," I whispered. "If you want me, I'm yours."

"I'm scared," she confessed, her voice trembling with the admission.

I pulled her closer, our noses touching now, lips centimeters apart. "I'm fucking terrified."

She laughed, the sound barely a whisper, but thick with emotion. Then, she pulled back, her blue eyes flicking between mine. "I'm sorry I ran last night."

I nodded, brushing her jaw with the pad of my thumbs. "It's okay."

"Are we absolutely insane, or just somewhat certifiable?"

"Oh, we're a special kind of crazy, that's for sure."

"Good," she said, pushing up onto her toes. "I never liked being sane, anyway."

Mallory pulled my lips to hers, and the way she kissed me was so desperate, so thick with need, I was sure I was her lifeline. The oxygen she needed existed in my lungs, the shelter and protection she craved was provided by my hands, the care and understanding she'd been searching for, she found in my embrace.

And I found all I'd ever wanted in her.

She was the spontaneous to my well planned, the art to my logic, the unexpected welcome to my day-to-day routine I didn't even realize was suffocating me.

In that moment, I took my first breath on a new life with her.

We stayed connected at every point as we floundered up the stairs — hands in hair, lips locked, legs and limbs tangling and claiming until her back hit the comforter of her bed. The only light was the soft glow from the lamp in her living area, and that warm light spread over her like the glow of the sun as I stared down at her. My fingers began working open the buttons on my vest first, then my shirt, all the while with my eyes devouring that diamond of a woman I managed to find in the rough of Stratford, Tennessee.

She leaned up quickly when I moved for the button on my pants, clamping her hand over mine. I stopped, and she peered up at me, scooting until she sat at the edge of the bed. "Let me."

My breath was heavy in my lungs, chest rising and falling as I watched her hands carefully, slowly, shakily unfasten the button on my jeans. She tugged the zipper down equally as slow, pulling the denim off my hips, down my thighs, letting them pool at my ankles. Her lips parted when she saw my erection under the black briefs I wore, and she ran her hand over the bulge, making my next breath nearly impossible to take.

It was too much already, seeing her below me like that — her blue eyes on my shaft, and then looking up at me, her lips parted, hot breath touching the sensitive skin of my abdomen. She pulled at the band on my briefs, glancing up at me through her lashes before her tongue slicked out and over the tip of me. I hissed, hands fisting at my side, and she gave me a wicked grin before pushing my briefs the rest of the way down, and wrapping her warm hand around my shaft.

It was ridiculous, the jolt of energy that pulsed through me at her touch. She pumped, and I flexed, and she grinned, and my eyes fluttered like I was being touched by Aphrodite herself. When she lowered her mouth again, this time swirling her tongue around the tip once, twice, a little lower, a little lower still, before taking me in completely — I lost it.

My hips flexed forward, sinking deep inside her mouth as my hands found a home in her hair. I gripped and pulled, earning me a satisfied moan from her that vibrated around my cock. I grunted my own approval, and she started to work — bobbing and sucking, alternating sinful, teasing licks with taking me so deep she gagged.

Mallory released me long enough to flip herself on the bed until she was lying on her back, head hanging off the edge, and then her hands reached around me, grabbing my ass and pulling me back to her. She took me in her mouth again, and this time, the new angle of her throat allowed deeper penetration, and the hottest fucking view I'd ever had in my life.

She was spread out on the bed, t-shirt hiked up so much from her flipping over that the bottom of her breasts peeked out from the hem. They bounced with every gentle thrust of my cock inside her mouth, and I reached forward, tracing the bottom of them before I squeezed. She moaned, making my eyes roll back, and I continued my trail down her toned stomach, dipping one hand beneath the band of her sleep shorts. My fingers skated between her lips, and I groaned, circling her clit and slipping one finger inside her easily.

"Jesus fucking *Christ*, Mallory," I said, and she hummed, her lips vibrating over my shaft. She was soaking, and I knew I didn't have to say it for her to know. She rolled her hips against my hand, rubbing her wet clit against my palm, taking my finger deeper — and my cock deeper in her mouth in the process.

When I looked down and saw the bulge in her throat — that bulge being *me* — I pulled out on another curse, stopping myself from coming and flipping her over on the bed before she could wipe the corners of her mouth and ask my why.

"My turn," I whispered at the hollow space under her ear. I licked her lobe, sliding my hands under her shirt and peeling it over her head before I made quick work of her sleep shorts. I bent her over the edge of the bed she'd just had her head hanging off, and then I lowered myself to my knees.

Her pussy was swollen and dripping, her round ass poking out, back arched. I ran my hands over her spine, down the crease where her cheeks met, and then I spread them wide, and buried my face in that sweet deliverance.

"Oh, God!" she cried out, her legs already trembling. She held onto the sheets like they were what was responsible for the torturing pleasure, ripping at them until one corner popped off the mattress, and then the other.

I ran my tongue around her clit, between her lips, diving inside her pussy before I repeated the cycle. She spread her legs wider to give me more access, moaning, writhing, her thighs quivering on either side of my face. And if I thought she was close then, when I ran my tongue all the way up, running it in a circle around her perfect little asshole, she shook so violently I had to use my hands to hold her up.

"Oh fuck, *fuck,* Logan," she panted. "Yes."

"Yes?" I asked, sucking her clit between my teeth once more before I ran the flat of my tongue up and over, hitting that sweet ass again.

She arched. "*Please.*"

With that plea still hanging on her lips, I lowered my lips back to her clit, keeping all my focus there while I pressed my index finger against her puckered asshole. She rolled her hips, gasping, moaning, and when I slipped that digit inside her, feeling her pulse so tightly around me I thought she might break my finger, she let out the most guttural, animalistic groan I'd ever heard in my life.

She came fucking my finger, fucking my mouth, her hips rolling and thrusting, ass bouncing. Every part of her wanted more, and I gave and gave until I was out of breath and she was limp and gasping for air.

It was the sweetest addiction, making that woman come. And I decided then and there that I wanted that pleasure for the rest of my damn life.

She seemed a little dazed as I withdrew, standing and helping her roll over and slide up the bed until her head was on the pillows. I carefully lay down on top of her, elbows propped on either side of her head, body nestling into the space between her legs.

"Who even *are* you," she breathed on a laugh, pressing a hand to her forehead before she let it flop back into the pillows.

"I think I can help you remember my name," I said, kissing her neck and rolling my hips against her. My hard shaft slipped between her legs, into the wet space, making both of us groan in sync.

Her lips were on mine in the next second, and she kissed me hard and possessive, claiming me, urging me into her with her heels digging into my ass. But I kept just enough space there, sliding against her wet folds without actually entering her, just to drive us both crazy a while longer.

I pulled back, balancing on my elbows again, watching her eyes flutter, her lips part each time I rolled. But when her eyes opened again and found mine, that hunger faded, and vulnerability seeped in, slow and sweet, her eyes flicking between mine as both of our movements slowed to a stop.

"What is it?" I asked.

She shook her head, and instead of answering me, she slid her hands into my hair, pulling me down until our foreheads met. She closed her eyes, and I closed mine, and for a moment, we were just there, breathing, existing. Her chest rose to meet mine on every inhale, and with every exhale of mine, I tried to answer whatever questions she had that she couldn't even ask. I hoped she felt my sincerity, my assurance that whatever fear she had, I was there to fight it with her.

"Condom," she murmured.

I nodded, rolling off her long enough to dig in the drawer beside her bed. The moment that latex was covering me, she rolled until I was sitting, back against her headboard, ass on her pillows, and she straddled me, sinking down on me without so much as a second to let me brace for contact.

And I needed to brace. I *needed* to prepare for that overwhelming sense of ownership I felt when she took me inside her. I wasn't ready, and I had no choice but to give, to submit, to surrender everything. She was tight and hot around me, her legs pinning each side, arms surrounding my neck, forehead to mine. She kissed me softly, tenderly, sucking and biting at my lower lip with each lift of her hips. Every time she lowered back down, I groaned, louder and louder, my hands holding her hips to try to get her to slow down.

"I'm not going to last with you going like that."

"I don't want you to last," she breathed, biting my lip so hard I knew she'd drawn blood. "I want you to *come*."

The words were barely out of her mouth before I succumbed to her request. Hot lightning pulsed through me, and everything went blank. The only thing I felt, the only thing I could *ever* feel again was the point where we met, the emptying of me inside her, the sweet tightness of her throbbing out her second orgasm around my shaft. I pulled her close, wrapped my arms around her, flexed my hips into her harder, once, twice, again and again until every drop was spilled. Our bodies were slick and hot when we finally ebbed, our breathing shallow, lips numb where they met.

Mallory fell limp in my arms, burying her face in my neck. I held her for a moment, one hand at the small of her back, the other running back through her hair — which had come loose from her ponytail at some point. I rubbed her scalp before running my fingers through the roots to the ends, and repeated it again and again as she hummed a sated approval.

"That feels nice," she whispered.

I rolled us over until we were on our sides, disposing of the condom in the trashcan and shutting off the lamp before I climbed in behind her again. I pulled her into me, spooning her, wishing I could crawl inside her mind and know everything she was thinking in that moment.

For a long while, we were quiet. I watched my fingers running patterns over her skin, content to sit in that secret silence with her for as long as she'd let me. Her breath evened out, her eyes closing, and she snuggled closer to me. Before she could fall asleep, I wrapped my arms fully around her, tucking her into my chest, and whispered into her ear.

"Mallory?"

"Yes?"

"Do you think there's a universe that exists where you could be mine?"

Her eyelids fluttered open, and she turned in my arms. Even in the dark, those blue eyes of hers shone, and she locked them on mine, one hand crawling up to frame my face, sliding back into my hair, pulling me closer, her lips brushing mine when she gave her answer.

"Let's make one."

# Chapter Sixteen

## MALLORY

That weekend was the best weekend of my life.

I woke the next morning with Logan's arms around me, his legs weaved through mine, my back to his chest. We'd kicked the covers off, but the warmth from his body alone was enough to sustain me. I'd rolled in his arms, watching him sleep and thinking over the promise we'd made the night before.

To make a universe — one where we could be together.

It didn't exist. That much, we both knew for sure. There wasn't a day anywhere in the future where his family or my family would be okay with us being together. But sometime in the last month, we'd decided it didn't matter anymore.

Logan had kissed my nose when he woke up, smiling and running his fingers through my hair as he watched me. I could tell he was just as worried as I was, that he was wondering if what we'd said in the dark still held true in the light. He'd told me to stay in bed, brought me coffee and made us breakfast, and then we'd sat there in the sheets we'd made love in, and we'd talked.

He'd asked me if I wanted to be with him, and I'd said yes. I asked him if he was ready for the consequences of being with me, and he'd said yes. And that was all it took. Neither of us were in a rush, we knew we had time before we needed to tell anyone. For a while, we wanted to keep it between us — mostly because we were selfish, but a little because I needed to find a way to talk to my dad before we told him.

Logan was sure his family would come around, that they would support him eventually — even if it took a while. And from what he'd told me about them, I believed it. They may never fully approve, but his brothers would stand behind their brother, his mom would stand behind her son. There was love there, and understanding, and communication.

All three of those things were missing in my family.

I couldn't imagine a day or scenario where I told my father I was falling in love with Logan Becker and he said, *"That's just swell!"* I needed to think, to figure out a way to prove to him that Logan wasn't whatever it was my father thought he was. I needed to show him that I didn't do this just to piss him and Mom off, but because I cared about Logan — more than I'd cared about anyone before.

If Dad found out before I had a plan, everything would crumble. He'd take my shop, kick me out of the apartment above it that I called home, and if I knew him well enough, he'd find a way to take it out on Logan, too.

That was what scared me most.

So, with a promise to each other that we were together, but that we both needed time before we told anyone, we ate breakfast in bed, and then Logan laid me down in those sheets and made love to me slowly, sweetly, with his eyes watching mine, his arms trembling on either side of my head where they held him above me.

And the best weekend of my life continued.

It was absolute bliss, playing house with Logan. It was the first weekend of the shop being open, so all day long on Saturday, I was downstairs, hosting classes and talking to potential customers who would stop in on their walk down Main Street to find out more about what we offered. Logan was there, too, for a while — helping restock supplies, ringing people up at the Square register, cleaning up after one class so that I could get ready for the other. But when Mrs. Brownstein came in with her children, casting us questioning looks, we knew it was a little too dangerous. Nearly everyone in town knew our family history, and we didn't need word getting back to either of our families before we were ready.

So, Logan went home for the day, working on cracking the password to his father's hard drive and — God bless — working on that perfect body of his, too. Then we met up for a late dinner at my place, and he told me about the Elon Musk book he was reading while I told him about the hidden art talent in Stratford. We spent Saturday night tangled up in each other, talking and laughing and never even bothering to get dressed, because we knew it wouldn't be long before we'd peel those clothes off once again.

And Sunday, we did it all over again.

Logan didn't leave my place until bright and early Monday morning, giving himself the day to shower and shop and get ready for our Christmas party at work. It was Christmas Eve, and the entire distillery was off for the next two days, but the Scooter Whiskey Christmas party wasn't exactly optional for the employees. It was always a grand affair, with Mom going all out with catering and a band just like she loved to do, and Dad giving himself an excuse to talk into a microphone, just like *he* loved to do. They'd both made it very clear that I was expected to be there, and Logan and his entire family would be there, too.

Even though the last thing I wanted to do was put on another dress I didn't feel comfortable in and play into the politics of Stratford, I knew it would be bearable with Logan there. I looked forward to stolen kisses in dark hallways, to watching him from across the room without anyone knowing I'd had him in my bed all weekend, and most of all, to coming home tonight and knowing he'd be coming home with me.

I floated on a high all day long, even when Chris dragged me an hour out of town to the packed mall crawling with last-minute Christmas gift shoppers to find me a dress to wear to the party. I didn't even complain when he had me trying on heels to match, or when he insisted on paying to get my hair and makeup done by one of the girls at the salon there. We stopped by his place long enough for him to put on a well-tailored, navy blue suit and a red tie that matched my dress, and then we were off, headed to the distillery.

"Logan is going to have to sit on his hands to keep from touching you all night in that dress," Chris said as we made our way across the parking lot. A hundred other cars were parking, too, and the clouds swirled with a threat of snow above us.

"I'll have to tell him to thank you."

"Oh, trust me, you wouldn't be okay with how I'd let Logan Becker *thank* me."

I poked him in the rib, and he laughed, holding his arm out for me to loop mine through.

"Come on. Let's see if your mom made any of that boozy eggnog we used to steal when we were teenagers."

The wind whipped cold against our faces as we huddled together and made our way inside the distillery. The party was being held in the only event space the distillery had, which was usually reserved for schmoozing possible partners or big clients. I gasped when we pushed through the doors, gawking and doing a full three-sixty turn as one of the pew boys from church took my coat.

"Whoa," Chris murmured, looking around with me. "Your mom really went all out."

And she had. It was a winter wonderland inside that old warehouse. Blue up-lights cast the walls and ceiling in a beautiful cerulean blue, and fake snow fell from the ceiling in the form of little foam bubbles. As soon as the flakes hit the ground, they disappeared, but there was scene after scene of wintery fun lining the room — a snow man, a little forest of trees, a small log cabin with the chimney churning out light smoke, an actual fire pit that had people sitting around it making s'mores. The dance floor was already covered with distillery employees and their families doing line dances to the country music the band was playing, and there were carolers making their way around the room, singing Christmas songs softly — just loud enough to be heard by those in very near proximity.

We made our way deeper inside with our mouths still gaping, and someone handed us what appeared to be champagne, but it was tinged a light pink. When we tasted it, Chris's eyes widened.

"Peppermint," he said in awe.

I shook my head, a small laugh escaping my lips. It was an incredible party, and I had to give it to my parents. If they knew how to do one thing well — it was this.

Chris and I claimed our seats at one of the round tables in the back corner, me dropping off my clutch and him hanging his suit jacket on the back of the chair. Then, he led me to the dance floor, peppermint champagne still in our hands, and we danced.

I was never a big country music fan, but I couldn't fight back a smile as I did the old line dances I'd used to love in high school with the rest of the employees at the distillery. In a way, it felt like a big barn party, like just another night at The Black Hole, and I smiled despite the fact that I was in a dress and heels.

When I did a turn during *"Boot Scootin' Boogie"* and saw Logan watching me from across the dance floor, I smiled for a completely different reason.

I stuttered, but he moved easily into the next move, giving me a wink and a crooked smile that had his dimple popping out on his left cheek. I smiled back, finding my place in the dance again, but unable to take my eyes off him. His own eyes swept over me, and he shook his head, mouthing a "*wow*" that made me blush.

*Blush.*

Who even was I?

We were still staring at each other when Logan's older brother, Jordan, narrowed his eyes — first at Logan, and then at me. I swallowed under the intensity of his glare, offering a small, noncommittal wave. Jordan lowered his brows more, turning his gaze to Logan, who finally tore his eyes off me and continued dancing, acting like nothing had happened at all.

My stomach sank, remembering the universe we still lived in, regardless of the one we'd promised to make together. But I didn't have time to stew on it before Dad was on the microphone, telling us to make our way to our tables for dinner to be served.

I wasn't able to steal away time with Logan like I'd hoped — not during dinner, and not after, when the white elephant gift exchange was happening between the employee children on the dance floor. When the band picked back up again and people started making their way to the floor, I caught his attention from where he sat at a table with his mother, Jordan, and Mikey, and I nodded toward the hall where the bathrooms were.

Logan nodded, and my stomach was a mess of nerves as I made my way across the room, like I was about to steal a car instead of talk to my boyfriend.

*My boyfriend.*

An audible sigh left my chest at that, and I shook my head, giggling to myself and looking back over my shoulder to see if Logan was following. I stopped short, frowning when I saw he'd been pulled aside by the other tour guides. They shoved him toward the dance floor, relentless, and he laughed and laughed, but his eyes were sad when they met mine.

"*Sorry,*" he mouthed.

I smiled, waving him off and letting him know it was okay.

Maybe I wouldn't get time alone with him at the party, but I'd have him all to myself when it was all over.

That was enough for me.

Chris and I made another drive by at the peppermint champagne table before we were back on the dance floor, too — on the opposite side of where Logan was. We exchanged glances now and then, shared a smile or two, and all the while, I counted down the minutes until the party would be over and I would be in his arms again.

"If I could have everyone's attention, please," my father said when the next song died out. Everyone on the dance floor turned to face the makeshift stage, where he stood behind a podium with a microphone, smiling and beaming out at his employees. Mom stood beside him, both of them dressed in pearly white — Dad in a tux, Mom in a gown — looking like the Groom and Bride or like the King and Queen, themselves.

I would have rolled my eyes if I wasn't in such a good mood.

As it was, Chris and I gathered in the middle of the dance floor with everyone else, holding our glasses out when a server came around to refill champagne glasses. That meant a toast was coming, and if I knew my father, he'd be toasting to how successful the distillery was this year.

AKA — how successful *he* was this year.

"Mrs. Scooter and I would like to sincerely thank each and every one of you for attending tonight," he said, putting an arm around Mom as they swept their eyes over the crowd. "This is the twenty-seventh year that we've had the Christmas Eve party — a tradition that my grandparents started that I'm happy to keep alive today."

There was a light applause, and my mom squeezed Dad's arm. I swore I saw him getting choked up, which was laughable — considering him and grandpa were fighting about almost everything up to the very day he passed away.

Dad went on to talk about how well the distillery had done, talking about new partnerships and advances. The entire room was abuzz when he revealed that my brother, Malcolm, had secured us a sixty-second advertisement during the upcoming Super Bowl. Dad said there would be filming happening at the distillery, because they wanted to show the faces that made America's favorite whiskey come to life.

I zoned out a bit after that, sipping my champagne that I was supposed to be saving for the toast while my eyes scanned the room for Logan. I found him over to my left, closer to the stage than I was, surrounded by his mother and two brothers. Noah wasn't there this year, since he was visiting the mayor's daughter in Utah. It looked a little strange, seeing the family without one of the brothers — like a puzzle with one piece missing right in the center.

Logan must have sensed me watching him, because he took a sip of his whiskey, casually glancing around until he found me, too. He smiled, tilting his glass toward me, and I tilted mine.

With just our eyes, we had an entire conversation in that moment.

*You look beautiful,* he said.

*I can't wait to get you home,* I said.

*Soon,* he said.

*Soon,* I echoed.

Then, my father asked my uncle to join him on stage, and the applause pulled both of our gazes back to the front.

It was always my father who had the charm to bedazzle a crowd. Uncle Mac, on the other hand, always looked like he was perturbed, like he was biding his time until he could be alone again. He gave an awkward smile at the applause, standing next to my father with rosy cheeks and a glass of whiskey in his hand.

"As you all know, my little brother has been instrumental in this distillery's success since our father passed away. It was his idea to implement a tour department — an initiative that continues to pull visitors in from across the country and the *world* every single day."

There was another roll of applause, and Chris nudged me. "That initiative has also brought a plethora of gay tourists into Buck's," he said, wagging his brows and taking a sip of his champagne. "*Thank you, Mac.*"

I chuckled, nudging him back as my father went on about all of my uncle's accomplishments. I was tempted to zone out again, to see if I could eye-fuck Logan from across the room a while longer, when I heard my name called.

Applause started again, but I stood there frozen, confused, wondering what I had missed. Chris cleared his throat, nudging me forward before he began clapping around his champagne glass, too.

I smiled, cheeks heating as I made my way to the stage. One of the pew boys helped me up the stairs, and then I was standing next to my mother, facing practically the entire town of Stratford. I found Logan, and his comforting smile anchored me, steadying me as my father beamed at me from the podium.

"We've been trying for a long time to get our daughter, Mallory, to take her role at the distillery. But, as many of you know, she is a colorful bird who likes to fly her own course."

There were a few chuckles, and I forced a smile, despite the fact that I wanted to roll my eyes at the backhanded compliment.

"When Mallory told us she was coming back home to Stratford after she wrapped up her masters degree, we were thrilled. Not only because — as many of you know — she was opening her very own art studio, but because it meant we'd have our family together again, too." He paused, beaming at me like we were best friends. "And we are so proud of her, of all she's accomplished." He turned to the crowd then. "What do you guys think? Do we love the new addition of *Dalí and Mal's* to Stratford?"

The applause roared then, and Logan let out a whistle between his teeth that had me *actually* smiling and blushing. I covered the smile with one hand, and Logan grinned up at me, tossing me a wink that I held for my own.

"What you might not have known was that while she was building that studio up during her evenings and weekends, she was *here,* working as a tour guide during the week days. And from what her uncle has told me, she has excelled at that — after a few minor setbacks, of course."

Those who knew of those *setbacks* chuckled throughout the room, and I found myself forcing a smile again, wondering when all this hoopla would be over.

"We've had more compliments for Mallory's tours just in the past month than we've had for any other tour in the past *year,*" Dad said, and that had my eyebrows shooting into my hairline — one, because it was news to me, and two, because I found it hard to believe — especially given how many compliments came in for Logan each and every day.

And that's when my stomach sank to the stage floor.

Because I knew, right then, that my father was up to something.

And I knew it was something I wouldn't like.

"She's put personal touches on her tours, telling our visitors about fond memories she had with her grandfather, about growing up around the distillery, about the history only our family knows. She's even volunteered to help out with tasks *outside* of her normal duties — like cleaning out an entire storage closet to make way for new equipment that will help our brand excel."

I frowned, opening my mouth to mention that I did *not* do that alone — or by choice — but my father kept talking.

"That's why, it is my absolute pleasure to announce to all of you tonight that my brother, Mac, is retiring after the new year. And it is my *distinct* pleasure to also announce that we are filling his position with another deserving member of our family — a member we weren't sure would ever come home, one we are so happy to have back in Stratford, and one who has already made us proud in her short time working at Scooter. We know she will have a long and successful career ahead, and we can't wait to see where she takes this instrumental part of our company. Please help me congratulate Mallory Scooter — our new Manager of Tour Guide Operations."

Dad started the applause, Mom teared up, Mac looked bored — and I tried my best but failed epically to hide my expression of horror.

*No.*

*No, no, no!*

Mom wrapped me in a hug, and Dad made some comment about me being stunned, a laugh rolling off his lips. All the while, I searched for Logan — and it wasn't hard to find him, because the entire distillery was watching him, too.

They were watching the entire Becker family.

Logan stood like a statue, just as stunned as me, his eyes on my father while Jordan held a firm hand on his shoulder. Their mother, though small beside them, was standing tall, head held high, a determined-level expression on her face. Their youngest brother, Michael, stood just as tall and silent on the other side of her, shaking his head, his brows furrowed over angry eyes.

I willed Logan to look at me as my father reached to pull me into a hug next. The room was a mixture of awkward applause and animated chatter. Suspicious eyes glared up at me, and I didn't have to read lips to know the things they were saying about me weren't flattering. I didn't blame them. I hated myself in that moment, too.

This job shouldn't be mine. It was never *meant* to be mine.

It belonged to Logan, and I wasn't the only one who knew that.

The man I'd had in my bed all weekend looked like a stranger under that pale blue light. And when his eyes found mine, he looked at me like *I* was a stranger, too — like everything between us was a lie.

I pleaded with him as much as I silently could to wait, to not draw conclusions, to let me think, to let me *fix* this. But he pursed his lips, shook his head, and then he was shaking his brother off him and tearing through the crowd.

I pulled out of my father's grasp, running down the steps and chasing after him. I didn't give a fuck what anyone said about me, about *us*, because at this point — they were talking, anyway.

The only thing I cared about was getting to Logan and making him see that I had nothing to do with this.

It was snowing lightly when I shoved through the doors that led to the parking lot, and my breaths racked through my chest painfully as I searched for Logan. I found him storming across the wet concrete toward his truck, and I ran, feet screaming in my heels the entire time.

"Logan!" I called, but he didn't so much as stutter or pause. "Logan, wait!"

He spun then, and I nearly crashed into him, skidding to a stop with just a foot between us.

I held up my hands, trying to catch my breath. "Logan, I am so sorry. I had—"

*neat*

"You had *what*, Mallory?" he fired back, standing tall. "You had no idea that was coming? You had nothing to do with it? You had no intention of hurting me?"

I gaped at him, because of course that was exactly what I was going to say. But when those words rolled from his lips, shame shaded my cheeks, because he knew as well as I did that somewhere, in the back of my mind, I suspected this might happen.

He suspected it, too.

And I did nothing to stop it.

"Do you know how long I've fought for that job, Mallory? How many hours I've put in, how many years of my life I've dedicated to this company, just *trying* to keep my own family's legacy alive, *trying* to fight for my father — who has no voice to fight for himself anymore?"

"Of course, I do," I said, reaching for him, but he pulled away like I was poison. I swallowed, letting my hands fall limp at my sides. "Logan, of course I know that. I know *so much* about you, and I want to know everything. I'm falling in lo—"

"Don't," he warned, his voice a thunderous growl. "Don't you *dare* say that to me — not right now. Not when you just ripped my fucking heart out on that stage in front of everyone in this goddamn town."

My throat closed in, emotion strangling me from the inside.

"I *trusted* you," he breathed. "I let you in like I've never let another woman in before. I told you things about myself that not even my *family* knows. And you know what?" He laughed, fist hitting his chest hard. "It's *me* I'm pissed at the most. It's me who was the fucking idiot, trusting a Scooter, giving myself to a woman who has showed this whole town time and time again that the only thing she cares about is herself."

I gasped. "Logan... you don't mean that."

"You're going to tell me you had *no* idea that this was coming?" he asked, stepping into my space. I took a step back. "You're going to look me in the eyes and say your father never hinted at this, that you never thought to talk to him about it, or to talk to *me* about it — especially after everything that's happened between us?"

I swallowed, body trembling as more snow fell down around us. Little flakes caught on his lashes, in his hair, and he looked so devastatingly beautiful in that moment that I had to cross my arms to keep from reaching out for him.

I wanted to pull him into me, comfort him, tell him I would never hurt him...

But he was right.

There *was* a part of me that suspected my father had this in his plan. I wondered why the timing was the way it was, why he wanted me in the tour department out of all the departments there were at the distillery. I was an *art* major — I should have been in marketing with my brother.

The truth was — I knew.

Deep down, I knew.

And I'd been too chicken shit to do anything about it.

"I can fix it," I breathed, sniffing against the cold. "Please, just give me a chance to fix it."

"You *can't*," he said, stepping into me again. This time, I didn't move away. I looked him right in the eyes as he gave me the lashing I deserved. "Your dad just announced that you're the new manager in front of everyone. You can't convince him to go back on that, and you can't do *anything* without him taking the studio away from you. Admit it, he played you, and a part of you knew it would end up like this." Logan shook his head. "It's actually kind of perfect, isn't it? Playing with me the way you have been the past month. Was it one last dig at your father? One last way to piss him off before he locked you into a life you never wanted?"

I choked on a sob that had no tears to back it, a result of years of me training myself not to feel. I would have given anything to cry in that moment, to throw myself into Logan's arms and beg for his forgiveness.

But I didn't deserve it.

"I was just another way to rebel, wasn't I? When everything else was out of your control, when you knew you had to play by his rules, I was the only way you could get your hits in, huh?"

I shook my head, bottom lip quivering, but I had no words to fight back. I had nothing but my bleeding heart in my hands — a heart I knew Logan wouldn't take. Not now. Not ever again.

I didn't deserve Logan Becker, because I was exactly the piece of shit he was describing me to be.

And the best thing I could do for him was let him go.

Logan sighed, pinching the bridge of his nose before he let his hand fall to his side. His eyes searched mine, and they welled with tears the longer he stared. He opened his mouth, closed it again, and then his head fell as he shook it. When he looked at me again, it was with a single tear slipping down his cheek.

"I was so blinded by you that I couldn't see," he whispered, his voice shaking. "All I wanted was to love you. Nothing else mattered. And now..." he swallowed. "Now, I've lost everything. Including you — and I never even had you at all, did I?"

My face twisted, again, all the signs of crying without the actual tears making themselves known. My heart ached so violently inside my chest I thought it would revolt and tear itself out of my body just to escape the pain.

He was *everything* to me.

But how could he ever believe me if I told him that, after everything that had happened?

When I didn't answer, Logan shook his head, putting his hands up as if it was his final surrender. Then, he turned, storming the rest of the way to his truck. He climbed inside, slammed the door, roared the engine to life, and peeled out of the parking lot, leaving me damp and cold in the falling snow.

And it was right where I deserved to be.

# Chapter Seventeen

**MALLORY**

On my phone, there were a dozen missed calls and texts.

There were texts from my mother, asking where I was, and from my father, warning me to not upset my mother on Christmas Day. There were missed calls from my brother, from my grandparents on my mother's side, and from Chris — who had left a few threatening voicemails that he'd beat down my door if I didn't answer him soon. There were texts from acquaintances and "friends," wishing me a Merry Christmas and a happy new year.

But there wasn't a single word from Logan.

I didn't know why I hoped for it, why my heart leapt into my throat every time my phone buzzed, or why I ever expected to see his name on the screen when I unlocked it. Last night hadn't been a small fight. It hadn't been a little misunderstanding that would feel silly and insignificant in the morning light. It had been the final blow in a fight neither of us even realized we were in. It was a total knock out.

And now, here I was, beaten and bruised on the cold floor of what I hoped my life would be, wishing I could go back in time and do everything differently.

If I had Doc's DeLorean, I'd set the dial to send me back a little over a month ago. I'd go back and tell my father to take his deal and shove it right up his ass, because I would have listened to that little voice inside me that *knew* he wasn't exposing all his cards. I'd known who my father was my entire adult life, and I'd been naïve to ignore what I knew about him just so I could selfishly pretend there was no reason not to take the deal he offered me, to get my dream if all I had to do was sacrifice a little time at the distillery.

If I hadn't realized it from the beginning, I *definitely* should have figured it out once I got on the inside.

Once I saw how everyone in that department looked up to Logan, once I saw how, effortlessly, he was the best on that entire team, and once I put two and two together that my uncle was retiring, and that I'd been sent to that department *despite* the fact that I was the least qualified in our family to give tours...

I should have known.

I should have stood up, found my voice, fought for justice like I always did.

I should have stopped it.

But I didn't.

Part of me ignored it because I didn't want to have my dream ripped from me when I'd only just had the chance to hold it in my hands. Part of me ignored it because I was scared, because I had nowhere to go, because failing didn't feel like an option for me — and I would avoid it all costs.

And perhaps the largest part of me ignored it because the more time I spent with Logan, the more I fell for him

— and I thought if I ignored everything else that wasn't him, I could live in a blissful little bubble where nothing could touch us.

I didn't think of him, of his dreams, of his happiness — when it seemed all he'd done the past month was put *my* dreams and happiness first.

My chest ached as memories of us working in the shop filtered through my mind. I longed for those long afternoons, laughing and listening to music and learning more about him. I yearned for a different last name, for a different family, for a different circumstance where I could have met Logan Becker and fallen for him and let him fall for *me* without any of this shit being an issue.

But that wasn't the world I lived in.

My phone buzzed on the coffee table again, but this time I didn't even move to check the screen. I knew it wasn't Logan, and I knew that whoever it *was*, I didn't want to talk to. I didn't want to talk to *anyone*. It didn't matter that it was Christmas Day — I was perfectly content being miserable.

And alone.

It was what I deserved to be.

I hadn't eaten since the night before, the thought of food so revolting I couldn't stomach so much as a piece of toast, so my legs were a little wobbly as I wrapped my thick robe around me and padded downstairs to the shop. Snow had covered the town last night, leaving us with a beautiful white Christmas that every little kid and mother, alike, had prayed for. Under different circumstances, I might have run out to play in it. I might have been having a snowball fight with Logan, or laughing as I got soaked making snow angels.

As it was, Main Street was empty, everyone home with their families celebrating the birth of Christ, and I found the vacancy comforting. It left me alone with my thoughts, alone with my misery, alone with my broken heart — and my ability to use it to create something.

It was the only thing I wanted to do, other than sit around and feel sorry for myself. I wanted to bring something to life — and before I could make a choice of how, my body made it for me. My feet carried me numbly over to one of the stools in front of a blank sketch pad, and I sat with my back to the store windows, letting the late afternoon light cast its light over the cream paper.

It was cold in the studio, but I didn't turn the heat on. If anything, I wanted to feel that cold down to my bones. I sat there, shivering, pulling the sketch pad into my lap and propping my feet on the footrest of the stool. For a while, I just stared at that blank sheet, vision blurring, heart slowing to an almost nonexistent beat within my chest.

Then, I drew.

Time slipped away easily, just like it always did when I lost myself in art. The afternoon light turned to evening light, a bright glow from the setting sun reflecting off the snow and casting the studio in a halo so beautiful it might as well have been sent from the heavens. I found comfort in the familiar scratching sounds of the pencil against the paper, in the way nothing slowly turned to something. Gray dust covered my hand, and my back and shoulders ached from poor posture, but still, I drew.

And blended.

And created contrast and depth and everything that was so challenging with sketching — that challenge usually the medicine that healed all my ailments.

But when the pencil fell limp in my fingers and I stared down at the face that stared back at me — the one that had haunted my dreams all night, too — I didn't feel any relief.

*neat*

I only felt the deep, all-encompassing, impossible-to-ignore urge to make everything wrong right again.

I'd brought Logan to life on that paper — the crinkle of his eyes when he smiled, that dimple on his cheeks, one hand seeming to hold the face of the person looking at the drawing while the other rested under the pillow he laid his head on. My sheets pooled around his waist, allowing me to bring the lean lines of his toned stomach to life. His hair was a mess, just the way I liked it, and he was looking at me like I was the only thing that mattered in this entire world.

Like the way I looked at him.

I sighed, dropping the pencil to the pad and scrubbing my hands over my face. I didn't even care that I was surely marking my face with pencil dust. I wanted to rub away the exhaustion, the headache, the stress.

When I lowered my hands again, I found myself staring at the photograph of him eating pizza and taking notes that first day we'd worked on the shop. My heart crawled into my throat, and I tried and failed to swallow past it as I looked at him.

I could only remember one life-altering moment in my life.

That night my father chose his reputation over me, the night he made it clear that my safety and wellness came second to the connections he needed to run business — I made a choice. I chose to never lean on my family again, to never abide by the rules they set for me, to forge my own path and forsake what anyone in this town ever had to say about it. I chose what was right over what was wrong, what was hard over what was easy, and what was just over what was *unjust*.

Now, I found myself sitting in that same, hollow, yet somehow exciting kind of moment.

I was on the precipice of making a decision that would alter everything. I would no longer be able to wake up in the life I'd known, in the comfort I'd made a home in, in the certainty I'd found peace in. Because once I made the choice that I was teetering on making, everything would change, and though it was the harder path to walk — it was the right one.

I stood, setting my sketch to the side and walking over to stand in front of the photo of Logan. My heart clambered in my chest, and I placed a hand over the spot where it ached, soothing it as best I could.

He was worth it.

He was worth everything.

And no matter what it cost me, I *would* do right by him.

That was a promise.

## LOGAN

*I told you so.*

It was the unspoken theme of that Christmas Day.

I felt those words floating in the air, could practically hear them coming from my mother, from my brothers, from my*self* — though no one spoke them out loud.

For all intents and purposes, it was a Christmas like any other. We all gathered at Mom's last night after the party at the distillery, and Mom made cookies that we decorated just like we did every Christmas Eve since we were kids. Her favorite Frank Sinatra Christmas album played on the speakers, we all wore matching flannel pajama bottoms, and though we were quieter than usual, and I was a fucking wreck inside, we all kept it together on the outside.

No one spoke about the promotion.

No one asked me about Mallory.

No one gave away that we were all hurting, that we were all upset, and that once again — our family had been disrespected by the Scooters.

Instead, my brothers and I put on our happy faces for Mom, and she put on her happy face for us, and we made cookies and watched old Christmas cartoons and then we made a big pallet in the middle of the living room floor. The three brothers slept there while Mom slept on the couch, and though it felt wrong to not have Noah there, it was still home.

It was still Christmas.

I wished it was a rainy, cold day in the middle of November that I felt this kind of pain. I wished I could be alone, in my bed, in my own home. It felt like a betrayal to my soul to open gifts that morning, to eat a lavish Christmas dinner, to pretend I gave a shit about anything other than running to the person who had caused me more pain than I'd felt since my father passed away, and somehow finding a way to make it right with her.

And perhaps more than anything else, I wished I could open up to my family about what I was feeling. I wished I could lean on my brothers, on my mom, on the ones who had always been there for me. But I already knew what they would say.

They'd say *I told you so.*

And I couldn't stand to hear it — not now, maybe not ever.

I'd been so sure that they were wrong about Mallory, that the acts of her father didn't speak for her. I was so sure she was different — not just from the other Scooters, but from every other person in this town, period. I'd seen this deeper side to her, this diamond she kept hidden from everyone else — at least, that's what I'd convinced myself.

And even now, even in the middle of the pain caused by her hand, by her father's hand — I still believed it.

I'd lashed out at her the night before, and shame heated my neck again at the memory of it. I was hurt, and unable to control my anger, and I'd taken everything out on her when I knew she hadn't meant to hurt me.

But she *had* hurt me.

And I didn't know if the intention *not* to even mattered anymore.

She had her hands tied. That, I could understand. She was out of college, without a job and without a home, and her father gave her the opportunity to have an art studio of her own, a home above it, a place and a purpose. Could I have said no, had that same opportunity been presented to me — even if the strings attached to it were sticky and dirty and suffocating?

I sighed, readjusting the pillow behind my back on the couch. Jordan, Mikey, and I were taking turns playing Madden while Mom cleaned up in the kitchen. Pie would be served soon, and then I could make an excuse to leave and finally be alone.

"You sound like a bull with all that huffing and puffing you've been doing," Jordan said, keeping his eyes on the screen where he was currently making an offensive running play against Mikey. Mikey's defensive end took the running back down easily, and the screens popped up for each of them to select their next formation and play.

"My back is aching," I lied. "Just trying to get comfortable."

"You know you can cut the bullshit anytime, right?" He hiked the ball. "I think we're all tired of pretending like last night didn't happen."

"I'm not pretending anything. I just don't feel like talking about it."

"Why? Because you're too big and bad for feelings?" His tongue jutted out as he pressed the buttons that sent the ball flying out of the quarterback's hands and down the field to a wide receiver. It was caught, and he ran it all the way to the ten-yard line.

"Bullshit," Mikey mumbled. "You're not getting into that end zone, brother."

"We'll see," Jordan replied with a smirk as they picked their next plays.

"No," I said, answering his assessment. "Because I already know what you guys will say, and I don't want to hear it."

"Oh, you hear that, Mikey? Logan's a mindreader now. Knows what we'll say before we do."

"Should sign him up for the circus," Mikey chimed.

I rolled my eyes. "Come on, like you're both not waiting for the chance to say you told me so, that Mallory is a Scooter and I should have known better? That I should have kept my distance?"

Jordan paused the game, and he and Mikey both turned, confusion on their faces. "What are you talking about?"

The color drained from my face. I realized then that the only person I'd told about my interest in Mallory — past the fact that she worked with me, anyway — was Mom.

I shook my head. "Nothing."

"I was thinking about the fact that the promotion rightfully owed to you was given to a Scooter, yes, but it doesn't reflect on you," Jordan said, one eyebrow lifted. "This was on them. There was nothing you could have done to prevent it."

"He's talking about the fact that he's in love with Mallory and feels like a sucker now that he realizes she was taking his job all along."

Jordan's attention snapped to my youngest brother, and I gritted my teeth, hands fisting at my sides.

"I'm not in love with her." Again, a lie.

"Wait," Jordan said, pointing at Mikey when he looked back at me. "What does he know that I don't?" He narrowed his eyes, pointing his finger at me this time. "Have you been hooking up with Mallory Scooter?"

I sniffed, crossing my arms over my chest without an answer.

Jordan let out a bark of a laugh, eyes wide. "Wow."

"She's not what you think she is," I defended.

"Clearly."

"She's not. She hates her father almost as much as we do. She knows the shitty things he's done, and she's spent her whole life trying to get away from that legacy."

"Well, obviously, she's doing a fine job of that."

"She didn't know he was going to do this," I growled.

"Then why are you so upset?" Jordan threw back. "If Mallory is so innocent, and you're so in love, then why are you moping around like someone rearranged the books on your bookshelf?"

"Because everything I was afraid of losing I lost in a matter of minutes!" I stood, glaring down at my brothers on the floor. "Because that job was the only chance I had of doing my part to keep the Becker name alive in that distillery. Because they're trying to wash Dad out of their history altogether, and it's working. Because I can't do anything about it. And yes, because for the first time in my fucking life, I thought maybe I could have what Mom and Dad did, that I could be with a woman who understood me, who challenged me, who made my life better instead of just making me roll my eyes at all the fucking town gossip that most girls in Stratford are obsessed with. She was different, and for the first time since Dad died, I was actually fucking happy." I didn't even bother hiding the tears that flooded my eyes, because with my brothers, I was never afraid to cry. "All I do, all I've ever done is try to keep the peace. I need steadiness — routine and dependability. And right now, I don't have any of that. Right now, I'm on a piece of fucking driftwood in the middle of the ocean without a paddle or a prayer in hell of finding land again." I swallowed, holding my chin high, though every part of me was trembling. "*That's* why I'm upset. Are you fucking happy now?"

Neither of my brothers could look at me then, and I took their eyes being glued to the carpet as an answer. Mom had peeked out of the kitchen, and the look in her eyes when I turned around was so heartbreaking, I couldn't hold it together any longer. I swiped my laptop off the kitchen table and barreled outside, not bothering to grab a jacket. I needed space, and fresh air, and to not have anyone's pitiful stare on me for a while.

Of course, I should have known better with my family. It didn't take long before Jordan and Mikey walked outside and sat on the porch with me. Jordan handed me my jacket, and I tugged it on without looking at him, keeping my attention on the laptop. They let me stew for a little while longer, but then my little brother got up from the rocking chair he sat in, flipped my laptop lid shut, and forced me to look at him.

"We're sorry," he said, leveling his hazel eyes with my own. We both favored Mom, and sometimes, when I looked at him, I saw a younger version of me. "I'm saying that on behalf of all of us. But you should know that we love you, and we would never judge you. Not even if you robbed a bank and tried to get away in a go-kart."

I sighed, smile tugging at the corner of my lips. "I know. I'm sorry, too. I just... I don't know how to handle all of this. I hate feeling anything negative, and right now, I'm drowning in *everything* negative."

"I know the feeling," he said, and Jordan and I exchanged glances.

Our little brother had been battling a broken heart for months, and here he was, ready to go to war for *mine*.

That was the Becker way.

Mikey pulled his rocking chair over so he could face me, and Jordan leaned against the porch railing, quiet for now.

"I didn't realize it until Noah got with Ruby Grace, until Bailey broke up with me, maybe not even until just now, when you said what you did inside, but..." Mikey shrugged. "I think we're all looking for what Mom and Dad had. And if I'm being honest, I think we're wasting our time."

Jordan shifted his weight, but kept quiet, watching our little brother as he continued.

"I don't know what happened between you and Mallory, but I can tell you now, if it's over?" He shook his head. "Just let it be over. Find a way to let her go. I know it feels impossible. Trust me — I'm *still* holding on to a girl who tossed me aside so easily, I got whiplash. But, the more time that passes, the more I see that... well... maybe the kind of love Mom and Dad had really is so rare that not everyone can find it. Noah did, and I love that for him. But, I don't know... maybe it's not in the cards for all of us."

My throat tightened, the grip so tight I couldn't swallow past it.

"That's probably not what you want to hear," he said. "But, it's what I believe to be true. And you know, there's more to life than love. We can find joy in other things, you know? Our careers, our family, our hobbies. Travel. Maybe live in a new city, a new place that doesn't have the same weight as this town always has for us."

He swallowed at that, and I narrowed my eyes, because if there was one thing our family always agreed on — it was that our place was in Stratford. We had a legacy here, and we would fight to keep it. But the way Mikey was talking, it was like he wanted to be free of it all. In a way, I guessed I couldn't blame him.

"You forget that I lost my career," I pointed out.

"No, you didn't," Jordan said from where he stood. "You lost a promotion, but that's all. And who knows, maybe Mallory will crash and burn and they'll have no choice but to give the job to you."

"Or to a rookie, since they seem hell bent on keeping Beckers out of leadership," I argued.

"Maybe," Jordan conceded with a shrug. "But, that's the fight we all knew we'd be in, right? When Dad died, when that company covered it up and made it seem like an accident, even though we know there's something more to it... we all agreed to keep Dad's memory alive in this town, in our own ways. You and Noah and Mikey knew going into jobs at the distillery that it wouldn't be easy, but you're still there. And you're going to tell me that because of one setback, you're ready to quit? To leave it all behind?"

I blinked, shaking my head as my gaze fell to the chipping wood planks of the porch. "I don't want to quit."

"Then don't."

I nodded, letting their words settle over me. They were both right, of course — another annoying trait of the Becker family. When one of us lost our cool, we found it hard to see clearly, but the rest of the crew was always right there to help light the way back to rationality.

When we fell, we fell hard. When we loved, we loved with all we had. When we fought, we fought until we dropped. And when one of us was knocked down, the whole team stopped everything to get them back on their feet.

That was the Becker way.

I sighed, deciding in that moment that there was nothing more to say. Jordan was right, there was no way I was going to walk away from the distillery. If anything, I reckoned that was what Patrick wanted me to do — and I'd be damned if I'd give him what he wanted. I was there to stay — even if it would suffocate me to see Mallory in that job every day.

And as for what I felt for her, maybe Mikey was right about that. Maybe what I thought we had, what I desired from her, from us... maybe it didn't actually exist. She had ties to her family, and I had ties to mine, and for that reason alone, it didn't make sense that we would ever be together. I'd lived in the apartment above that shop with her in a secret hideaway, a place where we could pretend we were someone different, that what we had could last.

Now, we were back in the real world.

And it just was what it was.

I stared at the laptop in my hands, and my chest ached for a completely different reason. "There's something else I need to tell you guys," I said, looking up at both of them.

Their frowns mirrored each other as I opened my laptop again, and I swallowed, turning the screen toward them.

Jordan squinted at it. "Username: Becker dot John at Scooter Whiskey dot com," he said, shaking his head. "I don't get it. Are you trying to break into Dad's old email?"

"I'm trying to break into his old laptop."

Mikey leaned in closer. "But his laptop is gone," he said. "They never recovered it from the fire."

"They did," I corrected. "They just never told us."

My brothers watched me for a long moment before Mikey pulled the laptop into his hands, and Jordan watched over his shoulder while I told them the whole story. I told them about the storage closet, the laptop, how I'd extracted the hard drive, but it was password protected. I told them that I didn't want to tell them at first, because I thought it was hopeless. But, I'd tried everything that I knew, and now, I needed their help trying to figure out the password.

"If we can get into it, maybe we can find something," I said. "I don't know what I'm looking for exactly, but maybe..."

"Maybe there are answers," Jordan finished, his eyes scanning the screen.

"Ky knows a little about hacking," Mikey chimed in. "She's big into gaming and computers, and one time she hacked into the school system and changed everyone's grade to an A in Mr. Zee's anatomy class because he was such a stickler and never taught us what was actually on our tests."

"Oh shit, I remember that. Your sophomore year, right?" I asked

He nodded. "Maybe she can help."

"Here," I said, reaching for the laptop. I safely ejected the external hard drive that now housed the one that had been inside Dad's computer and handed it to Mikey. "Take it. You guys can work on it for a while. I've been obsessing over it, anyway. Need a break."

"Okay. We need to tell Noah, too."

"I will," I said. "As soon as he's back. He's happy right now, I want to let him have that."

For a long pause, my brothers and I were quiet. I felt marginally better, though my chest was still tight. I figured it would be that way for a while, until time could do its work and heal me, my heart, my soul. It'd been that way when Dad passed away, too, and I'd survived.

If I could make it through that, I could make it through anything.

When we all stood to make our way back inside, Jordan nudged Mikey with a smirk. "So... you and Ky are hanging out again, huh?"

Mikey frowned with a noncommittal shrug. "So? We've been friends forever. Why is it weird that we're hanging out?"

"No reason," Jordan said, but he and I exchanged a knowing look. That girl had been in love with our brother since they were toddlers, and I had a feeling Mikey was going to discover that real soon.

I just hoped he could give her a chance, open his heart to that possibility after Bailey.

And I hoped that maybe, one day, I could do the same with mine.

# Chapter Eighteen

**MALLORY**

I shouldn't have been as angry as I was that Christmas decorations still lined Main Street when I woke up the next morning. Of course, no one was going to take them down over night. In fact, I knew they'd still be up for another week or so, spreading joy through the new year.

Damn them.

It was just that it didn't match my mood as I flew down the road in my old Camry, the one I had insisted on buying with my own money that I saved up before I went to college. It was a piece of shit. It needed a new air conditioner and a new radiator and a new everything.

But it was mine.

I wondered briefly why I never saw my situation now the way I saw buying this car when I was seventeen, but I tried not to dwell on it. What was done, was done.

I only had my actions and choices *now*.

It was a little harder to breathe when I pulled through the gate at the end of my parents' long driveway. I didn't grow up in a house, I grew up in a giant, southern-as-can-be Tennessee estate. It sat on one-hundred-and-fifty-two acres on the north side of town, which was entirely too much land for a family of four. Of course, my father needed land to entertain — to shoot skeet, have a driving range and putter course for business talk, and, for some reason, horses. I never did figure that one out, since he wasn't a rider, and neither was Mom, nor were Malcolm or myself.

And where Dad wanted the land, Mom wanted the large house. She wanted enough room to have servants' quarters, where those who worked for her could live and be readily available. She needed multiple kitchens, dozens of rooms to house guests who were too inebriated to leave, and, as she would tell anyone who would listen, "*Plenty of room for future grandchildren to have adventures and get lost.*"

It was always too much for me. I'd felt suffocated in that massive home, and when I parked in the driveway next to the elaborate fountain, I found myself struggling for air once again.

I pushed through the front door without knocking, handing my coat and scarf to Larry — one of our butlers — before I made my way into the dining room. Mom lit up when she saw me, clapping her hands together, whereas Dad just barely glanced at me over his newspaper. Malcolm was there, too, but he was on his phone, and I was pretty sure he didn't even realize I'd walked in.

"How nice of you to finally join us," Dad murmured. "Sit. I'll have Amada bring your breakfast."

"I'm not hungry. Can we talk in your office?"

Dad waved a hand over his half-demolished plate, not taking his eyes off the newspaper. "I'm eating."

"Looks like you're done to me."

*heat*

"Mallory," Mom scolded, in the sweetest, most unassuming voice. It annoyed me more than if she would have yelled at me. "You missed Christmas Day and now you won't even eat breakfast with your family? What has gotten into you?"

"Sorry I missed yesterday, I wasn't feeling well," I said, then I turned back to Dad. "Your office? Or do you want to do this here?"

Dad gave an exaggerated sigh, taking his sweet time folding up the newspaper he was reading before he grabbed his coffee, kissed Mom on the forehead, and assured her and Malcolm that he would be back.

Again, Malcolm didn't seem to notice any of it.

Dad followed me down the hall to the west wing of the house where his office was. As much as I hated the business done within those walls, I absolutely loved the office. Three of the four walls were covered with books — which was laughable, considering the only books my father had ever read were end-of-the-year reports on the distillery — and the last wall was a floor-to-ceiling window that overlooked the rolling hills of our property, the Smokies peeking out over the horizon far in the distance.

He closed the door once we were inside, taking a seat behind his desk.

I remained standing.

"What is it that you're being so dramatic about?"

"Stop acting like you don't know," I said. "What the hell was all that about at the Christmas party? I've worked at the distillery for a *month*, Dad. I'm still in training. I'm not fit to take that job from Uncle Mac any more than you're fit to be a good father."

"Watch your tone, young lady."

"That position was *Logan's*," I said, pressing my index finger on the top of his desk like I was pointing at indisputable proof. "And you know it."

Dad rolled his eyes. "Cut the theatrics. This was a business move. We can't have a Becker running an entire department, let alone the most important *local* one, lucratively speaking."

"*Why*?" I asked, tossing my hands up in exhaustion before they fell back to my thighs with a *whack*. "What is your vendetta against that family? They lost their father in the one and only fire our distillery has ever had. We owe them. Besides, Papa *loved* their grandfather. They were partners."

"They were *not* partners," Dad said, nose flaring and face reddening. "That was never officially written on any paperwork."

"It didn't *have* to be written. They knew it because they were friends — you *all* were. I remember Papa telling fond stories of Logan's dad, John. How much he saw him as a son. And I also remember seeing pictures of you and their mom, Laurelei, when you were high schoolers. You two seemed like friends then. What happened?"

Dad slammed his fist on the desk, his face so red I thought he'd burst a blood vessel if he didn't calm down. "That's *enough*. What decisions I make for my business are just that — *my* business. I don't owe my daughter an explanation."

"You do when it concerns me!" I argued. "When it's my life, my job, my friends—"

"Logan Becker is *not* your friend."

"You're right. He's more." I stood tall, swallowing down whatever hesitance I'd had before that moment. "I love him, Dad. And I don't care if that's not *permitted* in your mind. And I also don't care what you had in plan for me at that distillery, because I'm done. I'm quitting. And you're going to give that position to Logan."

Dad watched me for a long, slow moment, blinking several times before he let out a bark of a laugh. Then, he gave in to a whole fit of laughter, swiping at tears coming from his eyes before he spoke again. "Oh, child. Your spunk is so adorable."

"You will give that position to Logan," I said again, not backing down. "Because he deserves it. Because he's the right one for the job. Because it's the right thing to do."

"I will not."

"You *will*," I said again, folding my arms. "Or I will go see your favorite journalist at the *Stratford Gazette* and tell her everything about that night when I was fourteen, when our police chief sexually harassed me and my father did nothing about it."

All the color drained from my father's face.

Miranda Hollis loved to publish scathing articles about my father and the distillery. It seemed her mission was to get Scooter Whiskey out of Stratford, to disconnect the town from what she thought was a *garbage business*. Since her father was involved in politics, Dad had never been able to silence her.

Much to his dismay.

And he knew as well as I did that if she got this story, there would be a shit storm for him, for our family, for the police chief and the entire town.

He placed his palms flat on the desk, stood very, *very* slowly, and waited until he was towering over me to look me dead in the eye. "You will do no such thing, young lady. Now, I don't know what the hell has gotten into you, but if you remember right, it's *me* who pays the bills on that little studio you love so much. It's *me* who bought that apartment above it where you sleep every night. And it's *me* who can take all of that away," he said, snapping to illustrate the point. "Just like that."

"Fine," I said, shrugging. "Do it. Take the studio, take the apartment. I have my car, and my dignity, and that's fine by me."

Dad laughed, shaking his head like I was delusional. "You've lost your mind, little girl. You'll be excommunicated from this family, from our money, from *everything* — and that shop is gone. That's not a threat. That's a promise."

I shrugged, though my heart squeezed painfully in my chest. I knew this was how he would react, and I knew when I walked out of my studio this morning that the dream I'd built inside it would be gone.

It was a sacrifice worth making, because this was the right thing to do.

"That's fine, if that's your choice," I said calmly. "But this is mine."

Dad shook his head, face screwed up in confusion like I was certifiably insane. And maybe I was. All I knew was I could never live with myself, playing a part in his game just to have a studio that I could maybe have on my own someday. It would take longer. I'd need a loan, and a business plan, maybe some investors. It wouldn't be easy.

But nothing in my life had been.

I knew one thing for sure — I never wanted to be in debt to my father, and I never wanted to be a part of any plan that hurt the man I loved.

"I know you don't want another scandal rocking this family, and I *definitely* know that with everything in the news right now, with the way companies and celebrities are getting shut down by women coming forward with their stories, this is the kind of scandal you never want to leak. So, if you want me to keep my mouth shut, I will. But you have to do this for me."

Dad's jaw clenched, face red. I gave him one last pointed look before I turned and crossed the office, opening the door that led to the hallway.

"Make it right, Dad," I said. "You have until New Year's."

Then, I slammed the door on the devil, and vowed to never make a deal with him again.

**LOGAN**

A week off from work was too long when you were miserable.

Having Christmas off was a blessing. The distillery was the absolute last place I wanted to be after the party on Christmas Eve, and spending time with my family was exactly what I needed. But that night, when I'd gone home, I'd realized it was going to be a long, lonely week.

I was so used to filling all my time with Mallory, I didn't know what to do with myself. My usual routine felt stale and suffocating now, like I was wasting time instead of making the most of it. I longed to reach out to her, to talk to her, to hold her — even with the sting of the burn she'd left fresh on my skin.

My brothers said leave her be, let her go.

My heart said go to her, hold on.

I sat in that tornado of thoughts all week, trying anything I could to keep my mind off things and failing. Working out didn't help. Reading didn't help. Cleaning didn't help. Not even an all-day marathon of murder documentaries on Friday helped. The closest I'd come to feeling okay was Saturday night at The Black Hole with my brothers. Noah was back in town, and we'd taken him out to get his mind off leaving Ruby Grace. It'd been a night of Becker debauchery, and then we'd ordered pizza at one in the morning and sat up all night trying to crack the password on Dad's hard drive.

It felt like old times, like when we were kids staying up too late during winter break, dreading the time when we'd go back to school.

And that's what it felt like, dragging myself back through the distillery doors on Monday morning — New Year's Eve. As much as I couldn't wait to get back to work, to have something to keep my mind off everything, it was a catch twenty-two.

Because everything I wanted to forget about was inside those walls.

The sympathetic looks started in the lobby, with Lucy, and they followed me all the way back to my office. A few people stopped me on the way, shaking my hand and holding my shoulder in sincerity when they said they were sorry, that it was all bullshit, that they were on my side.

Like it mattered.

My stomach churned, even after I was in the solace of my office, because I knew at any moment, Mallory would be there, too. I didn't know if she'd walk in and go straight into Mac's office, start working on transitioning, or if she'd be doing tours with me — business as usual. I didn't know if she'd try to apologize again, if I'd be able to listen.

If I'd be able to stay away.

Again, I found myself at war with what my brothers had said at Mom's. They urged me to stay, to not give up on the career I'd built, the reputation I had, the legacy our father started that we were keeping alive.

But now that I was in my office, in a place that used to bring me hope, and fuel, and drive — I only found hopelessness.

I sighed, staring at my desk for far too long before I actually sat down at it. I pulled up my emails, whipped out my highlighters and schedule and clipboard, and tried to get into the groove just like I would have any other Monday morning. And twenty minutes in, I found myself slipping away, into work, out of my mind.

Until there was a knock at my door.

My stomach dropped, heart leaping into my throat as I stared at the door. I didn't know who was on the other side of it, only that if it was the person I thought it was, I wasn't ready.

But I had no choice.

"Come in," I croaked out, keeping my eyes on my schedule and pretending it needed my full attention. I started highlighting things that didn't need to be highlighted, just so I wouldn't have to look up.

"A word, Becker?"

My head popped up at the sound of Mac's voice, and now he was playing the same game I had been, looking at his clipboard like he was on a tight schedule and I was just a stop along the way.

"Yes, sir. Of course. Do you want me in your office?"

"No, this is fine," he said, closing the door behind him. He sat his clipboard on my desk, taking the seat opposite me. For a long while, he just looked at me — as if he were truly seeing me for the first time since I'd worked there. Then, he sighed, pinching the bridge of his nose. "I want to apologize for what happened at the Christmas party. None of us were expecting that, least of all me, but when my brother makes up his mind... well..." He shrugged, folding his hands in his lap. "I guess I don't need to tell you that there's no arguing with him."

I didn't answer. I had nothing to say.

"Anyway, I came in here today to tell you that we spoke this weekend," he said, shifting uncomfortably. Mac was one of those men who was easy to read. He always had been. I knew when he was lying, because he could never look you in the eye when he did, and he fidgeted uncontrollably. "I argued that Mallory wasn't ready for a leadership position, and after much convincing, he agreed. So, we're offering the management role to you."

My jaw dropped. "You're... what?"

"I don't know why you're surprised," he said, cocking a brow. "I think everyone in this town knows the position is rightfully yours."

I swallowed. "But, they announced at the party that the position was Mallory's."

"Are you deaf, son? Did you not just hear me?"

"I did," I assured him, shaking my head — because it didn't make sense. Patrick Scooter didn't go back on his decisions, especially once he'd announced them to the entire town. "I'm sorry, sir. I guess I'm just a little confused."

"Yes, well, that makes two of us," he murmured, standing. Apparently, the conversation was done. "Anyway, we've got about a month before I'm trading in this name tag for a life of golfing and fishing. So, we have work to do. Have Joseph take your tours today. I want you to figure out a transition plan, and then set up time for us to train."

"Yes, sir."

He nodded, but before he could make his way out the door, I called after him.

"Mac?"

"Hmm?"

I swallowed. "What does this mean for Mallory? I mean... is she... is she taking my spot, or?"

Mac shrugged. "Apparently, she's not working here at all anymore. Once she found out we were giving you the position, Patrick said she quit. And is selling her studio, too, I guess. Said she's done with this town, that she's leaving and never coming back." He shook his head. "I'll never understand that niece of mine. Go through all that trouble to buy and build a studio, have a grand opening, just to shut it down a week later?" He scoffed. "This is why women shouldn't run businesses. Too emotional, you know?"

I kept my mouth shut, offering him an awkward smile and a nod before he let himself out of my office. When I was alone again, I blew out a breath, mind racing as I tried to piece it all together.

Patrick Scooter would never go back on a decision he'd made. Never. Not without there being a *very* good reason.

And Mallory wouldn't give up her studio — not after all she'd done to bring that dream to life.

Something was off. Something was wrong.

I put an *out of office* email up before I stood, swiping my jacket off the back of my chair and practically running back out to my truck. Mac wouldn't miss me for a day, not if this really was the new direction we were going. Hell, I could make a transition and training plan in an hour.

And I needed to find out what the hell was going on.

I needed to find *her*.

If what Mac said was true, and the studio was being sold, I didn't have a clue where to find her. That was her place — her home, her getaway, her sanctuary. I didn't know where to even start, aside from hunting down her best friend, Chris. Maybe he'd tell me where she was.

Then again, maybe he'd spit in my face. After the way I'd talked to Mallory, I deserved it.

My stomach twisted into a tight knot as I threw my truck in drive and peeled out of the parking lot, wondering what had happened, what Mallory's father had done.

Suddenly, the only thing that mattered was making sure she was safe.

And finding her before she left Stratford — and *me* — forever.

# Chapter Nineteen

**MALLORY**

Crying was disgusting.

I remembered now why I had avoided it at all costs during my adult life. I was snotting all over myself, my eyes were red and puffy, lashes wet and clouding my vision as I added in the final details to the painting I'd been working on all day. I kept wiping my nose on the back of my wrist because I was too engrossed in what I was creating to get up and get a tissue, and besides, what did it matter? I was alone in the half-empty studio that would soon be completely bare again, just like I'd found it, and then auctioned off to the highest bidder.

I knew I looked like a complete wreck in my baggy black sweatpants and oversized Nine Inch Nails t-shirt, my hair piled on top of my head, and now, an ugly cry face, too. At least I hadn't bothered to put on makeup, so there was no scary mascara streaking down my face.

Again, not that it mattered, since I was very, *very* alone.

It was, perhaps, the loneliest I'd felt in my entire life, sitting in that studio with my hands creating art in an attempt to remind myself there was something worth breathing for. And as another wave of tears hit me, my face twisting with the gut-wrenching arrival of them, I tried to pinpoint what had set them into motion — but I couldn't.

It had all hit me at once.

I'd been holed up in my room upstairs all morning, *not* packing — though I should have been, and reading the end of *All the Light We Cannot See*, instead. Maybe it was because I wanted to escape my new reality. Or maybe it was because I wanted to feel some sort of tie to Logan again — no matter how small.

Regardless, when I finished, I closed the book, stared at the wall, blinked several times, and then, I sobbed.

I cried for Maurie-Laure, for Verner, for the horrors and tragedies of war and for the beautiful victories of life lived after. I cried for the man who had given me that book, who I wished I could call and talk to about it, who I wished I could laugh and play with like I had just weeks before. I cried for my art studio, for the dream I'd barely seen brought to life before I'd forfeited it. And I cried for my family — or rather, my lack thereof — for the little girl who had her innocence stolen and for the woman who realized maybe no family was better than the family she had.

Not that I had a choice. My father had made that for me.

Just like he threatened, I was excommunicated from the family. He didn't even let me talk to my mom or my brother again, and explained to me that they were already told what I'd done, and that they had no interest in speaking with me, anyway. I figured it was true for my brother, who believed whatever Dad said, but I couldn't stomach that Mom felt the same. And I knew even if she didn't, she was too scared of my father to come find me, to try to make it right.

*heat*

And so, I was alone.

I had roughly a week left to get out of the studio before Dad would have me formally evicted. Chris had offered his couch for as long as I needed, but past that, I didn't have a plan.

I didn't have anything.

Something inside me surged, like a warm, bright burst of morning light, because that wasn't true. I *did* have something — my pride. My dignity. My moral compass, pointing due north.

I had done what was right, even knowing it wouldn't be easy, and that was enough to ease the pain.

It was another cold night, and since Dad had already cut off the electricity, I was painting by the light of several candles, wrapped up in a blanket on one of the few bar stools left. My arm and hand were freezing, but I was almost done with the painting I'd started that afternoon, as soon as I'd finished the book.

It was the most powerful scene I'd ever read — the version that I saw in my head, anyway. It was my Maurie-Laure and Verner, sitting on the curb in Saint Malo. It was a young, innocent boy trapped in a war as a villain he never intended to play, and a young, innocent blind girl who fell in love with a world she could not see — even when it was at its ugliest.

That scene was one I would never forget. Just like the book. Just like the boy who *gave* me the book.

And I wanted to immortalize all of it with that painting.

Fireworks were already spouting off here and there outside, even though we were far from midnight and the hour that would welcome in a new year. The sounds were dull and distant, so when a knock sounded at the shop front door, I nearly jumped out of my skin.

When I turned and found Logan on the other side of the glass, I was paralyzed altogether.

Small bursts of fireworks were going off somewhere in the distance behind and above him, casting him in soft pink and purple and blue glows as he stood there, hands in the pockets of his Carhartt jacket, hair a mess under his navy blue ball cap. My feet carried me numbly to him, and it felt like someone else's hand unlocking the door, someone else stepping back to allow him inside. When the candlelight reached his face, I saw how dark his eyes were, how his beard was longer than usual and scraggly like I'd never seen it.

He didn't say anything at first. He just looked at me, at the blanket around my shoulders, the tears marking my face, the bird's nest of hair on top of my head. Then, he looked behind me — at the painting, at the book on the stand next to it — and then back at me.

My bottom lip quivered, and I sniffed, trying and failing to fight back another wave of tears. "I told you I'm not good with emotions."

Logan smirked, opening his arms, and I padded forward until I was in them. He wrapped me up in a tight hug, and I cried harder when I felt that embrace, when my head rested against his chest, his chin on top of my head, his distinct scent of whiskey and wood and old books surrounding me in comfortable familiarity.

He sighed, as if that embrace was all he'd been wanting, too. And for the longest time, he just held me there, arms wrapped tight, hearts beating in sync, me crying on his shoulder.

"I take it you finished," he said, voice rumbling through where my ear rested on his chest.

I nodded. "I told you not to make me cry, Logan."

"Well, you made me cry first, so I think we're even."

My heart ached at that, and I pulled back, looking up at him through my wet lashes. "You're right. I guess I deserved it, huh?"

He chuckled, sweeping the mess of hair that had fallen loose from my ponytail away from my face. His eyes catalogued every part of me, but he didn't look at me like I was the hot mess express in pajamas.

He looked at me like I was a priceless, one-of-a-kind, first edition of his favorite novel.

"I thought you were gone," he croaked, voice low. "I came by earlier this morning, and the shop was so empty, and you didn't answer... I've been looking all over town for you."

"You have?"

He nodded, that favorite wrinkle of mine making its appearance between his eyebrows. "Mac came to my office first thing this morning and told me he talked to your dad, that he convinced him they made a mistake by giving you the management position. He said it was mine, and that you had quit, that you were selling the studio and leaving town and..." He swallowed, shaking his head. "I just knew something was wrong, something was off. I had to find you."

I laughed, wiping my nose with the back of my wrist with a shrug. "Welp. Here I am."

A hint of a smile touched his lips, but it disappeared quickly, his eyes searching mine. "What happened?"

"I don't even know where to start," I said, blowing out a breath. My hands gathered at the center of his chest, and I looked at them instead of at his golden eyes. "I was sick all that night, after what happened. I wanted to run to you, to beg for you to believe me when I said I had nothing to do with what happened. But after our fight..." I shrugged. "You were right. I may not have played an active role in it, but somewhere, in the back of my mind, I knew what my father was capable of. I knew making any kind of deal with him was dangerous."

"I'm sorry for the way I spoke to you."

"You shouldn't be," I said, shaking my head. "I deserved it. And that next day, after wallowing in self-pity, of course, I came down here and I drew a sketch of you in my bed. And I looked at that picture of you on my wall. And I felt you in every inch of this room, of the room upstairs, of my *life*," I confessed. "And I knew I had to make it right somehow."

Another tear slipped down my cheek, but it didn't make it far before Logan was thumbing it away, and somehow, that made my chest squeeze even tighter.

"I told my dad he needed to make it right, that he knew as well as this entire town did that that position was yours — not mine. I told him if he *didn't* make it right, I would go to the *Gazette* with what happened that night when I was fourteen."

Logan inhaled. "Mallory..."

"I know," I said, glancing at him before my eyes fell to my hands on his chest again. "I know. Trust me, I didn't want to. I don't want to *ever* talk about that night with anyone ever again. But, I was willing to do it, if I had to. And I knew my father well enough that it wouldn't come to that. He doesn't want another mark on our name — not now, especially after everything that happened with Mayor Barnett this summer." I sniffed. "Anyway, the next day, he told me I had two weeks to get out of my apartment, that he was sending movers to take all the furniture and art supplies to auction, and that I was never to talk to anyone in my family ever again."

Logan shook his head, framing my face with his hands and forcing me to look at him. "Why would you do that?" he asked urgently, searching my gaze. "It's just a job, Mallory. I could have done something else. I could have—"

"It's not just a job, and you know it," I argued. "It's your family's legacy. It's the position you've worked your entire adult life for — and the one you damn well deserve, too."

"But, your family," he whispered, then he looked around. "Your dream."

"My family was never family to begin with. Family sticks together, no matter what. They love each other and understand each other and they would never, *ever*, do what my father did to me — not when I was fourteen, not now." I shivered. "And my dream is to bring art to kids. But, I don't need my father to make that happen. Maybe I'll go into education, or maybe I'll open up a shop of my own. Whatever I decide to do, I know one thing for sure — I don't need my father to do it. I don't want any part of his legacy, not with the way he's living it. I'm ashamed I even came back and agreed to that deal with the devil in the first place."

"You didn't do anything wrong," Logan assured me.

"No, I did. I did. And that's okay, I admit it, and I did what I had to do to make it right. When I came back, I was lost. I was fresh out of college and jobless with no money or career possibilities ahead of me. I fell right back into the trap I fought my whole life to escape. It was a moment of weakness, a moment of being on my knees. But, I'm standing again now."

The left side of Logan's mouth quirked up, and he nodded. "You are."

"On top of all that," I continued. "I realized something very important that day after I watched you walk away from me."

"What's that?"

"That if it means I can't have you, if it means hurting you, then it's not right. I don't care what *it* is." My hands began to tremble as I slid them up the rough fabric of his jacket, my eyes flicking to his mouth and back to those honey eyes. The blanket I'd been tucked under fell to the floor at our feet. "And I'm going to say something so crazy, you're going to want to commit me. Because I know it's too soon. I know that to most people, it would seem impossible. But..." I swallowed, shaking so bad I had to fist my hands in his jacket to keep from tumbling over. "I think I love you, Logan Becker. You poor sonofabitch."

Logan laughed, his eyes sparkling in the candlelight as he pulled me into him more, as if his warmth could stop the trembling that came with that admission.

"I can one up your crazy," he said.

"Oh, yeah?"

"Yeah. Move in with me."

My next breath didn't come, though my jaw dropped low enough to let in a giant gulp of air, had my lungs allowed it.

Logan smirked, chucking my chin with his knuckles until my mouth closed. "Move in with me, Mallory. We can figure everything else out together. Wanna know how I know?"

"How?" I barely whispered, still riddled with shock.

"Because I love you, too," he said, leaning down until his forehead met mine. "And I don't just think it. I know it."

"You're *insane*."

"As long as we can be crazy together."

Before I could laugh, his lips were on mine, hands sliding back to hold my neck and pull me into him. Two more tears slipped free when that man kissed me, and I leaned into it — into the pain, into the love, into the crazy. I leaned into the uncertain future that kiss promised me, into the man I trusted to get me through anything, and into the choices we'd both made that led to that moment.

He was my Romeo, and I his Juliet, and our families be damned — we were going to make it.

And this story *wouldn't* end in tragedy.

It was the wildest, most whirlwind of a month I'd ever experienced in my life — that month I spent falling for Logan Becker. When he took my hand and led me outside to watch the fireworks, bringing the blanket with him, I curled up inside that warmth with him with the most relieving sigh finding my lungs. I'd never felt so right, so sure, so... *at home.*

He leaned against the storefront of the shop — the one that we'd built up together, the one now empty once again — and I rested my back against his chest, eyes cast toward the sky. We watched those bursts of light fire off in the sky, talking about the week we'd spent apart and what each of us had been through. Logan promised me his family would come around, that he would find a way for that to happen, that somehow, we'd make it work. And though it scared the absolute shit out of me, I believed him.

For hours, we sat there in the cold, talking and holding each other and watching the town of Stratford say goodbye to another year passed.

When the clock struck midnight, Logan pulled me to stand, wrapped me in his arms, and kissed me into the new year, into a new future, into that new universe we promised to make — one where it was me and him against the world.

Then, he dragged me inside, up the stairs, and we made some fireworks of our own.

# Epilogue

## LOGAN

"**O**h, come on, Mom! It's his graduation," Noah pleaded, holding the shot glass filled to the brim with Scooter Whiskey. "Just one shot."

"Absolutely not," she said, pointing a finger at Noah in warning. "I said no, and I mean it. I'm not naïve enough to think you boys didn't drink before you were twenty-one," she said, waving that finger across all of us older boys. "But, I've managed to keep this one away from the stuff so far, and I intend to keep it that way." She said the last part pointing at Mikey.

"I don't know what you're talking about," Jordan defended. "I was an innocent, law-abiding child."

Mom rolled her eyes, taking the shot glass from Noah and slamming it back herself. A wave of whistles and cheers rang out when she slammed the empty glass back down on the table, cringing and shaking her head against the burn.

"Atta girl, Laurelei!" Betty yelled, throwing her hand into the air for a high five.

Mom slapped it, smiling victoriously. "Now that that's settled, who's ready for cake?"

A unanimous show of hands went up, and she laughed, waving us off as the chatter kicked back in and she escaped to the kitchen to retrieve the massive graduation cake she'd ordered for Mikey.

My younger brother sat on the opposite side of the table from me, an easy grin on his face — and the closest thing I'd seen to his full smile since the fall. He'd changed since he and Bailey broke up. He'd grown quieter, more serious, and he preferred to be alone more now than he ever had before. Still, he seemed relaxed that day, and happy — and he was surrounded by everyone who loved him most to celebrate his accomplishment.

His best friend, Kylie, sat to his right, laughing at a story Betty was telling. Betty was a relatively new friend of the family, one Ruby Grace had brought with her when she and Noah started dating. Ruby Grace had worked down at the nursing home where Betty lived, and through that connection, she'd become one of Mom's best friends — and like a grandmother to all of us.

Ruby Grace was there, too, sitting next to Noah, who had his arm around her and a soft smile on his face as he watched her listen to Betty's story, too.

Jordan was on the other side of Mikey, currently holding his shoulder firmly as he bent low and whispered something meant for just the two of them. I was sure it was something similar to the advice he'd given me on my high school graduation day — advice that I still carried with me every day.

*Fight for what's right, stand up for those who can't stand for themselves, give yourself permission to love and to lose and to be loved and lost in return, and above all else, family first — always.*

*neat*

And, perhaps my favorite addition to that family table at Mom's was the woman sitting next to me.

Mallory sipped on her gin and tonic, smiling at Betty while her fingers drew circles on my knee under the table. Her hair was a neon mix of orange and pink, bright colors that set her blue eyes aflame against her pale skin, and she had a fresh tattoo healing behind her ear. It was a small lotus flower, a symbol she'd told me reminded her that, like the lotus flower born from the mud, we must embrace the darkest parts of ourselves to become our most beautiful selves.

I reached down and covered her hand with my own, giving it a squeeze. She smiled, tossing me a wink before she turned her attention back to Betty, chiming in with her own story next. And I was content to sit back and listen, to watch her fit in with my family just like I knew she always would. It seemed she'd grown on everyone — even Jordan, who was perhaps the most hesitant. Once she moved in with me, they had no choice but to accept her as part of me.

That's what family did.

And it seemed like everyone was beginning to love her.

Well, everyone except for Mom.

She'd been quiet when I'd told my family that Mallory and I had made up, that we were in love, that she was moving in with me. She'd been quiet the first time I brought Mallory to dinner, too — but polite, of course. And though she hadn't warmed up much over the past five months, she hadn't disowned me, either.

I guessed that counted for something.

As for Mallory's family, they'd kept their word of disowning her. She hadn't spoken to any of them since that day she'd told her father off in his office, and though she tried to hide it, I knew it hurt her sometimes.

But *I* was her family, now. *We* were her family.

And unlike what she'd been used to before — we'd be a real one to her.

"Mallory, can you help me in the kitchen?" Mom called, and the table went silent for a moment.

Betty was quick to kick the conversation back in gear as Mallory stood, squeezing my shoulder. "Of course." She disappeared into the kitchen, and I worried my cheek wondering what Mom was saying to her.

"It's getting pretty serious with you two, isn't it?" Jordan asked, nodding toward the kitchen.

I couldn't hear what they were saying, but I kept my eyes on the women inside those walls, anyway. "Serious as the last two minutes of a tied Super Bowl."

Jordan chuckled, lifting his glass of whiskey. "Better hope Mom doesn't eat her alive, then."

I cheersed my glass to his, taking a long sip and letting it burn on the way down. Watching Mallory in the kitchen with Mom, I couldn't help but feel a surge of pride at the woman she was, the woman I loved, the woman who would someday be a part of our family. I knew it without a single doubt in my mind, especially after all we'd been through.

If the first month of our life hadn't been enough of a ride, the last five months would have sealed the deal. Between learning how to live together — her perpetually a mess, me perpetually a neat freak — and adjusting to a new way of life with each of our new careers, it had been a whirlwind. Mallory was spending every hour of her day creating, whether it was painting or sketching or crafting or photography. Anything she could make and sell at the craft fairs around the state, she made. It was all part of her plan to save up to buy a shop of her own one day, and I helped her in whatever way I could — even when she asked me to pose nude for an exotic series of black and white sketches she sold for fifteen grand at a romance novel festival.

As for me, I was working longer hours at the distillery, turning the tour guide department into what I'd always envisioned it could be. We had more tours being booked than ever before — more than we had people to *give* tours — which meant I had my hands full trying to figure out how to accommodate the new demand.

And while I loved chasing my dreams with her, my favorite moments with Mallory were the quiet ones, when we were on the couch, Dalí curled up in a ball between us, a book in our laps, soft music playing in the background. I loved reaching over to close her book, to kiss her, to pull her into our bedroom where we made love.

I loved sharing my life with her.

And I knew without hesitation that I wanted to do it forever.

Mom carried the cake in, setting it down in the middle of the table with slices already pre-cut. She distributed small paper plates and my heathen brothers dug in immediately as Mallory took her seat next to me again.

"Everything okay?" I asked.

She smiled, unfolding her napkin and putting it in her lap again. "Everything's fine. She was just threatening to hang me by my neon ponytail if I ever hurt her baby boy."

I blanched. "She didn't."

"Oh, she did," Mallory assured me on a laugh, patting my knee. "But, I don't blame her. And it was a good talk, one I'm glad we had. I have to prove to her that I'm not like the rest of my family, and I don't think that's an unfair request. It's also not a challenge I'm not willing to take on." She leaned in, pressing a quick kiss to my lips. "Especially for you."

I smirked, squeezing her hand where it grabbed mine under the table just as Mom called our attention.

"Now, before you go digging in," she said, swatting my hand where I was about to put the first bit of cake in my mouth.

"Hey!"

"I'd like to take a moment to say something," she said. She clasped her hands gently in front of her, and with the evening light pouring into the house, the silver of her hair shone a brassy gold. "Michael, this is one of the most important days of your life. It is a day you will never forget, a closing of one door and opening of the next. And no matter where this life takes you, I want you to always know that you have a home to come back to, and a family that loves you, very, very much."

"Hear, hear," Jordan said, lifting his glass. The rest of us lifted ours in unison.

"To Michael," Mom said, tears in her eyes now. "Our baby boy, a baby no longer."

We all cheered and whistled, taking a drink before digging into our cake. Mikey stood and wrapped Mom in a big hug, and as soon as they had both sat down, Noah stood. He seemed nervous, and when I realized he hadn't touched his cake, I narrowed my eyes, looking between him and the offending slice.

"Uh, while we're all gathered here," he said, clearing his throat. "I wanted to let you all know we have another cause for celebration."

The whole table went quiet, and we all knew before he even said his next words.

He reached for Ruby Grace's hand, and when she stood with him, it was the first time we'd all taken our heads out of the sand and noticed the rock on her finger.

"Yesterday, I asked Ruby Grace to marry me," he said, beaming at the red-haired beauty beside him. "And she said yes."

Betty was the first to jump up, wrapping Ruby Grace in a fierce hug as she went on and on about Richard Gere, for some odd reason. Mom was *really* crying now as she stood to hug Noah, and we all took turns embracing each of them and offering our congratulations.

"What an exciting day," Mom said when we were sitting again, dabbing at her eyes with her napkin. She laughed when Jordan offered his, too. "I'm just a mess."

"You had to know this was what you were getting yourself into with four boys," Kylie said.

Mom chuckled. "Yes, I suppose I did."

Kylie was a tiny little thing — maybe five-foot-two wearing heels. She had long, dark, chestnut hair and the classic girl-next-door face. She'd always kind of felt like one of the guys when we were younger. I remembered her playing man hunt with all of us out in the backyard, and had a distinct memory of her knocking one of Mikey's teeth out when he said something she apparently didn't like. Now, though, she and Mikey both looked like they were caught in some strange in-between — not yet a man and woman, but far from a boy and a girl.

It made my chest hurt a little to see them growing up like that.

She'd been around more that spring, trying to help Mikey break into our dad's hard drive. It apparently was more encrypted than we knew, though, and she said she could do it, but it would take time.

Michael took a sip of his water when we were all settled again, clearing his throat with his eyes on his glass. "While we're making announcements, I guess now is as good a time as any to tell you guys..."

"Tell us what, sweetie?" Mom asked.

Mikey looked around the table, and then he sniffed, eyes back on his glass. "I'm going to spend the next few months here in Stratford, enjoy one last summer in my hometown. But, after that, I'm moving."

Everyone stopped what they were doing — forks suspended in mid-bite, hands paused around glasses, all eyes on my baby brother.

"To New York."

There was a very, *very* small stretch of silence — and then all hell broke loose.

Mom started crying — this time, they weren't happy tears. Jordan immediately launched into not making hasty decisions while Noah argued that he couldn't leave the distillery. I opened my mouth to chime in, but Mallory squeezed my knee in warning under the table, and when I looked at her, she just shook her head.

"You guys can yell and holler all you want, but my mind's made up," he said over the chaos, standing and tossing his napkin down on the table. "I'm eighteen now and this isn't a choice that any of you get to make for me. So, you can either support me, or not, but either way, I'm going."

With that, he stormed across the house and out the front door, footsteps thumping down the porch steps.

Kylie grimaced, folding her own napkin and setting it on the table beside him before she stood. "I'll go talk to him."

When they were both gone, Mom's whimpers were the only sound at the table. Jordan reached over to hug her, and Betty smiled, turning the attention back to the good news of Noah and Ruby Grace's engagement.

"So, tell us how he proposed," she urged.

And, at least for the moment, Mikey's news was put aside.

I was still reeling from it all when Mallory and I pulled into our driveway later that evening, and I felt like a zombie opening the car door for her, carrying the leftovers Mom sent with us inside, and plopping down on the couch. Mallory sat next to me, running her fingers through my hair and watching me with worried eyes.

"You okay?"

I nodded, though I wasn't entirely sure. "I just... I can't believe he wants to move. To *New York*, of all places." I shook my head. "This has always been our home. I guess I never considered the possibility that one of us could leave it."

"Maybe he'll change his mind," she soothed.

"Maybe. But if he doesn't, I'll support him. That's what he would do for me in the reverse. I should put it on my work calendar now that I'll be out a couple weeks at the end of summer, just in case he needs help moving."

Mallory smiled, moving until she was lying on my chest. "You're a good brother."

We laid there like that for a while, both of us quiet, until a soft chuckle left her lips.

"What about your other brother? Getting married?"

I smiled. "That wasn't as much of a surprise. I knew when he first got caught up with that girl that he'd marry her one day."

"Oh, yeah?" Mallory asked, scooting up to look at me. "How'd you know?"

"He looked at her the way I look at you," I explained easily, moving her hair away from her face. "Like forever was sitting right there in her eyes."

Mallory made a gagging notion with her finger, rolling her forever eyes.

I laughed. "What? You don't like the sweet romance?"

"Not when it's cheesier than a pizza from Mario's."

"You'll let me cover you in all the romantic cheese I want to," I said, wrapping her in my arms while she squealed and played like she wanted to get away.

We both knew she didn't.

"And you'll like it, too," I said, kissing her.

She chuckled. "Fine. But when you and I decide to tie the knot, promise me one thing?"

"Anything."

Mallory grinned. "Let me shove cake in your face."

I blanched. "But then I'll have icing all over my face."

"Mm-hmm," she agreed, still grinning as she kissed my nose. "And probably all over your tux, too."

I wrinkled my nose. "Sounds messy."

"Well, you did agree to let me be the mess in your life," she reminded me.

And when she leaned in to press her lips to mine again, I held her there, deepening the kiss with a promise that I'd do anything she ever asked.

Because what a beautiful mess she was.

More from Kandi Steiner

**On the Rocks**
A small town summer romance following four brothers who are finding love and solving the mystery of their father's death.

**The What He Doesn't Know Series**
Charlie's marriage is dying. She's perfectly content to go down in the flames, until her first love shows back up and reminds her the other way love can burn.

**The Wrong Game**
Gemma's plan is simple: invite a new guy to each home game using her season tickets for the Chicago Bears. It's the perfect way to avoid getting emotionally attached and also get some action. But after Zach gets his chance to be her practice round, he decides one game just isn't enough. A sexy, fun sports romance.

## On the Way to You
It was only supposed to be a road trip, but when Cooper discovers the journal of the boy driving the getaway car, everything changes. An emotional, angsty road trip romance.

## A Love Letter to Whiskey
An angsty, emotional romance between two lovers fighting the curse of bad timing.

## Weightless
Young Natalie finds self-love and romance with her personal trainer, along with a slew of secrets that tie them together in ways she never thought possible.

## Revelry
Recently divorced, Wren searches for clarity in a summer cabin outside of Seattle, where she makes an unforgettable connection with the broody, small town recluse next door.

## Black Number Four
A college, Greek-life romance of a hot young poker star and the boy sent to take her down.

## The Palm South University Serial
Written like your favorite drama television show, PSU has been called "a mix of Greek meets Gossip Girl with a dash of Friends." Follow seven college students as they maneuver the heartbreaks and triumphs of love, life, and friendship.

Rush (book 1)
Anchor (book 2)
Pledge (book 3)
Legacy (book 4)

**Tag Chaser**

She made a bet that she could stop chasing military men, which seemed easy — until her knight in shining armor and latest client at work showed up in Army ACUs.

**Song Chaser**

Tanner and Kellee are perfect for each other. They frequent the same bars, love the same music, and have the same desire to rip each other's clothes off. Only problem? Tanner is still in love with his best friend.

# Acknowledgements

The Becker Brothers will be back this winter.

Sign up for Kandi Steiner's newsletter
**bit.ly/NewsletterKS**
so you don't miss the release of Michael's book –
*Manhattan!*

Didn't read Noah's book first and
want to know his and Ruby Grace's story?
Read *On the Rocks*
**amzn.to/2F6GgGg**
(available in Kindle Unlimited!)

Book two in the Becker Brothers story is complete, and as another brother finds love and the mystery of their father's death is slowly unraveled, I'm finding myself emotional and very, very thankful.

Momma, I want to thank you first, because even though you are facing so much in your own life, you are always here for me when I need you. It's because of you that I have chased this writing dream, and whenever I feel overwhelmed or scared, I hear your voice saying, "one step at a time." Thank you for always reading and loving my books, for giving me feedback, and for keeping me humble – always. I couldn't do anything in my life without your influence, least of all this. I am a better woman for having you as my mother.

Staci Hart, as always, you get a HUGE thank you. No one else is as active in EVERY step of my writing process. Thank you for letting me talk through issues when I get stuck, for listening to me ramble on about characters, for reading and providing valuable feedback, and for having my back no matter what. I love that I have you in my corner and that we lean on each other so much in our creative process. I can't imagine doing this without you, so don't ever leave me.

My beta readers were, as always, instrumental in the creation of Neat. Kellee Fabre, thank you for reading so quickly and always asking questions that help me see what I couldn't before. Trish QUEEN MINTNESS, I am so obsessed with your messages as you read. You make me feel like I'm not a complete screw up, and you keep the fire burning when I'm struggling. Thank you for your amazing feedback and suggestions on this one, and for always letting me inside your head as you read. Kathryn Andrews, your tough love is exactly what I need when beta rolls around, and I can't thank you enough for always keeping it real. Sarah Green, thank you for making time for my work even when you have so much of your own. Your words of affirmation mean so much to me!

I also brought on two NEW beta readers this round – Natalie Bailey and Carly Wilson. Thank you both SO MUCH for bringing fresh insight to my team and for providing quick, honest, and helpful feedback. I appreciate having your eyes on my work to help polish it to a shine!

To the most amazing friend/beta reader/assistant/ master of all hats in the world — Christina Stokes — THANK YOU. Thank you for always thinking of me, for foreseeing things I never think of, for reading my work and providing crucial feedback, and for just being one of the brightest humans in my life. I can't imagine a world without you in it.

Sasha Erramouspe, thank you for always being my last set of eyes before I release my books into the world. Your "Charlie" read is always so beneficial, and it helps me see if I've corrected the issues I faced in beta edits. More than that, thank you for being a sweet, kind, and caring friend. I adore you.

To Elaine York of Allusion Graphics, THANK YOU for always handling my last minute deadlines and changes, for making me a priority, and for petting my hair as you edit my book so I can smile from time to time as I fix all the mistakes. I consider you such a good friend and I'm so happy this book world brought us together!

I have the most amazing team on my side, and I want to thank all of them. Nina, Brittany, and the rest of my team at Social Butterfly PR — thank you for promoting my books like they're YOURS, and for making my life easier when it comes to release time. And to Flavia, Hannah,

Jackie, and Meire at Bookcase Agency, thank you for believing in my work and putting in as much heart and hustle as I do. I love you all so much.

Lauren Perry of Perrywinkle Photography is such a dream to work with, which is why she has done all the photography for every cover I've had since *A Love Letter to Whiskey*. Thank you for always pushing to see my vision and bring it to life, and for sharing your incredible talent with the world.

I want to give a huge shout out to all the bloggers and authors who read early copies, reviewed, promoted, and got everyone else excited about *Neat*. This book world is a community, and without all of you, my dreams wouldn't be possible.

Kandiland is my favorite little corner of the interwebs, and I swear, you all feel like my family. I love that I can go on a live video in my pajamas and we can talk all night long. I love that you get excited over my sneak peeks and teases, that you motivate me on writer block days, and that you're always excited to read what comes next from me. You are everything to me, and I am so thankful for your support. Let's be besties forever!

Finally, I want to thank you—the reader. If you've made it this far, even reading the ACKNOWLEDGEMENTS? Well, you're pretty freakin' awesome. Thank you for picking up MY book out of all the choices you have out there. I truly appreciate you, and I hope you'll find other books in my backlist that you love as much as this one.

# About the Author

Kandi Steiner is a bestselling author and whiskey connoisseur living in Tampa, FL. Best known for writing "emotional rollercoaster" stories, she loves bringing flawed characters to life and writing about real, raw romance — in all its forms. No two Kandi Steiner books are the same, and if you're a lover of angsty, emotional, and inspirational reads, she's your gal.

An alumna of the University of Central Florida, Kandi graduated with a double major in Creative Writing and Advertising/PR with a minor in Women's Studies. She started writing back in the 4th grade after reading the first Harry Potter installment. In 6th grade, she wrote and edited her own newspaper and distributed to her classmates. Eventually, the principal caught on and the newspaper was quickly halted, though Kandi tried fighting for her "freedom of press." She took particular interest in writing romance after college, as she has always been a die hard hopeless romantic, and likes to highlight all the challenges of love as well as the triumphs.

When Kandi isn't writing, you can find her reading books of all kinds, talking with her extremely vocal cat, and spending time with her friends and family. She enjoys live music, traveling, hiking, anything heavy in carbs, beach days, movie marathons, craft beer and sweet wine — not necessarily in that order.

## CONNECT WITH KANDI:

NEWSLETTER: bit.ly/NewsletterKS
INSTAGRAM: Instagram.com/kandisteiner
FACEBOOK: facebook.com/kandisteiner
FACEBOOK READER GROUP (Kandiland): facebook.com/groups/kandischasers
GOODREADS: bit.ly/GoodreadsKS
BOOKBUB: bookbub.com/authors/kandi-steiner
TWITTER: twitter.com/kandisteiner
WEBSITE: www.kandisteiner.com

Kandi Steiner may be coming to a city near you! Check out her "events" tab to see all the signings she's attending in the near future:

www.kandisteiner.com/events

CPSIA information can be obtained
at www.ICGtesting.com
Printed in the USA
LVHW111012121119
637105LV00002B/162/P